To Mis

Best Wishes,
Hope you enjoy!
Elizabeth Olivier Wooten
2009

Memories and Murders

This is a work of fiction. names, characters, places, and incidents either are the product of the author's imagination or are used fictitiously. Any resemblance to actual persons, living or dead, events, or locales is entirely coincidental.

Copyright © 2009 Elizabeth Oliver Wooten
All rights reserved.

ISBN: 1-4392-5520-2
ISBN-13: 9781439255209

To order additional copies, please contact us.
BookSurge
www.booksurge.com
1-866-308-6235
orders@booksurge.com

Memories and Murders

Elizabeth Oliver Wooten

2009

MEMORIES

Memories are heartbeats,
Of times gone by.
A picture, a poem, or a possession,
Bring bittersweet thoughts,
Of loved ones passed on.

Memories are treasures,
Held close to the heart.
They hurt, they comfort,
They are ours to hold,
To share—or let go.

Memories remain forever,
Dim scenes, faded photographs,
Bring joy and pain.
Forgotten at times,
They dwell always in our hearts.

Memories ride through time,
Love will remain forever.
While sorrows will pass.
They are ours to have and hold,
Memories, treasures, pleasures,
Forever.
                Elizabeth O Wooten

I

The road was bad, it had been neglected for many years. The first hundred yards ran between other people's properties, and then it followed the south property line of our piece of land. Next the road curved and went between the old cotton field and the garden spot ending at the house, which sat in almost the center of the twenty acres. This road was not the nearest point that Papaw's land touched the main road. The logical long driveway would have been there. The way we had entered was reserved on the deed as right-of-way and had been used for at least a hundred years. We certainly didn't plan on changing it. It was useable and could be repaired, for now, it would certainly discourage visitors.

It was a beautiful summer day, like many I remembered when I lived here with my paternal grandparents. No vehicle like our motor home had ever been here. David drove the motor home and I followed in his small Nissan pickup. As soon as we stopped and got out, David began to voice his doubts.

"Are you sure this is what we want to do?" David asked

"Sure, I'm sure, but not real sure."

"I know that you want to be here to write about your family," he continued as if I had not spoken.

"I've been thinking about doing that for a long time. Why not here?"

Elizabeth Oliver Wooten

David pretended not to hear me. He didn't answer so I took that as, "It's okay we can try."

Two years before my husband and I had bought Memaw and Papaw's old house and land. We planned to restore the house, barn, pasture, yard, orchard, and all the things I remembered from my childhood. This was the place I still thought of as home. The house was not only old but also rotten and rundown; rats and other critters had been the only inhabitants for years. Actually it was falling apart but to me the piece of property was beautiful. In years past, trees had surrounded two sides of the land, a neighbor's cornfield bordered one side, and the main road ran along in front of the property. We could see the public road from the house, although it was two hills and a hollow away.

I could see in my mind the way things looked some forty years ago. The apple orchard had been in a low-lying area near the stream that meandered through the pasture. Beautiful willow trees grew nearby offering their hanging limbs for climbing. A chestnut tree grew on the side of the hill. The pasture had green grass and wild flowers in the spring. The peach orchard was nearer the house. Oh, how good those big Elberta Peaches were. The vegetable garden was in front of the house. Memaw grew flowers all around the house. Maybe there are a few hardy flowers in the weeds. Those were some of the scenes I recalled and I just knew it could be that way again.

If we couldn't restore the old home maybe, we could build a new one. The nearby hill, a little bit isolated would make a perfect place to put our new house if we decided to stay. It was out of sight of the road and with no nosy neighbors nearby we could have peace and quiet. In reality, it was only two miles from town, a distance I had walked many times. The long driveway would start at the road, down the first hill, cross the creek over a bridge and up to the new house or the old one if it could be renovated.

Memories swiftly returned as soon as I saw the well shed. I recalled, drawing buckets of water from that deep well when I wasn't strong enough to lift the big bucket of water, but the windlass was always oiled and easy to turn. The well was in the yard in front of the house. It still looked as it had years ago when I lived there. It was the picture of how things used to be. The four- post set in a perfect square held up the old fashioned roof that was covered in wood shingles. No flowers were growing around it now. No bucket sat on the well tile. Things are different now. Time has changed everything.

If we could have known the events that were to come, perhaps I would not have been so happy and optimistic. These events would include drugs, bones, and murder. Granny, my great grandmother who had lived here with us in her later years might have been able to foretell some of these happenings in her teacup. It was said that she had 'the gift'.

I remember only once that she tried to please some neighboring visitors. They came asking her to tell them who had damaged the tombstone at the grave of their father and husband.

Granny said," I don't do that anymore."

"Would you just tell us what you see?" the ladies begged.

Granny refused at first but we insisted. My sister and I had never heard her read the tea leaves, so we begged her to do it. We didn't have any tea leaves so Memaw brewed up some coffee and poured her a cup. She drank a little and then poured out the coffee and turned the cup upside down. She then studied the lines and told them something that we were not supposed to hear.

Memaw explained later that it didn't matter what the ladies were told; they probably knew who shot his picture that was mounted in the headstone. It seems the dead man had been well known in the community since he sold many of the locals moonshine whiskey. Memaw said it could have been poison, or very bad whiskey and many people had it in for him. She thought the man died before they got their revenge.

Memaw had her opinions about a lot of things and often shared them with us. I recall her sayings often and wonder where she learned them. "A merry heart doeth good," I believe that one's from the Bible. At that time in my life, I had neither a merry heart nor the will to do well. The 'us' was three girls that lived with Memaw and Papaw for many years.

David and I did have a few problems awaiting us. The lack of water and electric power was probably the least of them.

৵⌘

Our plans were to live in the motor home, while we rebuilt the farm of my dreams. David and I had traveled over most of the states and thought it was time to do something useful and challenging, little did we know how challenging and dangerous this project would be.

The first disappointing things were about the water and electricity. A deposit with the Power Company should get one of these but not for months. It seems they had to replace some power poles, at our expense, and we had to convince the TVA that we would be here for at least two years. We had not tried to convince anyone of that because we didn't know how long we would be here. Anyway, we would have to wait for it to be done. They put us on their list of new installations.

Next, the city water didn't come to our place so we decided to use the well like we did in the past. It was a deep well. I remembered when concrete tiles were lowered into it to keep the water clean. We drew the water up with a bucket on a rope by turning the windlass. After the tiles were in place there was plenty of good cold, clean water for years. Why couldn't it work again? However, the bucket and rope were gone and we couldn't get any water out to test it. I felt sure we could find a well repairman somewhere around here. Digging wells and cleaning them had been a thriving occupation when we lived here. First, a person with the gift of witching for water had to help locate the stream of water and tell them how far under ground that they would find water.

I recalled when we needed a well dug at a home we built in a nearby county. The men who came to dig our well wouldn't begin until a man came to witch for water. The witcher used a branch cut from a live tree and walked around the area where we wanted the well dug. He held it in both hands and when it found water in the ground the branch would point down. I didn't understand or believe in that voodoo stuff. He sure showed me and he was correct. The men dug where he said and found water at the depth the witcher said they would.

Elizabeth Oliver Wooten

I hoped somebody knew of a person who would tackle the job of cleaning out the bottom of this deep well, check the amount of water, and install a pump. We shouldn't need a witcher. Our motor home tanks held enough water, if we were very conservative, for a week and the generator could run on gas. It was summer and no heat was needed, but air conditioning would have been nice.

It was time to level our motor home, get settled, and look around. Finally, after putting our home where the garage or car shed, as we called it, had been, we dressed in protective clothing, boots, hats, and gloves, got our scythe and guns and went exploring.

2

Joe came to us the week after we had setup the motor home as our home. He arrived in his pickup at ten in the morning looking as if he had just left his bed without getting ready for the day.

"I'm Joe and can do most anything. Are you the folks looking to pay me for some help?" He asked.

"We do need our well repaired, Joe" I replied.

I noticed that he had not asked for a job or inquired what we needed done. Joe had made it clear he needed to be paid, probably before he did the work. Since I answered him, David expected me to help decide what Joe would or could do.

"Joe, this is my husband, David Cotton, and I'm Jane."

Joe reached to shake our hands with a big smile. He seemed to be wide-awake now and more interested in how he could help. I asked who he was, what his job was, and how he learned of our need.

"Yes Ma'am, My full name is Joseph Horatio Burns. Mr. Cotton's daddy told me about you. I've worked for him a little in town."

"You must be talking about David's brother. He does help with the town's work. I remember a Preacher Burns and Mrs. Burns that lived down the road. That was a long time ago when my Grandparents owned this place. Are you a relative of theirs?" I already surmised that he probably was from that family.

Elizabeth Oliver Wooten

"Preacher Burns was my Uncle; I didn't really cotton to him and the Missus. Did you know them very well?"

"Only by his preaching and seeing him in town and on his porch. I'll tell you more about them later. Let's decide how you can help here. Have you ever cleaned out a well and installed pipes and a pump?"

"No Ma'am, but I can. I have tools to cut some bushes and weeds. It'll make this place more livable and scare off the big snakes. You'll have to still watch for their little uns."

David was listening and I could tell he felt Joe needed the money. David was always ready to help anybody. Joe was dressed like the old time poor farmer or a person who lived like a hermit and didn't have to please anyone. His hair and whiskers were partly gray and probably hadn't been cut for years. He was dressed in overalls and a shirt with holes, his boots were well worn, but they looked like they would protect his feet and legs. I remembered that we had a copy of a disclaimer that all workers had to sign. It agreed we were contracting with them for labor and they were not employed by us. If Joe would sign this, he could begin immediately. Besides we had heard of no one who would be willing to go down in our deep well and he said he could. So, it might be a start.

"We can pay you $5.50 an hour for cleanup and when you take a break we'll discuss the well. First read this form and sign your name," I explained to Joe.

He seemed to understand the content and signed it quickly above where I had printed Joseph H. Burns. I asked for his address and phone number, which he gave as Joe Burns, Route Two, Veeny, Alabama 59580. He did not have a phone. This didn't tell us where he lived, who he lived with or where he usually worked. It did appear that he had some education.

I quietly told David, "This man is willing to work; also I think he could be very interesting. Can he begin today?"

"Yes Jane, you tell him what to do" was David's answer.

3

Veeny, Alabama is located in the hills of North Alabama, not far from the Tennessee State line and only a few miles from Mississippi. David and I both were born in the area. He stayed in the area until he was eighteen and went north to find a job. My early years were not that stable. My parents were very young when they married. Dad, Papaw's son, was a timber cutter and was driving a log truck at age fifteen. In those years, timber cutters went to any place that needed them. After my sister and I were born, Mother and Dad lived in many different places and we were left with our grandparents. The only constant things in my life were Memaw and Papaw, and this home that I wanted to preserve.

David and I had been here several days. We had visited some of his brothers and family. They all were very surprised at what we were attempting to do. We had lived away for many years and we felt it really would be nice to see some of his relatives. I also had cousins in the area. One of them was building homes and I hoped to get him to give us an estimate on repairing the house.

People around here told where they lived in relation to how far it was to the nearest Wal-Mart. It was exactly thirty-two miles to Wal-Mart from our motor home. I had driven there a few times for supplies and also got groceries in that town. Besides the Wal-Mart, Tussellville, Alabama had fast food places and a restaurant. It was the county seat of Benjamin County. The best place to get a quick meal was only fifteen miles down the road from Veeny at Blue Pond. We ate there often since our home was still lacking water.

One day when I was at Trussellville I went to the County Archives building and looked at old land records. I found the records and dates when my grandparents had purchased this land—the first home and twenty acres they had ever owned. They had been married for twenty-three years and their two children were married. They also raised two boys from Papaw's first marriage who were married and out of the home. I also got some information about my mother's ancestors that I needed for my book.

While looking at records, I came across the cemetery records of who was buried in each cemetery in the county. It surprised me to find the listing of a small plot of graves on Mr. Cotton's land. That was near our little farm. David's family farm was just over the hill and through the woods from ours. We always looked at the few graves in their woods and wondered who had buried people there. Maybe we could find time to compare these records to the tombstones and contact their descendants.

The people at the archives talked about Veeny and what it was now compared to its beginning and the glory years from 1912 through the 1950's. The ladies at the archive office found three articles about Veeny. I had them make copies of several pages. I left with lots of information.

☙❧

One day David and I walked over the Town of Veeny and had a hard time believing the utterly neglected look of everything old. Nothing from the time we lived there had been updated or preserved. Old buildings were still there and most were solid enough to be used, but none were occupied. The highway that went through had only a few open businesses. The Masonic building was still useable. In the past, Veeny's only bank had occupied the first floor and the Masonic Hall was on the second floor of that brick building for many, many years.

A Stop-and-Go station sold gas, food, and drinks. A local café 'Norman's', a fix-it car place, a bank, and the post office, city hall, and jail were the only places open for business. The main road from Trussellville went down the middle of town and forked into two roads. The other road that crossed that one was from Blue Pond and continued on to Podges, Alabama. Blue Pond was still a busy small town and that's where the businesses were now.

We went to the café in Veeny for food and gossip most every day. The café had the same atmosphere as Moomaw's place of the 1950's. They served a good breakfast and lunch. I think the old Moomaw's café sold only sandwiches and drinks. I remember eating hamburgers there. At Norman's the evening meal was only sandwiches and visiting. The customers all seem to know each other and what was happening in the area. People asked questions of us that David and I answered; I briefly explained where we had been for the past forty years and why we were back in Veeny. Norman, the owner told us about many of the people we remembered. Most of the people who lived and worked here fifty years ago had died. Some of their children were now living in the area and a few of our classmates came to eat at Norman's café. It was easy to get conversations started about the old days. An entire afternoon and some evenings were spent at the café listening to tales about what certain people did and about things that had happened here.

Elizabeth Oliver Wooten

At the café, we learned about a square dance once a month in Blue Pond, a Hee-Haw program another Saturday night at another nearby spot, and an antique auction on the last Saturday of every month here in town.

David spoke up. "We like all of those things, and I know Jane will want to attend the next auction."

I asked, "Do you think it's possible the auction might have some of the old furniture we used?"

Norman answered, "It might, some of the stuff is old junk and some is new junk."

※

I really wanted to know what happened to this lovely little county town and it's folks. The old buildings still stood and I could clearly remember what had been in each. A few were missing. I could picture them all, the bank, the drug store, the big mercantile store, and another general store with farm supplies. Mrs. Wright had a ladies' goods store and there were two other stores that sold food and other things. The blacksmith shop, three gas stations that did auto repair, two cafés, the taxi stand, and the post office were all within walking distance of each other. The telephone exchange was in a home right downtown, and the three doctor's offices were on a side street. Later there was a makeshift movie theater behind one of the cafes and a game room was built much later. All of this was in an area of about six city blocks. The three churches were still located at the same places. There was a Baptist, a Methodist, and a Church of Christ. The churches were still an active part of the community.

Veeny was a very prosperous town for that period of time. My granddaddy, Papaw, was the country veterinarian.

His office was right along side the two medical doctors' office. One of the three buildings was still standing along that street; I thought it was the one Papaw's office was in. I think he rented it or the town may have furnished the three offices for the doctors. Dr. Thorn, the one who delivered me at the log house where my family had lived, was Papaw's fishing buddy. They rarely had time to go, but I remember that many fishing trips were planned and we knew where they would be and for how long.

My parents, sister, and I were living on a farm the year Dr. Thorn died. Our rural mail carrier gave us the news. I guess it was a heart attack because no one knew he was sick. Dr. Thorn, Dad, and Papaw had a fishing trip planned for the next day and we were to go stay with Memaw. Instead, we all went to his funeral two days later.

A filling station was across the street from the doctors' offices. Gas was purchased on credit and paid for when Papaw had the money. I remember gas was rationed during World War II but the doctors could still buy all the gas they needed. The owner of that station was Mr. Fulbright.

The school on the other side of the railroad tracks was in good shape. All of it was situated as it had been when we attended here. The football field, with banks on opposite sides, the street at one end and the high train tracks on the other end, was still between the town road and the school buildings. Next, the gym and then the school. The buildings had been replaced with new modern ones. Although the town was small the school buses picked up children from the surrounding area and this was one of the larger schools in this area. It was first through twelfth grades and now it is kindergarten through twelve. It has a football team and a basketball team for boys and one for girls.

I remembered the school, as it was when David and I attended school there. The gym was attached to a large two-story brick building. The first six grades had classrooms on the ground floor and most of the upper grades were on the second floor. Another brick building was for the girls' home economics studies and the boys shop classes. A wood building held the lunchroom. The outdoor toilets were quite a distance from the other buildings.

As a child I rode buses from two places my parents lived. One I remember was a long ride on very rough, bumpy roads. The farm that we lived on for two years was ten miles from town. Dad farmed it for two seasons. He hated it; I didn't like it either. My brother was born that year. I was seven years old and no one told me Mother was expecting. I sure was surprised. I remember going to school and happily telling my teacher about the new baby at our house. Maybe it was my fault for not listening. Or maybe I was too young to know about such things.

Another house I remember was past the next little town that didn't have a school. Dad was working cutting timber then. The house had only three rooms and there were five of us living there for about a year. The bus picked up my sister and me, for another rough ride to and from school.

Living at Memaw's was much easier. Papaw took us to school in his Ford pickup, we could ride a bus the two and half miles back after school or sometimes my sister, cousin and I walked. We always stopped in town and if we found Papaw he would give us each a nickel for candy. My best friend Margaret lived on the same road and she sometimes walked with us. She also got a nickel for candy. We could even buy an ice cream cone for a dime. Of course, this had to be approved by Memaw and the school.

Veeny, Alabama held many memories for David and me. We remembered the people that lived and worked here. Maybe we could learn where they went or where they were buried as we worked to restore my old home.

4

Joe was back three days after he first came to help us. He looked a little neater, but we could tell he wasn't feeling very well. When I asked, he insisted he was fine and ready to work on the well.

He said, "I used the money to put food in my kitchen and to buy something else I needed."

I didn't ask about the something else. It could have been beer, something stronger, or drugs since he looked like he had a hang over.

We had inquired about Joe Burns. The information we learned was sketchy but nothing bad. He probably lived alone; George said he didn't know where. It seems his wife left a few years back and he quit his job and disappeared for a couple of years. Since he had been back, he only worked when necessary. George, David's brother said he was a good worker when he agreed to do something but didn't stay at it very long.

We knew Joe's work had pleased us the one day he was here. He had cleared around the house, around our motor home, and the path to the barn. He was willing to go in the cellar under the house and look under the house to see if it might fall. After that, we all ventured into house to have a look. I was so upset about the condition that I cried.

"Oh Lord, we need your help or at least your guidance in this project" I quietly prayed. David looked but said nothing.

It was now time to devise a plan to check out the well. Joe told us that morning that he knew of a Mr. Calbetter who had at one time cleaned wells. He had already found out that his equipment was useable. Mr. Calbetter would not help with a well cleaning job, but would loan his windlass. I asked Joe if he had found a helper. He did not know anyone who was willing to help with the well. Joe and David talked about how the two of them could do the well cleaning. I had my doubts but didn't voice them.

"First we have to get the stuff," Joe said.

"I'll clear my pickup" David replied, "Will it be big enough to carry it all?"

"I think it will. We'll need new rope or chain for it to be safe."

"Where is his house?" David asked.

"Up the road a few miles. I can show you. He may want us to buy his stuff."

"We'll see and then go to Home Depot for the new stuff we need," David added sounding very confident.

I quickly decided I would stay home. Maybe locked in, but I could spend the morning thinking about my writing. My computer worked well. I could start with what I knew about my ancestors. Our cell phones worked here some of the time or they would if we went to town. I begin to wonder just how far back we had gone. Was it the distance or were we really back in time.

This was the first day I had time to really stop and think about things from my childhood. Sitting there looking at the land behind the house, I could visualize what it had been fifty years ago. The field was planted in cotton. Since it was a sloping hillside, Papaw had terrace ridges about twenty feet apart. These kept rain from washing gullies down the hillside. The terraces and rows went around the hillside making very long rows. I was too small to help then, but I knew how much work there was to farming. There had been lots of rocks on this back section. My grandparents, parents, or maybe even the owners before them had picked them up and stacked them. There were still huge piles of rock not far from where I sat.

Looking in that direction at the edge of our property, I could see the land that was still owned by a timber company. It was now planted in pines. As I stared at the trees remembering, one of them seemed to move! Was it my imagination? As children, we were told to never go into the woods, even with an adult. Memaw explained that there might be Indians still hiding there, wolves, or wildcats. She never mentioned bears. I learned later what she meant by the Indians hiding. Wolves and wildcats were in this area at that time. We always had a dog. Fido was supposed to watch out for wild animals and keep them from eating the chickens at night.

My mind kept remembering other things. The barn was a favorite place to go to when cousins came to visit. There wasn't much to entertain them so it was a place to get away from the adults. Papaw always had a mule, a cow, some hogs, and lots of chickens. Most of the time we had baby animals to play with. The pigsty was farther away than the barn. We always went there to see the little pigs but didn't stay long because of the odor. The barn loft was a great place to play; the hay there always smelled fresh and clean. We could climb the ladder. It was attached to the outside of the stable wall so we did not go in the stinking stables. We shared lots of secrets before our parents found us. They knew where we were and probably listened from below. None of us ever fell out, as the adults kept worrying that we would.

The barn had three stables, one each for the mule and another for the cow, and a third for a calf. The corncrib, where we shelled corn to be taken to the mill, was clean. The corn was ground at the water powered mill into meal to be made into cornbread. Cornbread was one of the first things I learned to cook.

It was amazing how well the barn had weathered the years. Someone must have replaced or kept the tin roof in good repair. I had looked it over but didn't climb the ladder yet. David had said it needed fixing. Maybe Joe would do that.

The sound of the pickup returning made me get busy with making a late lunch. I really hoped David and Joe had already ate lunch, then we could get busy with the first big project.

❧

The stuff they unloaded looked ancient; it really was. The windlass, so called because you wind it up to get water or a person out of a well, was all wood. When setup it stood about four feet above the ground. The ends were big wood Xs with braces from one to the other across the back. A huge round log lay across the top from one X to the other X in the top vee of the Xs. Iron cranks were in each end of the log so two people could wind down or up the rope attached to the log. We all knew how but I didn't know if we could. They assured me that the new rope would hold. They had bought grease to make things turn smoothly. It had been decided that Joe would be lowered into the well with David and me using the old windlass to help hold him as he went down inside the cement tiles. David assured me that two people could easily turn the windlass. Joe was a big man, so I began to worry about how we would get him out. They were enjoying this challenge so I agreed to help.

First, they had to remove the three-foot high, heavy, concrete tile that was above ground. It was thick cement but the two of them got it out of the way. Next, the thick wood windlass was placed over the well hole. We had checked before and could hear water when we dropped a rock in the well. Now with the new rope and bucket they could draw up a bucket of water. David remembered that a weight had to be attached to one side of the bucket to make it turn over and fill with water. It worked! The first water was dirty. Now the dilemma was whether to try to get most of the water out or go down and check how much water was there and how much trash and mud there was to remove.

"I'm ready to check it out," Joe said with a big smile.

"Are you sure, Joe?" I immediately asked. "Are you insured? Remember you are not working for us, you contracted to do this."

"Don't worry Mrs. C. I'm a veteran, I'll get fixed up if something goes wrong."

David agreed, "What do you think, Jane, that we might drown him in the well?"

"Who knows, but okay I'll help. Not to drown him but help with what I can. Should we wait until tomorrow morning or start now?"

"Now," Joe and David both answered.

5

Getting Joe ready for his dissent into this thirty or forty foot hole, with an unknown amount of water in it, was fairly simple. One end of the rope, which would support five hundred pounds, was attached to a large bucket. We checked again to make sure the other end of it was firmly tied, stapled, and nailed to the log. We even did a trail run, with me at one crank and David at the other. The bucket seemed to go a long way down. We were able to pull it up full of water very easily. We were all ready to begin.

Joe got over the well opening, straddled the rope with the bucket beneath him, and was ready. The large bucket had a very short handled spade in it to remove the mud from the bottom of the well. Joe held onto the rope as he went down. We unwound the rope as he disappeared below ground. We worked with almost no sound coming from below. So far so good, I'm thinking it's going to work.

Then it happened, Joe yelled loudly a curse word or two. We heard the sound of the bucket bouncing off the concrete tiles and hitting the water, then we heard Joe hit bottom. We waited—- I screamed for Joe to answer. What was probably only a minute seemed like an hour to us.

Joe yelled up to us, "The god-damn bucket slipped off the rope and unbalanced me. I'm standing on bottom now. My head got banged up but it's not bleeding. One leg and foot is hurting bad and my hand is probably broken." Then Joe added, "Don't worry Mrs. C. I'll be fine."

David, as usual, was thinking of what to do. He answered him; "I'll lower the rope down to you. Can you tie it around you and hold onto it while we pull you up?"

"I'll try." Joe's voice sounded too far away.

"Joe, I'm praying for you and that we have what it takes to pull you out." I yelled down to him. I tried to keep the panic I felt out of my voice. Joe had only one hand that he could use and one foot probably broke.

"I can't seem to tie a good knot with this hurt hand. I'll get it around me and hold it with my good hand." Joe was sounding worried.

"Joe, you will have to help us anyway you can and hold the rope tight with your good hand" David told him. "We may or may not be able to pull you up but Jane will go for help if this doesn't work."

"How deep is the water and how cold is it?" I asked.

"It's below my waist. I'm standing on one leg, and the water is cold enough to keep me awake. There is a hell of a lot of stuff at the bottom. I haven't felt any snakes; it's much too cold for them."

He sounded more like he could take this. The water was deep enough to cushion his fall and not deep enough to drown him.

"Joe, tell us when you are ready," David told him.

"Okay, I've tried what you said and I think one leg and foot are good but it's my right hand that's hurt. Let's try it."

After the first three turns it became impossible for us to turn the windlass again. I looked at David and started to cry. I thought I was too weak or too scared to help. The look he gave me said "Hush."

Memories and Murders

David spoke quickly and quietly to me. "The keys are in the truck. Hurry, get ready and go to town for help. Call the Blue Pond Fire Department."

As I rushed off to get dressed, I heard Joe yelling to David.

As David went to Joe's truck, he said, "He wants something for pain."

I got the Advil and gave it to David before I left.

I already knew that the town of Veeny had a volunteer fire department but no emergency medical equipment. The town of Blue Pond fifteen miles away had a real fire department as well as doctors and a hospital.

I drove the two miles to town as fast as the truck would go. I knew we needed more help than volunteers. As soon as I had a phone signal I called 911 and asked them to connect me to the Blue Pond, Alabama fire department. It took them minutes to get through; they also wanted to know where the fire was. "Just get them for me and I'll explain," I tried to sound reasonable.

"Fire Department" a female voice answered.

"Do you know where Thaxton Road is, out from Veeny?" I asked, praying I had the right fire department.

"Oh, yes, madam. What's burning? Are you all right?"

"I am now. Nothing is burning. We have an injured man in a well."

"Did you say in a well?'

"Yes, my husband and I can't pull him up. Can your men help?"

"We'll be there in twenty minutes. Can you meet us in Veeny and lead the way to the well?"

"Yes, I'm in a white pickup."

Nolan, the café owner, started calling the volunteers when he heard Joe was in our well. He also filled a thermos with hot coffee and asked if Joe needed medical attention. Then he said "Never mind, I'll go and see."

Twenty minutes later I got back to the well with the fire truck and emergency medical van right behind me. I got to the open well and yelled, "Joe, how are you doing? Help is here!"

He answered immediately; "I'm okay but ready to get out of here."

David already had help from Norman and six other men from the Veeny Volunteer Fire Squad. David had used the smaller bucket to lower whiskey and Advil to Joe. Joe couldn't get the bottle open. David pulled it up, unscrewed both tops, repositioned, and stabilized them so they would not spill and unwound the windlass again. Norman sent him the thermos of coffee to warm him up. They lowered the bucket several more times and each time Joe used his good foot and hand to retrieve some of the stuff that was at the bottom of the well.

The trained EMTs took over. The female I had spoken to at the Blue Pond Fire Department was Mattie Hornsby, a fire person, and a trained EMT. Roy drove the van and was also an Emergency Medical Technician. They talked to Joe trying to assess his condition and how to get him up without causing him more injury.

Joe was evidently feeling the effect of his previous drugs, the Advil and whiskey, and said, "I can do whatever you need me to."

Clyde, the fireman in charge, asked Joe if he would be able to put himself in the harness chair if they lowered it down to him. They were ready to send it down.

"I'll try. I think I can. I hope I can." Joe said from within the well.

"If this doesn't work we'll send our smallest man down to help you." Clyde told Joe. "I'm sure we can lower and pull up safely with our men at the windlass."

I decided that everything was under control. I could now have a nervous breakdown. It certainly didn't help my condition when I heard the men talking about what was in the bucket and what they had already pulled from the well.

One of them said, "They look like bones. Let's wash them off and see."

"I think they are human bones," One of the volunteers from town added.

I ran to my motor home wishing I had some of Joe's whiskey!

୧୶

Joe was able to buckle himself in. They pulled him up easily. He was checked over by Mattie. She quickly gave orders, "You men put him on the stretcher. We're taking him to the hospital. His foot or leg may be broken and he needs to be seen by a doctor."

The emergency vehicle left with Joe. Mattie was administering first aid and probably cleaning him up. He sure looked a mess but I didn't see any blood. I hope they shave him, maybe a haircut too. I would like to see what he really looks like. He may resemble his uncle. That reminded me that I promised to tell Joe about Preacher Burns, his uncle.

Elizabeth Oliver Wooten

Then I begin to think of the medical bills and who would take care of Joe. Maybe my nervous breakdown was for real.

The others, about a dozen men by now, were all excited about the bones. Clyde agreed to let Pete, one of the firemen, go down in the well and see if there were more bones on the bottom.

David said, "I think Joe said the water was waist deep. That's about three feet. Should we try to draw some of it out?"

"No, I can find the bottom. I'll take a grabber." Pete said. He seemed excited about finding somebody's bones.

I again escaped to our home. David told me later what happened next. A dozen more bones were pulled up from the well. Then the men closed off the well. It might be a crime scene. Someone had called the Sheriff to come take a look.

David wanted to believe that those bones were not human but an animal or two. After trying to calm me and assuring me that things were not so bad, David left to go to the hospital in Blue Pond to see about Joe.

ౌ

The county sheriff arrived after dark to pick up the bones. He saw what he thought was a part of a human skull and *warned me not to leave*. He said he'd be back.

ౌ

The news was good. Joe's hand was not broken. It was badly bruised and scraped. He could probably use it in a week. It was his right hand and Joe was right-handed. The bone in his left leg was broken. His leg below the knee was in a cast and he wouldn't be able to walk on it for weeks. He was being held in the hospital overnight.

"My first question was, "David, who will take care of him?"

"I asked him if I needed to call somebody to let them know he was injured and tell them where he was. Joe's answer was NO!

"I thought it was best to wait until tomorrow and try to get information about family and friends. Forget it all for now. Let's get to bed; it's late." David said.

6

Maybe David could sleep but I couldn't. I thought about Joe being hurt. Was it our fault? Would he be mad at us? Who is going to help him for weeks? The next big question I thought about was 'if those are human bones how did they get in our well?' What next, will we have to solve a murder? The sheriff would be back tomorrow. He might arrest one of us.

What will we do about water? We certainly can't use that well water even if they turn out to be animal not human. In the past fifty years nothing like this has ever happened here that I know of. I also thought of the tree that moved when I was watching the tree line at the back of our property. I got up and made sure David had locked the door. He was sleeping; I knew he was very tired. I was resting my physical body but my mind wouldn't rest. Tomorrow we must look over everything. Maybe the stream has water. There might be a spring of water where the pigsty was. The pigs had mud to play in. We haven't checked out the barn. We need someone to look at the house. It may be safe to go in but I don't think it can be saved. That well is very near the house. How do you get rid of a well? How do we get water?

I thought of a plan or what I thought we should do next. Tomorrow David can talk to his brother, George, about city water. I will call the power company and see what it will cost to get temporary service here. I will get in touch with Denny, my cousin, and ask if he will look at the house. We will take care of Joe if there isn't anyone else to do it. With these decisions made I finally went to sleep.

    David and I were up early the next morning. We didn't have much food for breakfast. I made coffee and made sure David was wide-awake before I told him of my decisions. He agreed but said getting Joe settled had to come first. David also wanted to go to Norman's Café for breakfast and find out what people were saying. I didn't want to know. David said we were taking Joe's truck to the hospital to pick him up. He needed me to drive his truck and follow him to Joe's place. When we got him settled in and found someone to help him, we would start on my ideas or plan to leave. That sounded so easy and sensible, but somehow I knew it wouldn't work that way.

7

David and I arrived at the Blue Pond Hospital before nine o'clock the day after Joe was injured. "Is this Joe?" I exclaimed.

This morning he looked entirely different. What has changed him so much? Those were my thoughts as David and I walked into his hospital room. Maybe I had never really looked at him before. When he first came to work for us, I tried to get to know him and had looked him over suspiciously. I knew questions made him very uncomfortable so I had not really asked anything else or appraised him since. The first day I saw him he looked very slipshod, unorganized, dirty, tired, and a little hung over. He had not shaved for probably two months nor had a haircut for even longer. His clothes were adequate for working but nothing else could be said about them. The next time Joe showed up to help, he didn't look any better. That day I had only tried to make sure he was sober, which he was. His speech was much better and his plans for our well were very well thought out. I had learned that he was a veteran, probably divorced, and living by himself. We didn't know any more than that about him.

Now here he was looking like a different person since he had fallen into our well. His whiskers were gone, his hair was cut, his dark eyes were bright and clear, and of course he was clean; he looked like a different man. I could now guess about his age, height, and weight. Joe was smiling.

He was very glad to see us and very much wanted to get home.

"David, did you bring me any clothes?" Joe barked without saying good morning.

"Can you leave today? Has the doctor dismissed you yet?" I spoke up to find out if he really could leave the hospital.

"I have to go home to see about Bear." Joe answered.

"Who's Bear? Is he a friend? You have to have someone to help you before you can go home. Slow down and tell us about your family or friends." David begged.

"David, please get me some clothes, then we'll talk on the way home. I think they threw away the ones I was wearing."

"Joe, you look like a new man. Who did your hair? Are you in pain?" I asked

Joe answered my questions; "I've had pain medicine and a sleeping pill. I feel good this morning. When we got here last night Miss Mattie and a nurse put me in a shower, threw all my clothes out, and gave me this."

He was wearing a hospital gown and not very happy about it. I could see why, but decided not to say anything. Didn't they have any pajamas for men?

"She trimmed me up while we waited for a doctor to come set my leg. She actually shaved off my beard. I told her to cut my hair, too. Guess I was under the influence of something. She's kinda nice."

I think he meant Mattie that I remembered from the well rescue. He was really communicating and looked so much better. He must be getting great pain medicine.

"David, I have some money. Go buy me a pair of jeans and shirt, I'll pay you back."

"Okay Joe, I'll go as soon as the stores open. What size do you need?"

"How do I know, haven't bought anything for two years."

"Joe I think you need a size medium shirt and a maybe a skirt. How can you get pants up over that cast?" I was kidding Joe. He did stop to think about the problem.

"You know, David, get what I can wear, maybe two sets of gym clothes, socks and shoes, or maybe just a shoe. No, don't get shoes yet." Joe had lightened up some.

"Hey, Joe, that's good. Ask the nurse when she thinks the doctor will be in. I'll go talk to someone in the business office. When David gets back we'll discuss your needs and make some arrangements. We'll take you home but only if you tell us about Bear and your family."

On my way to the front desk of the hospital, I met Mattie, the EMT that had assisted with Joe's rescue from the well. She was on her way to see Joe. So I only spoke and said I would be back shortly. Is she the reason Joe is smiling today? He sure is different, looks different, acts different, and sounds much more positive.

ಹೇಸ

Mrs. Smith, the person responsible for finances, was very helpful. We discussed Joe's problem and she agreed to contact the Veterans Administration about his status as a disabled veteran and try to get them to pay for his care.

"This was an emergency, not something that would wait for him to go to a VA hospital" she said.

I'll try to get them to pay for everything including the doctor."

Elizabeth Oliver Wooten

Joe had given them his address and said that he was a veteran of Vietnam. He had been treated at the Veteran's Administration Hospital in Florence, Alabama.

"I'll make sure you get his account number and identification number. Is there anything else you need?"

"Just have him call me with that as soon as he can. Here's my card with the hospital phone number."

I assured her that the charges would be paid and left her office. We needed some time to discuss this with Joe. I was hoping the Veteran Administration would cover most of the charges.

When I got back to the room, Mattie was leaving. She reminded Joe to get a phone and call her with the number. She said they needed to check on him daily.

"Joe, we came in your pickup it's bigger than David's. I hope that leg cast will fit in. You need to try walking with crutches or will you need a wheel chair? I see you are ready to get up and go."

"I'm waiting for some clothes," Joe answered.

The doctor arrived and began checking Joe's record and medications. His vital signs were all good. Joe told him the leg and foot did hurt but that if he could have pain pills he would be okay. The doctor's instructions were specific.

"Mr. Burns, do not put any weight on that leg for three weeks. You can try crutches, but I think a wheel chair is best. You need to keep the leg elevated and straight. I'll give you a prescription for pain; do not take more than prescribed." The doctor continued his instructions. "I want to check your hand in about five days; call my office for an appointment. The nurse will tell you how to care for the hand. If it looks red and more swollen you need to call me and come in sooner." He asked Joe if he had any questions.

"Are you letting me go today and where can we get a wheel chair?"

"Yes, you can go. I'll see you next week."

The nurse was standing by, and began to fill Joe in on the care of his injured hand. She told us where we could rent a wheel chair.

"Joe, the doctor is signing your release and you can go soon. Please listen!" She asked about his pain and did he eat his breakfast. The nurse explained. "It's very important that you have food every time you take these pills."

What the nurse said about food made me realize that I needed to buy food for Joe's house.

David had returned with clothes, including underwear and socks. "Joe, this is not going to be easy for you. We need to go rent the chair, go get your prescription, and then pick up some food before we put you in the truck. The nurse will help you get your new clothes on and see how well you can manage in their wheel chair. I don't think you have been able to get yourself to the bathroom yet. Learn how to do these necessary things while we are getting the supplies."

"Do I need to get bandages to dress his hand?" I asked the nurse.

She answered quickly. "We'll give him the supplies he needs for that and show him how. I'll work with him on how to use his other foot and body, not putting any weight on his bad leg. He will need help, because the cast is heavy. The medicine may make him unsteady and I'm afraid he might fall."

She was concerned about his care and so was I. Who would come help him?

~~

We had accomplished all the tasks and picked up Joe at the hospital. He was able to get in the pickup from the wheel chair and the leg was straight. He did ask us to stop and see about getting a phone. That was no problem since he had a credit card that had been left in his truck. They came out to Joe and got the information they needed and then demonstrated the phone. He now had a phone number to go with his Route 2, Veeny, Alabama address.

On the way back to Norman's I began immediately to ask Joe about his house, his family, about Bear.

"Where do you live? Who is Bear?"

"My house is about seven miles from Norman's, out Highway 19 toward Clark County. Bear is my watchdog; he's a chocolate brown Lab. He is also my best friend and he loves me. I leave him on a chain with water, near the house and a shade tree. I am never gone at night. I sure hope he's all right," Joe was really talking.

"We'll be there soon. Do you have food for him? I didn't know to buy dog food." I asked.

"Joe, tell us about your family or anyone who can stay with you a few days." David interrupted.

"I have food for Bear, not much for me. My wife left. We don't have kids. I have a sister who lives in Arkansas. She has three kids and I don't think she can come. I will call her and tell her about this accident. My buddies are not really friends that will help. I think Bear and I can manage."

When we stopped to get David's pickup, Norman rushed out to see how Joe was. He also told us the sheriff was looking for us.

"I explained where you were and told him that he could find you at your motor home later today. I told him you were not planning on leaving. Is that the truth?" Norman asked.

David assured him, "Yes, we'll be around. It may take a while to get Joe settled. If the Sheriff needs us, tell him to come there or to the motor home in a couple of hours."

I followed David and Joe. About six miles out Highway 19 we turned off to the right on a much smaller road. It was paved but narrow. I remembered that road very well. My sister and I had walked it before. Once when Daddy was escaping the farm we followed him and caught up with him about here. We all three then walked the seven miles to Papaw's house.

"Oh my, where are we headed?" As I talked to myself, I wondered if Joe lived in the big old house my family had once lived in for two years. I was sure that I was going to see that place again.

When the trucks were parked, I rushed to tell David and Joe how excited I was to see this house.

"Joe, do you own this?" was my first question. "I can't believe this old house is still standing. I was only seven when we lived here and I thought it would be long gone before now."

The basic house make of logs was still good. The long porch across the front had been rebuilt, but it was still high off the ground. Seven wide steps led up to the porch and front door.

Elizabeth Oliver Wooten

"What do you mean you lived here? Slow down and let us catch up." David quizzed me.

"Oh, David, you remember I told you about us living with Mother and Daddy and farming two seasons. This is the place, the big barn was out there. We had two horses that Daddy plowed with. He would hook them to the wagon and we took everything, his tools, and our lunch and went on down the big hill to work in the bottom along the creek. That's where I cut the gash out of my knee, in the corn patch. I remember crying a lot. It should have had stitches, and then I wouldn't have this scar. See it's higher up now, my leg grew since then. I think we all hated farming and this place.

"I remember when the law came and searched the house. Daddy was drunk. I guess they were looking for moonshine. Mother had gallon jugs of blackberry juice. She finally convinced them they were not for wine.

"Oliver, my brother was born in January of the second year. It was 1943 during World War II. After we moved from here Mother and Daddy left all three of us with Memaw and Papaw again. They worked in Mobile, Alabama building ships for the war for the next two years. I remember my sister taking Oliver and me to visit them. We rode a bus and it was very hot. We enjoyed seeing our parents. Seashells that I had never seen before were used as gravel on the streets. I thought that was terrible waste of those beautiful shells. I guess we saw the ocean; I don't remember it. We have pictures of Oliver, who was two, Mae, and me taken in Mobile.

"Okay, I know I'm rambling with my memories, but I am happy to be here. Joe, tell us why you live here." I asked again.

Joe tried to explain everything in one sentence. "My wife was born in this area and like you, she wanted to live here. We had plans to restore the house, the barn and raise horses here. We bought it about seven years ago. Did this much before she left. I haven't done much more, but I will."

David had unleashed Bear and he was trying to jump in the truck with Joe. It looked like Bear did love Joe. He was a big dog, but very friendly with us. I thought he could really scare strangers and would probably bite them. Joe had trained him to protect the place.

David had been looking around and finally said what he was thinking. "Joe, how do you think you can get in that house?"

"The kitchen door is much lower to the ground; I can sit on the steps and pull myself up without standing. Then if you put the chair inside and help me to get in it, I think I can manage everything else." Joe had been figuring it all out.

My next question was "Where do you get your water?" Not from the spring like we did."

"It does come from that spring; we have a pump in it and a bathroom in the house." Joe quickly added, "Oh, darn, darn—the pump isn't working right now. I forgot about that. I've been getting water in my camper and using that for a week now."

"Well, now, do we put your groceries in the house or in your camper?" I asked.

David had gone to feed Bear and didn't hear about not having water in the house. When he got back to the truck I asked him to take a walk with me to see the spring. He wanted to get Joe settled first.

I said "Joe will be fine here for a little longer, he has Bear to talk to."

I explained to David on our way to see the spring. We really had to figure out what to do. Joe didn't have anyone to help him. He didn't have water in the house. The camper probably wasn't big enough for the wheel chair, Joe, and Bear.

David was slow to answer. "Could we get the pump fixed, I don't think Joe can take care of himself alone. Jane, you need to think of something!"

"Give me a minute. Do you think I can fix everything? I'm glad the food is in an ice chest this may take me three minutes to come up with something. We agreed we would take care of him until he's on his feet again. That's at least three weeks. We don't want to come here every day for three weeks so I guess we take him home with us."

David exploded, "We don't have room for him. What do you mean suggesting that?"

"Wait, I have it! We take his camper and put it near ours. It will be perfect, Bear can be the watchdog. I think we need one. You can watch and help Joe and I can write. Let's go tell Bear and Joe."

David thought about it and looked surprised that I had a solution. He got back to the truck, asked Joe if we could hook his truck to the camper, and move it.

Joe said "Sure, I take it to get water once a week." David explained to Joe what I had in mind. He didn't ask him; he just told Joe that's what we had to do. He went to look at the camper.

I asked Joe if he was in pain and was he getting hungry. I was. I had enough food to make us a snack so Joe could have another pain pill. He was quiet thinking about how this idea was going to work.

He finally said, "I think that will work out fine. Can Bear go with us? We need to go by town and fill my water tank. I can probably use the chair in there and everything is very handy."

"Yes, Bear can go with us. We need a watchdog. What do I need to get from the house besides Bear's food? I'll get his chain and leash."

"I have a lot of stuff in the camper and I have new clothes and a phone." Joe told me. "Just get Bear's stuff."

David, Joe, and I ate from the food I had bought. Joe took his medicine. I took a quick look in the camper and wondered about power. It had a stove and refrigerator; maybe they worked off propane like ours.

As soon as he could manage, David had the camper and truck hooked together and was ready to go. I locked the door to the house and followed them again.

They stopped in Veeny to fill the camper's water tank. I headed home to our motor home that didn't have much water. When they arrived, I directed David on parking the camper near ours. As soon as it was stabilized, we managed to get Joe inside his camper and on his bed. The wheel chair would go from door to sofa, to kitchen, to bath, and to bed. Joe was ready to rest; so were we.

8

The next morning we all were feeling much better. Joe said he slept well. He was strong enough to move from bed to chair and take care of himself. He thought the camper was just what he needed. I made sure he had eaten breakfast. David and I were restless. The Sheriff had not showed up yesterday. We wondered what he wanted. He had already told us not to leave. We would like to hear his report on the bones.

We decided to take a walk.

David asked, "Will Joe be alright by himself?"

"Oh, we both have phones. Let's get his number and we'll try them out. He can call us if he needs us to come back."

We got our walking boots on and started our walk by going through the barn first. I stopped and climbed the ladder while David watched to see if it would fall. It didn't so he followed me up into the hayloft. Nothing much there, a little old hay and dirt. Then we looked toward the end of the loft, it had a window, and we saw something unusual. There in the loft were about three dozen pots and cans filled with dirt and dead plants.

"Who in the world would try to grow something up here? Looks like it didn't work, they must have forgotten to water them."

David finally spoke, "I think they tried to grow marijuana."

"Who would do that? Oh my gosh, I bet that man I thought was a tree was trying to get that out of here. This place has been deserted so long no telling what has happened here. Maybe even murder!"

David said, "Let's go, we need a long walk."

We headed for the old pigpen, to check for water. We didn't find any there so we went on to the branch. The line of heavy brush and trees showed us where it had been and it was still there almost on our property line. This was late summer and the thin stream of water was not moving. It was not going to be possible to get water from that little trickle.

We decided to keep going. Up the hill and through the woods, we were now on somebody else's land. We both recalled that we had done this when we were dating. We would go from Memaw's house to his home. The old road went past what was now a pine timber growth. At one time, it had been cleared land that was used for growing cotton.

The little cemetery that we always looked at was just in the edge of the growth of old trees. I wanted to check it for names and the number of graves I had found listed. We found the old stones and counted the six graves. Three of them had markers with names and dates. I read them, trying to remember each one, so I could check my list. I wished I had brought it with me.

David and I both noticed something very odd. There were two new graves. They had been covered with leaves, and were level not a mound, as if somebody didn't want them found.

"I think we better go on to George's house and ask him. This is land your brothers still own isn't it?" We had been enjoying our trek through the woods. Now I felt as if something was wrong.

George and Beth were home. They were surprised that we came from the hillside behind their house, but welcomed us in and asked what we doing there. David explained what we were doing and quickly asked about the graves. They had no idea what could be buried there, said they would ask their son. He lived nearby in the house David's family had lived in for many years.

George had heard about the accident and the bones they found in our well. He wanted to know how Joe was and what the Sheriff had found out.

David explained what we had done and how well Joe was cooperating, and how he looked now. "The Sheriff hasn't been back, although he was looking for us yesterday."

George and Beth agreed to drive us back. We talked about our water problem on the way back. George said that the town would put a water meter near the road where the main water line was. We could let him know if we decided to put in a temporary pipe or permanent one the rest of the distance to the house.

"Please have the meter installed in our name. We need to have a place to fill our tanks. I just don't know how long we will be here." David said.

Joe and Bear were fine. Joe had been wondering where we were. I had forgotten to call him. He also seemed glad to have visitors. They noticed the change in Joe. I still wondered if the pain medicine was making him talkative. Joe showed them his phone and gave George his number in case he could help him when he got better. He also said he called Mattie and they had made an appointment with the doctor for next Wednesday afternoon.

After George and Beth left, David and I discussed what we had found in the barn and the new graves. We decided not to tell Joe. I still had my doubts about him. I knew he drank and possibly used drugs. We didn't know much about his recent activities. I was glad he had not asked for beer or alcohol, maybe because he was taking drugs. David decided he would tell the Sheriff about the pots in the barn and the possible graves.

David and I also talked about what we should do next. I wanted to be left alone to write but with David and Joe there I knew that was not going to happen. We agreed that it was time to go check on everything at home. It was a three-hour drive back to Georgia where we had lived for the last fifteen years. David didn't think I could be left here with only Bear and a very crippled man. He mentioned that we were not supposed to leave. I thought about that and agreed that I should go. I could ask Jewel, my cousin, to go with me. If we left Sunday and returned on Wednesday, nobody would miss me, since he and Joe were still here.

ಆ~ಲ

I found Jewel at home when I went to ask her about going with me to Georgia.

"Yes, I would love to do that. When do you want to go?"

"Sunday after church. Pack your bag and bring it to church with you. Since we live near there we can get started sooner. David and I will be at church on Sunday. Would you please leave your car with David? I plan to drive his pickup and he would be left without a vehicle except Joe's truck. I guess Joe isn't going anywhere in his yet. He has a doctor's appointment Wednesday. David would like me to be back by then."

"That's a short visit, but that's fine. Sure, David can use my car. I want to see two old friends while I'm there. I'll call them before I leave. Who is Joe?" Jewel replied.

"Joe is a friend that has a broken leg. He has his camper near our motor home at the old home place. I'll tell you about it later."

9

David and I decided it was time to visit the church I had attended as a child and into my teen years. His parents attended this same Baptist church for many years. Two of his brothers and their wives still attend there. Today we dressed in our best clothes and arrived early in our pickup truck. We first went to the cemetery near the church where David's parents were buried. We placed a wild flower bouquet between their graves. Jewel's husband, Jay, was buried here. His grave had a military marker, since he had served in the Army. Several other markers had names of friends we had known in the past. We knew that some people we remembered had passed on to their heavenly home. It was going to be exciting to see some faces from our past that still attended church here. It would be interesting to see the changes made to the church. The church we remembered was a one room wood building, with a large tree near the entrance. The old wood building was gone and so was the tree. The church building had been replaced with a much larger modern building with air conditioning.

When I attended there as a child the tree was the only place we could play. There was no playground and not much level ground. In the summer, a lady, elderly to us, would take the children outside under the tree to read us Bible stories. That was my first teaching about Jesus. It took me another twelve years to fully understand the love Jesus has for us all. At age fifteen I believed completely all the stories and teachings Jesus taught his disciples. I accepted Him as my Lord and Savior on a hot August day at the altar of this little church. I was baptized in a cold creek nearby.

David attended this church as a teenager, partly because I did. He also became a member here when he was eighteen. His parents or some of his family have been sustaining members ever since.

Back then revival services were held every summer after the crops were 'laid by'. That means the fields had been planted and worked to kill the grass, briars, and weeds that grew in the cotton and corn rows. After the last plowing and fertilizing, the corn and cotton were left to grow and the family had a break from working in the fields. There were vegetables in the gardens that had to be picked, canned, dried, or cooked for dinner. The temperature would be in the nineties and no rain. The prayers were for rain at the right time and not during harvest. Church leaders invited a visiting evangelist to preach during the revival. Members and visitors came each evening and again at eleven in the morning. This revival was an outreach to the community and a social time for all that came. Most of the time a few people were 'saved'; they confessed their sins to the Lord and committed their life to do His will. After baptism by immersion, they became members of the church.

The preacher and evangelist and his family were invited to a different member's home for the noon meal. The wives cooked the fresh vegetables from their gardens, had fried chicken from their flock, and always, baked pies and cakes. We certainly enjoyed these special meals, even if we had to help prepare the food. They tried to do the cooking early in the morning so the kitchen and house could cool off before the guest came. None of us had air conditioning and August was very hot.

This Sunday morning lots of people began to arrive. Some we had seen recently, like the relatives, others were glad we came and made us feel like we had come home. Many of them knew us but we could only guess who they were and not admit we had forgotten them. Before the services was a social time. We had wondered if we would be accepted as part of them or made to feel like visitors. The people did make us feel welcome, but another couple that was visiting for the first time that day was not included in the visiting. The man was very friendly and introduced his wife as Sally. I did not hear their last name. The pastor was very friendly to the other new couple and us. It had been a very long time since I attended here and perhaps they didn't trust strangers, not even us.

The service was very different from the ones at our home church. It began after the Sunday school classes were finished and everyone had assembled in the sanctuary. It began with requests for prayer for anyone sick, bereaved, hurt, betrayed, or deserted by their spouse. The request could be for anyone in this community, or for relatives or anyone they knew anywhere, and for the leaders of our country. The prayer was led by one of the deacons. Songbooks were opened and ladies went to the piano and organ. Since they had no elected song leader, the deacon asked for anyone who would come to the front and direct a song of their choice. Several people did, other members suggested songs to sing. This was so different from our church; I begin to wonder what next.

Elizabeth Oliver Wooten

The minister preached a familiar sermon on salvation and the danger of not obeying the commands of Jesus. That reminded me of Preacher Burns, Joe's uncle that I had promised to tell Joe about. I needed to find a good time to talk to Joe about Preacher Burns.

"Are you keeping the Ten Commandments? Have you broken one today?" Brother Burns asked these questions every time we saw him. I needed to know Joe's thoughts on these questions.

"David, how did you like the service?" was my first questions as we drove the three miles home.

"I liked it fine. Did you?"

He seemed to be waiting for my complaints, so I said "Fine. Did you know those people? I remember only two ladies about my age, and can't remember their names. I have never met their husbands and they didn't introduce them."

David replied. "I only know my brothers and wives, also Jewel, and one deacon."

"I doubt if we will see any of them in our Square Dance class," I added.

Jewel followed us home. Joe was sitting outside when we got there. I had to find something for our lunch. I sure did wish for some of those vegetables and fried chicken I remembered. It was too late in the summer to plant any. Maybe we could find a farmer's market next week, or visit somebody with a vegetable garden and beg for some home grown food.

10

It was a hot Sunday afternoon when Jewel and I left. We had eaten sandwiches in our motor home after church. Jewel and Joe, both very friendly, had gotten acquainted quickly. Later she did ask questions about him that I couldn't answer.

"He is related to Preacher Burns. No, I don't know who his wife was," I told her.

Since it was an hour later in Georgia, we needed to drive without stopping if possible. I wanted to get home and attend church at six that evening. I didn't want our friends to forget us. We coveted their prayers and I could pay our tithes for this month.

"Your church seems to be doing well in attendance and finances." Who was the couple visiting today?"

"I don't remember seeing them before and don't know who they are." Jewel answered.

Jewel loved to talk. I had not been around her very often for the last five years. She talked about her family and what her three children and their children were doing. She told me about her life since her husband had died four years ago. Jay, her husband had cancer and only lived a year after it was found. He was buried in the church cemetery and we had visited his grave before services began. One of her sons was Denny, the builder that I had contacted for advice on the old house.

Elizabeth Oliver Wooten

I interrupted her to say, "Denny promised to come one day this week and look at the house. I know he's busy right now but we need his opinion of what we can save of our old home place."

"I think you two are crazy to even try to fix that old house," was Jewel's reply.

We were getting near the town my brother lived in. I told her we could stop to see them on our way back. I asked if she had called, Mae, my sister who lived in Rowling where we lived. Jewel said she had, and planned to stay at her house. Jewel asked if I wanted to meet her and the friends for lunch on Tuesday. I told her I couldn't meet them this time. It really would take me two days to get our mail and newspapers to take back to David, get our medicines refilled, and go see our daughter and her family in Atlanta. Today I had just enough time to go by home and then to church, after I dropped her off at Mae's house. I told them I would be back Wednesday morning, have breakfast with them, and see Mae's grandkids before they went to school. Her youngest son, and his family, lived near her and her husband. Then we could head back to Alabama.

I decided that all my family needed to know was about the well and accident. Jewel would tell about Joe. Maybe she didn't know about the bones. I certainly didn't plan on mentioning that to anybody except my brother.

❧

Most everything went as planned. I did turn in a temporary change of address to have our mail sent to P.O. Box 5, Veeny, Alabama 59580. I hoped we could rent that post office box when I got back there. I also asked the newspaper office to send our daily paper to that address. I figured if we got our mail I could make payments and not have to be back at any special time. Neither David nor I had any important medical appointments scheduled. My kids were all well and interested in what David and I had been doing. I told them we were having a great time seeing relatives and explained how bad the house was. I didn't tell much else. I promised my daughter that I would call her more often.

I tried to explain, "No, we don't know what we will be doing to the house, and don't know how long we will be there."

৵৵

Early Wednesday morning, after picking up Jewel and saying bye to my sister's family, we were on our way back to Alabama. Jewel had enjoyed the visit. The weather was perfect that morning. We could see white clouds floating over the top of the mountains and a blue sky that didn't look like rain. The foothills of the Appalachian Mountains surrounded the area of Georgia we called home. I loved seeing them in the distance. It was really the dry part of summer. Another month or two and we would have fall weather. I wondered if we would be back home before the coldest weather arrived.

I had called Oliver and they were at home. He and his wife always had either children or grandchildren at their house. My brother worked as an ABC Agent for the state of Alabama and I had questions for him. ABC is the Alcohol and Beverage Control Department. That department also does drug enforcement in Alabama.

I realized his wife and Jewel were listening as I talked to Oliver, no secrets from them. The accident, the bones in the well, the pots in the barn loft, and two possible graves nearby had certainly made our task of restoring the home place an interesting project. Oliver told me that the area we were in was most certainly a haven for drug dealers and users. About a year ago, a group of agents including him had visited the area we were living in. They arrested about a dozen people but could not connect any of them to the big distribution ring they thought was in the area. None of those arrested would talk, they just had to charge them with possession of illegal drugs, and some of them were out on bail waiting for a trial. His advice was for us to get out. They were dangerous and probably had killed to keep certain people from talking.

"Oh boy, what next? The Sheriff has told us not to leave. He must know we have nothing to do with this, but we do own the property, so maybe he can stop us. Besides, we have to get Joe Burns well enough to return to his farm. He broke his leg helping with the well. I am still deciding what he may know. We have him, his camper, and Bear as a watchdog, at the home place. David wants me back this afternoon so we have to get going."

Jewel had other things to tell me on our drive back to Veeny. She first told about the family that rented our house. That was more than five years ago when she and her husband still lived in our community. It seemed that besides the elderly couple and a disabled daughter there was a younger son that lived with them. She and others thought the son was selling drugs. He looked and acted like he was using drugs. His driving was dangerous and his friends hung out there. None of them seemed to have a job. Their name was Toler; she thought the son's name was Petro or something like that. No, she didn't think they were Hispanics.

When I asked, Jewel said, "Yes, I'll talk to the Sheriff. Tell him to call and he can stop by my house if he wants to. I think the son was arrested so he can get his name. I have no idea where the family is now."

She next talked about a family named Sanderson. She tried to describe the three sons that had gone to school with us. I almost remembered them.

"I really don't remember. Tell me, who are the Sandersons?"

"They lived, and still do, down below Veeny near the Mississippi State line. There were three of the boys in school with us. They had unusual names and were kind of homely looking."

"Oh, yes I do. Their names were, or we called them, something like Rabbit or Squirrel."

"Yes, that's the ones I'm talking about. Well, two of them have kept the home place and restored it as a kind of lodge. Real nice, I hear, for the hunting and drinking crowd. The older one that we called Squirrel is now know as Squire Sanderson. He built a real big house, an estate really; barns, white fences with beautiful gates. Pastures are all over those hills that had been in trees and farmland. I think he has horses and cattle."

"Where did he build that? I only remember where they lived near the road."

"On their property, back on a pretty hill. I've seen it in passing. Well, the talk is that they are somehow messing with drugs to have the money to do those things. Maybe the sheriff needs to investigate them."

"What other business or work do they do to explain having money? I doubt if raising cattle on those hills makes much profit. The lodge and hunters don't sound like big money."

"Squire's family works at some things. They have a big antique store in Jarmore—you need to go there. They say it's huge and fixed up very different."

"I'd like to do that, maybe next week. Would you go with me?"

"Sure, I'll call you or come over to the house."

≈≪

David called when we were about an hour away. "Joe and I are going on to Blue Pond. We want a good meal for a change. Then we'll see the doctor."

"Are you using Jewel's car?"

"No, we are in Joe's truck."

"I'll take her to get her car first so she can go home. We are tired. Call me back if you need me to come to Blue Pond."

"I think we can do this. I'll buy food before we come back. See you later. I think Bear knows you. He is chained. You have a key to the motor home on the truck keys."

≈≪

The doctor was pleased with how well Joe's hand was healing. He had showed him how to exercise it, and said Joe could probably use it soon. It should be good as new in a couple more weeks.

David said, "I've had to fix all of our meals. I'm sure glad you're back. One day, when I went to Norman's to get our dinner, we had visitors."

"Who? Did the sheriff come back?"

"They didn't announce who they were. Joe was in his camper and his truck was parked behind it. We believe they thought no one was here. They had started to drive to the barn but left in a hurry when Bear got near their pickup. Joe didn't come out of the camper. He told me later that he thought he recognized the driver. He thinks they were trying to destroy the pots and any evidence that they had ever been here."

David continued, "The Sheriff was back. The bones from the well are human. He said they were possibly a young to middle age man who was killed before he was dumped in our well. It will be weeks before they have an official cause of death. He thinks it might be a homicide."

"What, he thinks it might be a homicide? Or maybe he thinks the man jumped in our well and stayed there until he died."

David didn't try to answer me.

"The Sheriff took some of the pots. He plans to check out the little graveyard after he gets permission from the owners of the land. His last words to us were, "*Don't you leave, we need more information on this.*" I guess He thinks we know who put the bones in our well."

I told David about our trip, the friends I saw, and what I did. "We stopped to see Oliver on our way back. He wants us to get out of here. He warned me about the illegal drug traffic in this area. The State Agents have been investigating it, but haven't found out who they are. He thinks any deaths or murders are related to drugs. I also told David what Jewel said. "The sheriff needs to talk to Jewel. She knows about the last people that lived here, about five years ago. She thinks their son was using or probably selling drugs. He had lots of visitors. She knows the sheriff and said tell him to call her."

"I'll call the Sheriff, and give him that information. Does she know their names?"

"Sure, everybody around here knows everybody's name. Did Denny come to look at the house? Since we have to stay here we need something to keep us busy."

"He is coming Friday morning. Joe wants to hear what he thinks. Joe plans to work for us so he can pay his doctor," David said.

11

Jewel showed up Saturday morning to go antiquing. She thought the weekend was the time to shop. I was willing and explained to David what we had planned.

"Joe and David, would you like to go with us?"

"No!" David assured us. "Joe and I have things to do here, or at least we have to plan what we are going to do. You two can take my pickup but Jane better not buy anything yet."

"Okay, we'll take your truck; Jewel might want to buy some antiques. We'll be gone most of the day. Joe, please watch David; he gets hurt often. Since your phone works here, you can call me or 911 if he does get injured."

After we got started in the truck, I told Jewel that Denny had come to check over the house. His suggestion was to tear away everything but the original two rooms. Even the kitchen area needed to go. Then we could take another look. That would leave two large rooms; one of those has the fireplace. Of course, the well is going to be covered or filled in later. It probably won't look like the home we remember. It will give David and Joe something to do for the next few weeks. It looks like we will be here for a while.

We took a less direct route to Jarmore, Alabama. I wanted to drive past the Squire Sanderson Estate. Jewel knew the way from there to the antique place. The estate was exactly like she had described it. I knew it took over a million dollars to build that beautiful house and landscape the grounds that surround it. The decorative, wrought iron gates told me an excellent designer and architect had planned this place. We both wondered where they could have gotten that much money. I suspected drugs were involved.

The Jarmore Antique House was in an old cotton warehouse. I could still recognize the old building, but the change inside was dramatic, interesting, and expensive. There were several cars and trucks in the parking lot. Some were being loaded with good-looking furniture. Inside, about a dozen people were looking at other pieces. Jewel and I went in and shopped for a while. I became so interested in the stuff I saw that I wanted to talk to the owners. The pieces were so different, a large phone booth, an entire mahogany bar setup that was huge, and other very big furniture pieces and lots of unusual chests. None of this was going to enhance our old home, but I was curious.

A very attractive lady came out of a corner office. I stopped her with a question and then introduced myself. She was nice, answered my question, and seemed willing to talk. I explained that I had studied interior design and was interested in some of the pieces. I asked where they had purchased them.

"We go to auctions, we travel abroad, some of the pieces are from Italy and some from Germany. Sometimes we go to Chicago or New York and buy at their antique stores. What can I help you with?"

"I didn't get your name?'

"I'm Betty Sue Sanderson, we own this place. We love to remodel these old buildings and put new businesses in them."

"That's wonderful, that's what we like to do. Are you familiar with the little town of Veeny?"

"Oh yes, why do you ask?"

"We are living in that area now and I would love to see that little town restored to the way it was forty years ago. Maybe put shops and tearooms, or restaurants in some of those old buildings. They are still sound. If you and your people are interested and would help, I think we might be able to do it."

Betty Sue told me they would talk about it and if that was something their company would consider, she would get in touch. I gave her my phone number. Jewel gave me a signal that it was time to go find some lunch. We left with a promise that I would come back to Jarmore Antiques in a few weeks.

As soon as we found a small local restaurant and had ordered our lunch, Jewel began the questions.

"When did you start planning to revive Veeny? I didn't know you wanted to do that.

"I didn't know it either. I needed a reason to get to know those Sandersons, that seemed like a good idea. Please don't tell David yet. Let's wait until they contact me, then I'll explain my plan."

We stopped at several other small antique stores. There were a few old pieces that I might need later. Then we headed back home by the shortest route.

David called before we got home. "Joe and I are going to eat at Norman's. Are you two going to be back soon?"

"We're on our way. No, thanks, we won't join you. We'll be at home when you get back."

Elizabeth Oliver Wooten

When we got back to our place, I parked under the one tree near the old house. We were facing the house the way Papaw had parked his pickup. Jewel and I sat talking about the way it looked when we lived there.

Jewel described the way it looked when she first remembered it. "The porch went across the front of the main room. The door to the dining area, a part of the kitchen add-on, was on the front also."

"I did not like eating in that room, it was always dark. It only has one small window. I remember the porch. Didn't it have a large seat made from the headboard of a bed? Memaw didn't like it; she fussed until it was moved." I added to her memories. "I also remember being in the bed sick, near the front window that looked out on the porch. I think I had the measles."

I asked Jewel about when the addition was put on the front. "That room was added after I came here to live with you all. Mother died the year before when I was twelve."

"Oh yes, I do recall that. The truck bringing her furniture broke the bridge."

Jewel began to reminisce about her Mother and Dad, "I wonder where and what I would be today if Mother had lived. I liked where we lived in Georgia. Dad had a good job at the mill but he changed shifts every week and I could not stay by myself. He said I had to live here for a few years. Those few years lasted a long time. I had graduated high school before I left and then I went to Illinois with your Mother. If I had stayed in Georgia, I probably would have married someone else and I might not be a widow today."

"My Mother," Jewel continued, "wanted another child. The baby boy she conceived was partly the cause of her death from kidney disease. She did not agree to them taking the baby early in her pregnancy. In the seventh month of her term, she became so ill that when she went to the hospital they couldn't save her life or the infant. Mother was only thirty-five years old when she died."

Our reminiscing included memories of the death of Granny, our great grandmother, in 1943. I told Jewel, "I remember that she died on the bed in the room with the fireplace, I was in the room to stay warm. It was December and that was the only fireplace. The thing I most remember is that she talked just before she passed. Her hand reached up toward the ceiling and she said very clearly, 'I see angels. Don't you hear them singing?' I also stayed in the room when Mother and Memaw bathed her body and put clean clothes on her. Then the undertaker came and got her. The next day they brought her back to the house in a casket. Neighbors stayed all night or came with food to pay their respect. The funeral was the next day."

Jewel said, "That was two years before Mother died. We were living in Georgia then."

We also talked about Papaw dying in 1948, two years after his only daughter, Jewel's mother, Aunt Sue had died. He had been in bad health several years and had used all of their money for doctor and hospital bills. After his death, Memaw had to accept help from family, friends, and the government. The house and land was paid for and she continued to live here for many years.

I asked Jewel to describe the house in the years she lived there.

She talked about the addition; "The added room took away the porch. A small porch was put on the front; it's gone now. The porch on this side made the way from the well to the kitchen much easier. We drew and used a lot of water from that well. The original well shed was pretty, it just had four posts and the wood shingle roof, there were no walls to it, just a top shelter over the well."

"It's in good shape. I think we can save it. Memaw planted vines on the eastside that shaded the well and made the porch cooler. Memaw really loved her flowers and vegetable garden." I helped describe what we remembered.

"My sister and I were happy to have you live here. It was also a sad time. We girls were glad to have the new room with the nice sofa and chairs from your home in it," I told her, "Everything changes with time. You must come back and see what it looks like when David and Joe get it torn apart. We'll have to decide what to do with the house, or what's left of it."

Jewel had her doubts. She left soon after our talk.

When David and Joe returned we talked about what had happened. The consensus was that we might or might not hear from the sheriff next week.

David said. "What we do next depends on what he reports."

12

Fred J. Moore, Sheriff of Benjamin County, returned on Wednesday of the next week. David and Joe were glad to see him. They wanted to know what he had done and what he had learned. I looked at this man and didn't remember him from the day Joe was hurt. He had dark hair, he was a pound shy of being fat, and he wore a cowboy style hat, boots, and jeans. Not handsome, but nice looking and much more friendly than the first time I saw him.

The Sheriff reported on the contents of the pots first. "Those pots did contain dried up marijuana plants. We are trying to get fingerprints from the pots. They had been there a long time and are dirty. They probably won't get any legible prints."

David explained what we had learned, "The people that lived here last may have had a drug problem. Jewel Ray can tell you a little more about them. She said call or come by her house. Do you know her and where she lives? Jane can give you her phone number."

"I'll certainly talk to her. I knew her husband and I do know where she lives."

Sheriff Moore continued his report, "I've talked to the funeral directors all around this area and none of them have buried anybody in that cemetery. They don't even know where it is. I've come to ask the owners of that land for permission to dig there. Do you know where they live and can you show me the place?"

David said, "Yes, I know. My brother, Rory Cotton, owns the land. I'll go with you. I'll call Rory to meet us there. Do you need shovels?"

"No, I have shovels and two deputies waiting at Norman's Café. They are ready to do the digging. How many brothers do you have? I have met George Cotton."

Just three, George is my older brother, and then Rory, then me, and Lee came last.

ॐ∽ॐ

After the Sheriff and David left, I had a chance to talk to Joe. He had a chair outside in the shade of his camper and managed quite easily to move from his steps to it. I got two tall glasses of ice tea and joined him. It was another hot dry day. I still had questions for Joe but decided to talk about his Uncle first.

"Joe, I promised to tell about your uncle, Preacher Burns. I believe you said he was your dad's brother. Are your parents living? I haven't heard you mention them."

"They died a long time ago. I was in my late teens when Dad died and Mom only lived two more years." I think that Uncle died before Daddy. He didn't come to either funeral."

"Preacher Bill Burns and his wife, Carrie, lived on this road. I think they were only about one-half mile from Veeny. He would walk to town, as long as he was able, and sit on the porch or steps of one of the stores. He asked everybody if they were keeping the commandments. I remember him doing that when I was too young to know what he was talking about. He also wanted to pray for anybody who would kneel with him. Later when we were older and would walk to town, we tried to get past his house without him seeing us. If he did, we always had to answer his questions. Many times, we would kneel by the side of the road and he would pray for us. It was a nuisance to us then, now I realize that he was being faithful to God's commandment '…To love thy neighbor as thy self…and to tell others of God's love.' That's what we all should do.

"Preacher Burns died about ten years before his wife, Carrie. She found him dead in bed; he had died in his sleep. What a peaceful way to go. Jewel told me Mrs. Burns was very lonely after he died. They had not been attending a church, so she didn't have many friends. Joe, are you a Christian?"

"My folks were and they took me to church until I was about twelve. I know what the Ten Commandments say. I try to obey most of them."

"That's not what being a Christian is about. Among other things, you have to confess your sins to God. Believe Jesus is the Son of God and turn your life around. We'll talk about that later if you'll listen. Maybe you can go to church with us. The people there are very friendly. "Tell me a little more about yourself, Joe. Don't answer if I get too nosy." How long were you in Vietnam?"

"I joined the Army when I was nineteen. I really didn't have a home, wasn't married, didn't have a job, and didn't even have a girl friend. I was in that hell of a war for three years before I was injured. It took me a long time to forget or simply not remember what I saw there. The VA doctor gave me medication for a long time. I don't usually talk about that time. I'm well now."

"Did you get in touch with your sister?"

Elizabeth Oliver Wooten

"I called her, now she calls me most every day." She wants me to come visit them as soon as I'm able. I really want to help David as soon as I can. David sure is a nice guy. I really like him."

"I agree. I'm lucky to have such a good husband. I did train him, so I should get some of the credit for that. Did you know we were married when he was nineteen and I was only sixteen? We have two daughters and four grandsons, two from each daughter. They both have very nice husbands."

"David told me most of that. I haven't told him about my life, I don't think he would approve of what I've been doing lately."

"One more question, tell me about the men that were here the other day."

"I'm not sure about who they are. I was inside and did write down the license number. I think the driver might be one of the men who sold me drugs. I was afraid to tell the Sheriff. He would start questioning me."

"I think you will have to tell him what you know. You haven't done anything illegal, have you?"

"No, I don't think I have," Joe spoke sharply. "Is using illegal drugs instead of pills a crime?"

When David got back, he had more bad news.

"After I called Rory and explained he met us at George's house. Rory readily gave them permission to dig in the graveyard. We took George's jeep and Fred and the deputies followed us to the tiny graveyard. The road started from our old home and was in pretty good shape. The people who cut the pine timber a few years back had used it.

"David, please tell us what they found," I impatiently asked.

"Two more bodies!"

"Oh, my God, what next?"

"The Sheriff has called the county coroner to come and bring two body bags. The deputies, Shane and Bubba, are staying with the graves. Sheriff Moore is waiting at Norman's to show the coroner where they are. I hope he doesn't mention what they found. Norman will probably see the coroner's vehicle and figure out what's happening. George, Rory, and probably all the others are watching by now."

"Maybe I better tell you and Joe the details before we get lunch," David continued. "When we got there, it was easy to find the soft ground under the leaves, Bubba started to dig in one place and Shane in the other. They had to go about two feet down. Bubba found clothing first and then the body of a man. Shane hit something; rocks had been placed over that body, and found a man's body that was more decomposed than the other one. That's when Fred stopped them. He used tape to mark off the crime scene.

"Before I left the Sheriff warned me again. *"Don't you leave town!"*

"Oh, my Lordy, Lordy, as Memaw would say, what have the Indians done now." was all I could think of. "Of course she didn't really think there were Indians here or maybe she did. She liked to blame every bad thing that happened on them."

13

The time spent waiting for reports from the Sheriff was put to good use. David started tearing apart the additions to the house. Joe watched and advised. I actually started writing some of the things I had done research on. First, I needed the history of this area where my ancestors settled.

The Alabama Territorial Legislature organized three counties in the northern part of the state on February 4, 1818. Benjamin County although not the size it is today, was one of those. Before 1776, the North Carolina Territory extended to the Mississippi River. This covered what is now the Southern part of Tennessee, and the Northern part of Alabama and Mississippi. Prior to 1819, Pontotoc, Mississippi had a land office for early settlers to buy land. Alabama was admitted to the United States as the twenty-second state on December 14, 1819.

After the 'War of 1812', or 'Creek Indian War', many early settlers came from Virginia, South Carolina, and East Tennessee to make Benjamin County Alabama their home.

Until the 1830's, two areas of Alabama were listed as Indian Lands. For many years after Alabama became a state, the Chickasaw Nation lands abutted Benjamin County on its Western boundary. Their lands extended over into Mississippi. It wasn't until 1832 that the Chickasaws tribe ceded their part of land in Alabama to the State and it was added to Benjamin County.

Elizabeth Oliver Wooten

> *Papaw's grandfather, Henry, came from Lincoln County Tennessee about 1850. He had a wife and several children at that time. They settled in the northern part of this county. He was granted one hundred sixty-four acres just north of here. Four more children were born to them after they arrived here; Papaw father's was the last born in 1862. I believe they were farmers or possibly timber cutters.*
>
> *Papaw was born on January 30, 1881 and Memaw on June 12, 1892. Both of their parents and grandparents probably talked a lot about the Indians in this area. The 'Trail of Tears' which was the removal of the Cherokee Nation to Oklahoma took place in 1836. Many of the Cherokee stayed behind and hid in North Carolina and Georgia Mountains. So it is very likely that many of the Chickasaw Indians were still in Benjamin County, Alabama long after the 1832 treaty was signed. I could now begin to understand why Memaw talked about Indians.*

I had actually written something that might be a part of my book.

I certainly didn't think the person I saw near the edge of our land was an Indian. Somebody has to figure out who that was, who was in the pickup trying to visit our barn, and what happened to these three dead people. Maybe the Sheriff will call in help from the State and Federal Government. I think we need US Marshals, Secret Service, and or DEA (Drug Enforcement Agents), and the State ABC (Alcohol and Beverage Control) to help him and the county law.

Memories and Murders

The articles I had from the archive office were history of Veeny. (I might need this information to share with Betty Sue Sanderson.)

(Information from the Benjamin County News- September 24, 1931)

Years ago the little settlement that is now Veeny, Alabama was known as Jones Crossing. The four principal public roads in that part of Benjamin County intersected here. In 1906, the first general mercantile store was established near the crossroads. In the early 1900's two large lumber companies moved here.
This little town was granted a post office in 1907. About this time, the Illinois Central Railroad Company began the task of putting a track through this part of the county. More businesses were added to the growing village, another general merchandise store, and a firm that dealt in railroad materials, ties, and rail car stock. On February 10, 1908 the first passenger train ran through Veeny over the Illinois Central tracks. According to some of the oldest citizens, the town received its name from a friend of one of the engineers in charge of the railroad work.
The citizens purchased eighty acres of land and the town was incorporated in 1908—thirty-one votes for and none against.

(The following is an article from "Benjamin County Heritage")

Whistles blew, saws hummed—-Veeny was a boomtown in the heyday of the lumber industry. For fifty years, the town and surrounding area were busy producing timber products and hubs for wagons. In the early 1900's two large lumber companies were owned by Nute Massey and J. C. Williams. At both mills, lumber was sawed, planed, and kiln-dried. The White Oak Hub Company was owned by Nute and Ross Massey.

On the north side of the Illinois Central Railroad was a big general store owned by J. W. Rogers. The main part of town was south of the railroad. Fred Massey operated a grocery and merchandise store, which was later owned by Harvey and Ross Weatherford. The Drug Store was owned by J. H. Martin. Charley Massey had Massey Hardware until 1927 when it was bought by L.E. Osborn. E. L. Davis had a market, grocery, and concrete works. W. G. Wright had a large general store. Other stores were owned by Bailey Kennedy, Cleve Shotts, C. R. Baker, Julius Reid, Hosea Scott, Hoyt Davis, and Bill Shotts who also had a gin. William Arthur Barksdale had a store, grist mill, and theatre. There was a barbershop and other businesses. A building supply and hardware store was owned by Carl Massey from 1946 to the 1950's.

Tom McKinney had an early blacksmith shop. Cafes were owned by David Shotts, Henry Brooks and William "Little Boy" Moomaw. Garages were owned by Pony Nelson, Elf Albright, Raymond Orrick, and Stencil Reed.

The Banking Company served the financial needs of the area from 1920 until the 1960's. Burleson Masonic Lodge and Charity Chapter #1 of the Eastern Star are the oldest in the state.

North of the railroad, Ross Massey built the "potato house" for the curing process. In 1949, his son, Fred Henley, used the building to start Massey Seating Company, which he moved to Nashville in 1950. Churches were Baptist, Methodist, and Church of Christ. Dr. J. A. Thorn and Dr. Reid attended to the medical needs of *residents and those of the surrounding area until the early 1940's.*

E. T. Boling and Victor Wood were early principals of The High School, a consolidated school, which was accredited as a senior high in 1926. A manual telephone switchboard was operated by Tommy and Flossie Dedman until about 1950.

Oil and gas exploration near the town from the 1950's until the 80's saw two or more gas wells drilled nearby. Eva Wallace bought oil and gas leases and was instrumental in this endeavor.

Roger and Gloria Brown had a meat processing plant from the 1950's until the 70's. This was built by John Denson of Belmont.

Presently there is a mobile home plant. Thorn and Thorn Lumber Company is located north of the town

Now the town waits for new industry or business pursuits to help it experience good times again.

Yes, I agree Veeny sure needs to experience better times than what I see now. I could remember many of these people. I would be able to identify the buildings that were still standing and what business had been in each. Maybe restoring this town was more doable than restoring my old home. If the Sandersons were interested and had some money to invest, this project would keep us busy a long time.

I recalled many of those shops and stores as they were in the 1940's and 1950's, and many of the people who owned them.

Mrs. Wright had a ladies' goods store. She had fabric, lace, hats, and linens. I remember that she had a big, mean, pet parrot that stayed in the store with her. The only thing I ever heard it say was, "Polly wants cracker." When Mr.

Elizabeth Oliver Wooten

Wright ran the store earlier, it was said they sold undertaking supplies. I still wonder what undertaking supplies were, caskets maybe.

Fred Massey still ran a hardware store, on the road that went to Papaw's house. One day when David was working there, my mother and I passed carrying our suitcases going to visit Memaw. He told Mr. Massey that he was going to marry that girl.

Papaw had a favorite store that he often sat in to talk to the owners and other men. I liked the owners very much. Mr. Shotts let us buy candy on Papaw's credit. Mrs. Shotts taught history at school. I remember that she liked to give us information about all the previous presidents, even at the store.

The bank had a longtime employee, a lady that had not married. She adopted my friend after both her parents were deceased. I remember going to her house to visit and being served Jell-O for the first time. My friend and I had no idea how to eat that funny looking stuff.

The telephone switchboard was in the home of the operator. It was right downtown and we could go in and see how Flossie Dedman handled the calls. Mrs. Dedmon was the first to hear any breaking news, since all calls were connected at the switchboard.

The eating places, movie theatre, drug store, post office, and Masonic hall all held special memories for me. Once a year, near Christmas we were invited to a party in the Masonic hall. Since Papaw was a Mason, we were included and given presents.

These were all facts I could use when I did find time to write about my life here. Perhaps the Sandersons will want to hear more about the people who lived and worked in this town. Since Squire Sanderson and his brothers grew up here and attended this school, I think this reformation of Veeny will certainly appeal to them. Betty Sue, his wife, likes to save the antiques and likes to design the old buildings for present day use. She will be a positive influence on all of us.

14

We were waiting for news from Sheriff Moore. David was still tearing apart the house, with Joe supervising, when an interesting visitor showed up at my door.

"Hello, Mrs. C, may I come in?" A voice interrupted my writing.

I looked to see who was there, "Of course, Mattie, come on in?"

"Mrs. C, that is what Joe calls you isn't it?"

"It is but you may call me Jane and I'll call you Mattie."

"I've been here a few times to see Joe, but didn't get to talk to you or Mr. Cotton."

"They are busy as usual, so we can visit," I tell her. "Please sit down. Can I get you a coke? We are low on water."

Even before Mattie has sat down, she was talking. "Jane, I am thirty-two years old and I want to get married. I hope you can tell me how to have a long and happy marriage like yours. I want you to tell me all you can about Joe. I really like him, but we've only talked a few times and I realize I don't know much about him yet."

"Mattie, you do ask a lot. I'll try to answer some of that; but first tell me something about yourself."

"I'm Martha Lou Hornsby, born in Blue Pond, lived there most of my life except for college. My degree is in marketing and public relations. There are no jobs around here that I could find for that profession. I tried to live in

Elizabeth Oliver Wooten

Nashville for a few years after graduating but really did not like the job. So I trained to be a Medical Technician and was able to get the job I have now. I really like the work and time has passed so quickly. I volunteer to help non-profit groups and use my marketing knowledge to help them. I haven't met the guy I've dreamed of; maybe I'm looking too hard. What do you think?"

"Let me answer your questions in order. I would be glad to share about our long marriage if I knew the answer. We married young and both were Christians. We really did have a lot of quarrels those first years. With two little girls and not much money, we had to depend on our Christian teaching and the Lord, to know what to do. I guess that works; we're still together after the girls have married and left home. One lives in Houston, Texas; they have two boys. The other one and her husband, who is from Blue Pond by the way, lives in the Atlanta area. They also have two boys. We feel very blessed with our family."

I continue to talk. "Now, for what I know about Joe's character. I think you know the basics. He was working for us when he got hurt. I think he has done marvelous with that broken leg, don't you? He has been so agreeable since he left the hospital. We felt like we needed to bring him here since there wasn't anyone else to help him. I hope he isn't abusing the pain medicine. I do think he might have been drinking too much or maybe using drugs at one time. What do you think?"

"Joe says he has not had a lot of pain and only uses the pills at night. I think he is healing nicely. He will have an x-ray when he goes to see the doctor next week. If the bone is healing, the doctor will remove this cast and he'll have a lighter one for walking with a crutch.

"Joe has not told me about his wife, he does talk about his sister and his parents. I thought you might know more about him." Mattie added.

"No, that and the fact that he was injured in Vietnam; that he was in the Army for three years, and has been treated for some problem since he returned, is all I know. David and I both think he wants to make a better life. He admits his buddies aren't really friends. I've asked him to go to church with us. We also think you have had a good influence on his personality." I told Mattie.

"Would you like to go to the Saturday Night Antique Auction with us? We can ask Joe and David out to an early dinner and then attend. It's here in Veeny and I love antiques. I think we need to go find those two. I bet they are wondering what we are doing. You're welcome to come back to see me and I'll tell you what I know about Joe."

15

The Veeny auction was held once a month on the last Saturday of the month. It began at eight and was not over until eleven at night. Most of the attendees had things to sell. David, Joe, Mattie, and I didn't bring anything to sell. The auctioneer thought sure we would be buying. The attendance was good for a town the size of Veeny. About seventy-five came to the auction the evening we were there. Norman and all the regulars showed up after the café closed.

The things that were auctioned could be any item from razor blades, to boxes of books, or surprise boxes that you had no idea what was in them. Some furniture pieces were sold; most of those were newer stuff. A few broken and dirty pieces that the seller said were antiques did sell well. Many of the things didn't get a bid of what the owner wanted, and therefore they were not sold. The owner of those items still had to pay the commission. Ten-percent of the price of the things sold was collected by the auction people, when the buyer paid for them. I learned all of this so I could compute what this business might earn at a monthly auction. I might have to auction some of my flea market and yard sale purchases if I couldn't use them. The old building was full of people and a lot of them were buying.

Hot dogs, drinks, popcorn, and candy sold well. I wondered what else was being sold outside the building. I learned that sometimes they also had entertainment.

Elizabeth Oliver Wooten

The auction seemed to be a sort of a town meeting. We met the mayor of Veeny and some of the other citizens that didn't know us. I'm sure they had heard of the things that had been happening so we didn't mention any of that.

Rex Arnold, a councilman, did want to know more about us. He didn't ask direct questions. His first two statements made me feel like he wanted to accuse us of something. "I saw the Cottons here about six months before they moved in that trailer. They were driving a big new Honda van then." Rex injected into the conversation. "Somebody told me they saw them in the woods not far from where those two bodies were found."

I didn't want to answer him so I waited for David to explain. David was shocked. I thought it really would be interesting to know who else was in those woods the day we found the two graves. Maybe that somebody was Rex.

Joe spoke up, "Yes, David and Jane were out walking the way they did years ago. The trail went through the woods near that graveyard on the way to David's bother's house. David's home place is just down the hill from there. His brother owns that property. It all had belonged to their parents."

David added his explanation; " I was the one who told the Sheriff about those suspicious graves."

"The Honda is my vehicle, it's at home now." That seemed to answer Rex's statements, but I thought we would probably hear more from him.

Some people arrived at nine-o'clock and had a trailer load of furniture and antiques. Their pieces were more interesting but had to be sold last since they arrived late. The most interesting thing was who they were. I had already met Betty Sue Sanderson and tonight she was with her husband, Squire, and others. She noticed us and immediately came to sit by me.

"Hello, Jane, I remember you were interested in old pieces. We brought a few; maybe they are what you need."

After I introduced her to David, Joe, and Mattie, I told her, "David has warned me not to buy a thing until we have a place to put it. So I'm just looking and listening tonight."

Betty Sue found her husband and introduced him to our group. Squire Sanderson was dressed very differently from the other men. He wore a tailored suit that fit so well it must have been tailor-made for him. He wasn't very tall, a little too heavy for his height, but the light colored cowboy style hat made him look almost handsome. I still had not told David or Joe what I thought about the Sandersons or what Jewel had told me about them. We did discuss the fact that Squire and his brothers had gone to school at Veeny when we did. We did tell them what we were attempting to do at my old home place, but not how it was going. I was glad they didn't ask Joe about his leg.

While the others were watching the auction of some of their pieces, Betty Sue and I went outside. It was a nice evening and the smoke inside was bad. That gave me a chance to tell her some of the history of Veeny. She was not a native of the area and had no idea that it was a very busy little town in the 40's and 50's.

"What happened to the thriving town? When did it die?" She asked.

"I'm still working on that. We've been gone for forty years."

Elizabeth Oliver Wooten

"We have talked about needing another large unit to store some of our purchases. It's possible we can work together and restore some of these buildings." Betty Sue informed me.

My quick reply was, " I need to talk to the Mayor, I met her tonight. I'll find out who owns the buildings and what help we can expect from the town. If you'll call me, we can get together here after I have more information. I have already started writing the history of this area for my book. I'll print it out for you. My book will be about my family that settled in this area over a hundred and forty years ago."

The auction was almost over when we returned. My group was ready to go home. Mattie said she had to work the rest of the weekend. She reminded us that Joe had a doctor's appointment next Wednesday.

16

Monday we had a visitor that none of us expected. David said he looked familiar so he stopped work to welcome him. Reverend Harry Parke explained that he always visited the people who showed up to worship with his church family. I quickly brought out more chairs so we all could sit near Joe. We introduced Joe, and told him our names were Jane and David Cotton, just in case he had forgotten our first names. .

Reverend Parke said, "I tried to get here last week but didn't have time. I tried to find the other couple that visited the day you did. Neither of you came last Sunday, but George had asked them where they lived so I found them today. They are Sally and Butch Sanderson, very nice people. They have two children, a boy about twelve and a two-year-old little girl. Mr. Sanderson is looking for work. Mr. Cotton, do you have any work for him? He's willing to do anything honest."

"We met some Sandersons Saturday at the auction. Is he related to them?" David asked.

"I don't know. He seems to be new to this area."

I decided this was a good time to tell David, Joe, and Reverend Parke what Betty Sue Sanderson and I were planning. I did not mention that I was trying to find out where their money came from.

"The other Sandersons, the ones we met last Saturday evening, and I have big plans for restoring some of the buildings in Veeny. We think one would be an antique house, another could be a country store, another one a restaurant or tearoom, and one a museum. The Sandersons have one Antique House in Jarmore that has done well and has helped that town," I informed them all.

"Perhaps we could use Butch to help with that work. When you see him again ask him to come see us, Reverend Parke."

"Please call me Pastor Harry. Joe, how is your leg? I heard about your accident."

"It is almost well. I will get an x-ray on Wednesday. I think I will be able to walk and help David after they change the cast."

"Joe, I'd like to invite you to our church. Please come with the Cottons next Sunday. We have our first Sunday meal together at five-thirty. Jane, you do not need to bring any food; you all will be our guest."

Pastor Harry left after saying he would have Butch come to see us.

This had been interesting. To hear of nice people named Sanderson was confusing to me. I wanted to meet them. Of course, Squire and Betty Sue Sanderson were nice friendly folks also.

෴

David had lots to say about my ideas and none of it was good. I begged him to listen and started at the beginning. "First, Oliver talked about the drugs in this area and said he believed the bones in our well was part of a drug deal gone bad. Then Jewel told me that people were talking about the Sandersons being involved with drugs. She explained about their beautiful house, a clubhouse, cattle, and an antique house. We decided to go see the home and visit their restored warehouse in Jarmore. When I met Betty Sue that day I wanted to know them better so I came up with the plan to ask their help in restoring Veeny."

I continued with my explanation, "David, you know we will have to help find out what happened to these dead men. Rex Arnold is already accusing us of something."

David was thinking about all this. He finally said, "So you think you can question Betty about drugs. Find out if Butch Sanderson is related and what he knows. Then solve three murders, so we can leave."

"No, and yes. We won't be allowed to leave until the authorities learn who is guilty of those crimes. Besides I knew you wanted to find work for Joe and now for Butch. If Butch comes here about work, I can ask him questions. Maybe restoring Veeny will give them both a job."

"I think Jane is right, somebody needs to help our sheriff," Joe commented.

༺༻

The next day Fred, the sheriff, came back to tell us what he found out about Preston Perry.

"Preston J. Perry is a stepson of the man who rented your house some years ago. Mrs. Ray gave me enough information to find out who lived here. She was correct in thinking the son had been arrested. I got his name from the step-dad and found his record and a photo."

Sheriff Moore kept talking, "Preston Perry was charged with possession of a controlled substance, distribution of crack cocaine and conspiracy to commit a controlled substance crime almost five years ago. He served two years and is still on probation. I asked his probation officer about him.

He said Mr. Perry reports on time and lives out from Blue Pond. His probation is over at the end of this year. I'm looking for something to tie him to the bones in your well."

I jumped in with my thoughts; "He did live here. He knew the place was deserted until we showed up. Are the marijuana pots two or five years old?

"We think they are a year or two old, the cans aren't rusty. I have no evidence that Perry did that, except he probably knows how to grow marijuana."

Joe asked, "Sheriff, do you have his picture with you? I'd like to see it."

"I do, but it was taken five years ago when he was arrested. He may look a lot different now. I'll get it. Jewel Ray has already seen it and identified him as the one who lived here."

"I can't give you a description of the tree that moved, but I just know it was a man watching this place," I added.

"Sheriff, is smoking marijuana a crime?" Joe inquired as soon as the Sheriff returned with the picture.

"Not unless we catch you doing it and you have some more illegal stuff on you or in your possession."

Joe, David, and I all looked at the photo of Preston J. Perry.

Joe answered immediately. "That is one of the men in the truck that came here two weeks ago. Bear ran them off. They tried to drive to the barn. I was inside my camper and I did write down the tag number. I think he has sold me drugs but I can't prove it."

"Get me the number. I'll check out who owns that truck. I can also go talk to Mr. Perry about illegal trespassing. I won't mention drugs right now."

17

The following Sunday morning it was raining. David was looking for containers to catch the water in. He knew we needed it for something. Joe was restless but would not agree to go to church with us. He had two reasons, no clothes for church and he and Bear needed to watch our homes.

David and I arrived too late for bible study and social time. The songs and worship service were about the same as the last Sunday we were there. Pastor Harry mentioned an elderly member that needed visits since he was disabled. He lived alone and near the church. His name was Preacher Fredericks and he had been a part of this church for many years. I remembered that name from the long ago time when I attended here. We did see the Sandersons sitting in a pew in the back of the church.

After the closing prayer, Pastor Harry managed to get us together with the Sandersons and introduced them to us. He had already told Butch that we might have some work for him. I talked with Sally and the kids. Matthew was in the sixth grade. He answered my questions shyly.

"Yes, I like school. I don't know the kids very well."

. Kaylee, was having a birthday next week. She told me about it and that she was two years old. She talked like she was at least three years old. She was so lively and happy, a sweetheart and very pretty. I also liked Sally and asked her to visit us when Butch came to talk about work. I briefly explained our situation, or at least why we were living on Thaxton Road. They were very interested in finding work. Sally had a part time job and Butch had only been able to get temporary work at different jobs.

※

After church, we decided to take Joe and go to Tussellville for lunch. Joe seemed depressed. I asked if Mattie could join us. He said she had not called.

"Well Joe, maybe you need to call her." I suggested. "Most women of her age still expect the man to call and ask them out.

"Do you think that's why she hasn't called me?"

"Could be she is waiting for you to call her. When we were dating, I waited to hear from David. The months before we were engaged he called me long distance. I was working at this home that had a phone. My job was to watch their two kids while the parents, who worked nights, slept. He also wrote me letters that I still have. That worked, I accepted the ring he gave me in early August and we were married in September."

"I'm not interested in a ring, but I do like her," Joe answered.

"Okay, Joe, are you ready? David said. "You should get that big leg reduced on Wednesday, just think how much easier it will be to hop in your truck and go. Jane and I are riding with you, and I'm driving today."

Tussellville's one buffet lunch that was open on Sunday was crowded. Joe had learned to use crutches for very short walks. We found a table, got him settled, went through the long line for lots of food, and was enjoying it when friends found us. Maxine and Anthony Scott were family friends that lived in Tussellville. We had seen them several times in the last few years. They knew what we were doing in Veeny. After the hellos, introductions, and "How are you," Maxine asked "When are you going with us to the Hee-Haw show we told you about?"

"I'm ready to go, when and where?" I answered her.

"It's every Saturday night at Frog Town. Can you three go next Saturday? We haven't been for three weeks and we plan to go next Saturday."

"I think we can; give me your phone number and I'll call you. We will probably meet you there. I'll call you for directions later."

Finally, they left to get food, so we could enjoy our lunch. No one else bothered us until we finished eating. I did see some of my cousins and talked to them before we left. My Mother's family had lived in this part of Benjamin County and many descendants of her large family still lived around here.

Joe spoke up on the way home, "Guess I can make a date with Mattie to go to this Hew Haw event. Do you think she would like that Mrs. C?"

"I think she might. She seemed okay with us all going to the auction. If she isn't scheduled to work we can all go and get some dinner in Frog Town. I recall Maxine saying the only food at that event was hotdogs and popcorn. I've never been there and really don't know what we'll find. Joe, are you expecting us to go with or just you and Mattie on a real date?

"Oh, I want you and David to go with us. I don't think I'm ready to begin romancing a lady. She will want to know what it is and what to wear."

"Tell her it is country music; we'll all wear jeans."

"I will need to buy some new ones if they will fit over my new cast. David, will you take me to the doctor Wednesday and then shopping?"

"Yeah Joe, I'll take you, then after that maybe you can help me and not just comment on what I'm doing wrong." David was kidding Joe, but then he sounded real serious when he asked me, "Jane, could you stay home tomorrow and look at what I have done to the house?"

18

The rain had stopped by Monday morning. I was hoping that I didn't have to make any decisions about the house. David and I had not talked about it for two weeks. I asked first about the power and water.

David answered, "We are still on the list to get power out here. George got the water meter installed out near the road. I am going to talk to him about what pipe we need to get the water here. We'll only have an outside faucet with a hose to fill our tanks. That's better than we have now."

"That sounds great. When will we have water? I have tons of laundry."

"Jane will you stop talking and come look at the house?" David was impatient.

"Sure, I look every day but I kept seeing it the way it looked when I was little. I know I have to get over that. Is the trap door still in the floor of the back room? Is the fireplace and chimney good?"

"Come on inside and see for yourself."

The room and both porches that had been added to the front had been torn off. I could again see the a-frame roof of the original house. It just needed the porch across the front and rock steps going onto it. The cute well shed was still over the well in the yard. This might look right after all. I stepped very carefully over the old lumber and went inside with David. The rooms were cleared of all the debris and old furniture. I could see some of the original linoleum on the floor, as well as other layers that had been put on top of it. The walls showed various layers of different colors of wallpaper. I could remember some of them that I helped put on. I remember Memaw wanted the rooms papered to make them warmer. I think the first layer was a thick paper put up with tacks. Then we used flour and water to make paste to put up the wallpaper. It sure was hard to paste it on the ceiling.

"This is working; what you have done looks great. I'll help tear off all the wallpaper if you will remove those old floor coverings. Then we can see what the original wood is like. The fireplace looks good, even the original mantle shows up now. I know the fireplace had been converted to coal use. Later it was covered over completely to install a freestanding coal-burning heater. Did you find the old iron cold grate?"

"No, it wasn't there. What about the next room? I still have to tear off the old kitchen. We need to look at the rafters and roof next."

The next large room needed to have the wallpaper removed and the old linoleum taken off the floor. I could see that the trap door was still there. That had been fun sometimes when we were playing hide-and-seek as well as an escape to the storm cellar underneath the house, during a thunderstorm and hard rain.

This room had two windows, one on each of the outside walls. We all wanted to sleep here when the summer nights were so hot. A cross-breeze from those two windows helped a lot. Some of the window sashes needed to be replaced but I asked that he leave any original ones that were good. "David, can you find these old style four-panes to a sash windows."

"I don't know but we'll try. I want to make you happy. What are we going to do with this house?"

"I'll find a good use for it. Give me time to make plans." I was almost in tears again.

୨୦୶

Joe was yelling for David. He said that David's phone had been ringing. David got his phone from the outside table and checked the missed calls. He thought the call was from the Sheriff so he immediately called him back. After a long conversation, David told us the news.

"Sheriff Moore had a little more information about the bones. The subject, had been dead approximately four years, a male, age about thirty or younger. He was most likely about five and half feet tall. Size nine shoes would have fit his feet. No clothes were found and they wondered why. The Sheriff is checking back years for any male reported missing from this area. So far he has not been successful."

"The county law is getting help from the state." David continued. "Two detectives have been assigned to work on the murders of the two men found in the graves. They have asked Sheriff Moore to not talk to Preston Perry, since he may be involved in the killings. They also think drugs are part of it. They plan to watch Perry very closely, trying to find out who else is selling drugs in this area and where they are getting them. If Perry doesn't know he is suspected they hope he will lead them to others."

The Sheriff had said he would keep us informed and he was doing that. We didn't know if we could mention any of this to the locals. We thought we could tell them part of what he had said but not about the drugs since no one knew if that was part of it. We didn't want any drug dealers to get scared off.

༄༅

Butch, Sally, and Kaylee Sanderson showed up after lunch. I asked Sally and Kaylee to come in our motor home. I felt that was the safest place for them. I saw that Butch went to work immediately helping David stack up the old gray lumber I had asked him to save.

I had made a large banana pudding for us and a smaller one to take to Preacher Fredericks. We bought groceries and got water for the motor home the day before. I offered dessert and coffee to Sally. I even had cookies for Kaylee. Sally said they had eaten and refused my dessert. She said Kaylee loved cookies and, yes she could have some. I asked Kaylee, "When is your birthday party?"

"My birthday is two more days. Come to my party?"

I looked at Sally before I answered this little sweetheart. She tried to help me answer her by explaining about her party. I stopped her and found something for Kaylee to do. Crayons, paper, and her cookies were all she needed. Now that she wasn't listening Sally told me, " I did plan to have a little party with just my family and us but they have gone on a vacation. I don't know many people to invite especially children her age. I got the items for a birthday cake and balloons. We can't afford much."

Sally kept talking, "Butch and I lived here until six years ago. Then we moved to Texas, he worked with his family until six months ago. We've been back in our house here three months and haven't made any friends yet. We do think the church is the place to meet some nice people and get acquainted. They are friendly people, especially the Pastor."

"Could David and I come to Kaylee's birthday party? Joe might be with us. He wants to go to his house Wednesday afternoon. His home is not far from yours. Pastor Harry told us where you live."

"That would be great if you could. What time should I plan her party."

"I think we could be there by four. Is that too late for her? She will be excited."

"No, Butch can come home by then. I'll have her take a nap after lunch. She will sleep a long time if she stays up late the night before."

Sally and Kaylee seemed happy with that plan.

I needed to take the pudding to the old Preacher. I explained to Sally that if I didn't do my good deed when I thought of it I might forget all about him and not do what Pastor Harry had asked on Sunday. I told her that David and I remembered Preacher Fredericks from years and years ago.

When we went outside, we found David and Butch still working stacking pieces of lumber. I offered them some tea and pudding. Then explained that Sally, Kaylee and I were taking some pudding to Preacher Fredericks. David could deal with hiring Butch or not. I told him where the file of forms was, in case he was contracting with him to dig the ditch for the water. He was telling Butch what happened with the well when we left. That would explain what happened to Joe's leg and why he was here.

I knew where the Preacher lived. It was the same place where David's youngest brother took us to attend his wedding years ago. Preacher Fredericks was the pastor at Lee's church at that time, the same one we had attended yesterday. Since Lee didn't want a big wedding, his young fiancé agreed to be married at the Pastor's house. The bride's family didn't have money for a church wedding. His fiancée was working for us in a café. I think that worked well for them. They are still together so it doesn't require a big wedding to ensure a long happy marriage.

Preacher was sitting on his porch. He was surprised to see us. He told us, "Not many people stop at my house anymore. There are a lot of pickups and cars going by. I don't know why, only one other family lives on this road."

I introduced Sally and Kaylee Sanderson and told him who I was. He remembered the Cottons and David. He even knew who I was, and remembered my family. He certainly wasn't senile as his conversation was clear. He asked about the church and some of the members. He told us that his wife used to play the old pump organ. I recalled that and the fact he preached loud and long. He said she died fifteen years ago. Now he was not able to go preach but sometimes he just preached to the trees. His health just allowed him to get around the house and fix some of his meals. His sons and their wives checked on him and brought groceries. He had a cat to pet and talk to. There were three kittens in the box near him. He asked if he could show them to Kaylee.

"Of course," Sally said.

"I brought you something to eat. I'll fix you a dish to eat and bring it out to you," I told him. "It's banana pudding and I didn't add much sugar in case you are diabetic. Can I put the rest in your refrigerator?"

"That sounds good, I can eat most everything. The Lord has blessed me greatly. I praise Him every day for my health and my other blessings like children, grandkids and friends like you."

When Sally and I went inside, we found that the kitchen was extremely messy. The refrigerator needed cleaning out, the dishes were all dirty, and the floor needed scrubbing. Looking out the window, we could see Kaylee sitting in the Preacher's lap holding two kittens. Sally started to work on the refrigerator while I washed a dish, fixed his pudding, and went back outside.

Kaylee, Preacher, and the kittens were all good friends by now. The three kittens had been named Shadrach, Meshack, and Abed-nego. It was so funny listening to Kaylee repeating those names. She had invited Preacher to her birthday party. He wanted to know if she would have banana pudding at her party.

Kaylee squealed, "No—Birthday Cake!"

I suggested that I would also invite Pastor Harry to her birthday party and maybe he could bring Preacher Fredericks with him. "Here's your dessert; it's covered and setting on the table behind you. We really need to go but Sally is cleaning for you. That does need to be done. Could you afford to pay her something if she comes in twice a week and cooks and cleans for you?"

"Will she bring Kaylee to see me and the kittens?"

"I bet she would." I'll get her out here and you two can talk."

On the way home I told Sally about the two preachers that might come to the birthday party. She was so happy about that and about having another job. She said that Preacher thought her help would allow him to live at home and not have to go to a nursing home. That made us happy for him.

When we got back, Butch, David, and Joe were finishing the job of sorting out the lumber pieces that could be used and loading the rotten stuff on the two pickups to be discarded. The old house was looking much better.

As the Sandersons were leaving Butch said, "I'll be back tomorrow to help you get the water line in."

19

David was up early on Tuesday to go see his brothers. He wanted to see George about the pipe he needed. He planned to see Rory about using his ditcher and he wanted me to help measure the distance that they needed pipe for.

"Boy, give you a job and somebody to help and it gets done." I said to him. "Let's have breakfast before we start. I bet you also want me to go get the pipe."

"Would you? I'll find out from George what we need and where to get it."

After breakfast David measured a length of the well rope and cut it at fifty feet. We proceeded to walk and measure along the side of the driveway, where he felt they could bury the water line. It was quite a distance but David said digging the ditch would be simple with Rory's ditch buster behind his tractor. He even assured me that the pipe could be taken up and used somewhere else if we decided to abandon this project.

When David returned, he said, "George told me what pipe to use and he went to see if the city had enough and if they would sell some to me. If they have enough George will bring it out here. You need to call me before you leave Blue Pond in case we need more. You will need to pay for it and get them to deliver it. You did say you would go and do this, didn't you?"

"Sure, I will. I'll probably stop to shop for birthday presents for a two-year old before I get the pipe. Kaylee's party is tomorrow. You won't need the pipe until later will you?"

Butch was already cleaning up the yard. "Rory and George are coming to help and with Butch helping we might get the pipe down today. Bring us sandwiches and drinks for lunch."

"Okay, big subs for five workers. I'll get ice and make ice tea and lemonade. I have plenty of cookies for you all. Guess my shopping can't take very long."

"You probably won't have any water until tomorrow, David explained. I have to get things for the outside faucet. We won't cover the pipe until we try it all out. That way we can check for leaks."

I asked Joe if he was feeling better and offered to get him some groceries. He was much like himself and looking forward to seeing the doctor tomorrow. He insisted that David take his wheel chair back when they go to the doctor at Blue Pond. "Remember that it's only three weeks since your accident, you're not quite ready to run any races or work yet. Did you get your VA account number and Service information to the hospital?"

"Yes, Mattie made sure I did that. I did call her. She is meeting us at the doctor's office tomorrow."

"That's good, maybe she'll help you shop while David gets our plumbing supplies. Do you want me to get a gift for you to give Kaylee? We're all planning to go to her birthday party at four o'clock on Wednesday."

Joe said, "Get her something fun, like something to ride. I like her Daddy. He seems to be about my age. He sure worked hard yesterday."

"Joe, she isn't a boy and not very big but I will look for something fun."

I returned at noon with food and gifts. The city had the pipe they needed and George got it delivered. Rory came with his equipment and with all those men helping, they got the pipe in the ground before dark.

"Hurray! We'll soon have water and can take a long shower. Then I can do the laundry," I happily told David.

20

It has been a busy two days. The pipe was in the ditch after a hard day's work by the four men. David and Joe went to Blue Pond for lunch and to Joe's doctor appointment. David got what he needed for the faucet at the hardware store. Mattie met them for lunch and took Joe shopping. She thought he would have a walking cast on his leg and would be able to wear jeans. She did agree to go with us on Saturday evening.

The doctor's visit only took one hour. They had made an x-ray first. The doctor was pleased that the bone was healing very nicely. He then sawed the big cast to remove it. He did put another one on Joe's leg but it was much smaller and the foot was free to walk on. The doctor warned Joe to take it easy for another two weeks and then he would check his leg again.

Mattie had to go do her job and couldn't go to the birthday party. They returned the wheel chair and got back home in time to go to Kaylee's Party.

I had called Pastor Harry the evening before and told him about Kaylee's party and that we would like him to come. I told him about our visit to Preacher Frederick and how well it went, and that Kaylee invited him to her birthday party. Then I asked "Would you consider picking him up and bringing him to the Sandersons at about four on Wednesday? We won't be there long. I have several gifts for this precious little girl so don't worry about a gift. Sally didn't have anyone to invite. Her family is on vacation, so David, Joe and I are going."

Pastor Harry agreed to do that.

☙❧

With all those things accomplished, it was time to go take Kaylee her birthday presents. I had four pretty gift bags with things like clothes, toys, some games, and a small riding tricycle in a box. The games could be shared with her older brother. We were all acting like kids. David insisted on taking the ice chest and getting ice cream for the party.

Sally and Kaylee were watching for us. We arrived on time and gave her the gifts to open while we waited for Butch to get home. Next Pastor Harry and the Preacher got there. Preacher had a small box with him. Kaylee was so excited about her gifts. We had got the box open and she was sitting on the tricycle, not moving just looking at everything. Then Preacher gave her the box he had brought and helped her open it.

"Shadwach, Oh! Ooh, Oh, you came to see me! Kaylee exclaimed. "I wove you, Sha."

She was holding the kitten to her face and it was very calm. The kitten was definitely her favorite of all the gifts.

I immediately asked Preacher if he had permission, from Butch and Sally, to give her a kitten. He told me he did. Sally was by his house yesterday and they talked about it.

Another person came with gifts for Kaylee. I recognized her immediately. It was Betty Sue Sanderson.

Butch left the group as soon as he saw her. Sally seemed surprised and didn't say anything.

Betty Sue said, "Hello everybody I knew it was Kaylee's birthday but didn't know she was having a party. Here Doll, open this present from Auntie Betty."

Kaylee opened the box and found a beautiful doll. It was so big she didn't know what to do with it. Sally spoke up, "Betty, you shouldn't have. Can Kaylee play with it or should I put it away for later?"

"It's hers, but do what you think is best." Betty replied. She had seen the kitten and was talking to Kaylee about it.

"It's name is Sha, Mommy says its mine."

Butch called us all to come inside for cake. David got the ice cream and went to help serve it. The candles were lit, we all had sang 'Happy Birthday' and Kaylee blew out the two candles. When that was over Betty Sue said 'Bye' and left.

The party was soon over. Matthew had come home and was playing with Kaylee and her presents.

I asked him, "When is your birthday, Matthew, maybe we can come back for your party?"

Matthew answer was, "Mom will let you know. Thanks for coming to Kaylee's party. Boy, she got lots of gifts."

Butch said, "Betty Sue is my oldest brother's wife. I am not speaking to him these days, so it was a shock to see her here."

I told them "I met her at their Antique place in Jarmore. Then they came to the auction in Veeny and we met Squire. I did wonder if you were related. You must be the youngest. We knew two of your brothers in school many years ago."

Butch and Sally didn't say anything else about the family, so I thanked them for inviting us. "We enjoyed the cake and watching Kaylee with her gifts. You have two precious children."

Pastor and Preacher had already left, since there was church that evening.

We went to Joe's farm and helped him get the things he wanted. I warned Joe, "No liquor and no drugs."

Joe said, "Of course not Mrs. C. I've quit that stuff."

We decided to go home and wait to see what would happen next.

21

It sure didn't look like I would ever get to write about my family. I did believe planning a new Veeny and researching what was there in the 1940's and 1950's would help my story when I did write it. I decided to go find the current Mayor of Veeny and ask about any old records that the city had on file. Written records could confirm what I thought I remembered.

Marlene S. Finks, her Honor the Mayor, was in her office at city hall. She knew who I was and made me feel welcome. We sat down for a friendly visit. Before I could ask my first question, Rex Arnold came in. He was the city councilman that questioned us at the auction.

"Hello, you are David Cotton's wife, aren't you?"

"Yes, I have been for over thirty years and I hope it lasts another thirty."

"Tell us what's happening at your place. The well accident and bones didn't get a story in the newspaper. The two bodies dug up only rated a small article that didn't say who they were or how long they had been dead." Rex was again digging for information about what we were doing here.

"We don't know who they are or who buried them there. State officers are now handling the investigation. We're just working on restoring my home place. We have Joe Burns with us until his leg gets well. His dog, Bear is a good watchdog. If anyone comes around he lets us know."

Elizabeth Oliver Wooten

That was all I had to tell Rex, so he soon left. I had to decide if the Mayor would tell him what Betty Sue and I had in mind for Veeny. I just knew he would not support the plans if he knew I was a part of it.

Mayor Finks tried to explain about Rex. "He likes to get people angry and I don't know why. Sometimes it's embarrassing and sometimes it helps get to the heart of a problem."

"Mayor Finks, one of the reasons we are here is because I plan to write a book about my family and the place where I grew up. I feel it is very important that we record what life was like in the 1940's and 1950's. History doesn't record what our lives were like in a personal way. I remember Veeny as a busy, thriving little town during that period, but I would like to see any records the town has. I know that was over forty years ago but they should be here somewhere."

"Okay Jane, may I call you Jane? We already have two Mrs. Cottons."

"Sure, please do."

"We thought there was more involved than just trying to save that old house. Although we do hope you and Mr. Cotton will decide to live here. We think the Cottons who live here are wonderful people."

"I hope we can help this town. Betty Sue Sanderson and I have talked about trying to save the old buildings and put shops and small businesses in them. This is still in the talking stage so I hope you won't tell the town councilmen yet. I do need to know about any grants that could be applied for. If we plan a museum or something historic, I think government funds might be available and would help a lot.

Then, after we have a plan, you can present it to the group and see if the town will help. Can you tell me who owns the buildings that are still standing?"

"That's sounds great. I have worked to bring in some industry. We have two plants that have helped our tax base and provided some jobs. The town has bought some of the properties that were to be auctioned for back taxes. I do know who owns the others. I'll list them for you with the owner's names and their phone numbers. Are you only interested in the ones in the heart of the old town?"

"Yes, those and any homes nearby that are in good shape and not being used."

"Some records are here in boxes. When you have a day or two, I'll help you look at them and maybe I can file what we need to keep. Just let me know when we can plan on doing that. I'll have the property owners' names for you. No one else needs to know what we're doing, I'll say it is research for your book."

"Let's set a time. Is next Monday at ten o'clock all right with you, Mayor?"

"Yes I think that's good, give me your cell number and I'll call you if I have to change the time."

"We are getting water to our house. The city would only put a meter near the road and we are piping the water to the house. Our address for sending the bill is: P.O. Box 5, Veeny."

I went to the Post Office after leaving City Hall. I paid the rent on the P.O. Box. Got our mail and hometown newspaper. It had worked very well, having our mail and papers sent here.

Elizabeth Oliver Wooten

We had settled in very well on Thaxton Road in our motor home, but had no plans to stay there. We had planned to enjoy the work and attend any events that sounded like fun. Now, the finding of bones in our well, dead bodies in the cemetery, and marijuana pots in our barn had created a mystery that I felt like we had to solve.

22

It was Saturday and we were all ready to go to Frog Town for dinner and then find the Hee-Haw Show. Joe had invited Mattie and she arrived in her jeep ready to have David, Joe, and me ride with her. She first came inside to see what I was wearing. We all had on jeans and casual shirts. Mattie looked very pretty; she seemed excited and happy to be going somewhere with us.

Her first question for me was, "Do you have anything new to tell me about Joe?"

"Not much. I talked to him about his wife. He realizes that his depression and the way he handled it caused her to leave. Neither one of them has tried to contact the other. He said he would try to talk to her. Please don't say this to Joe, but I think he doesn't know what he feels right now. Not about her or his feelings, of whether he is guilty of doing wrong according to God's rules, or if he has broken the legal law."

"I'm willing to wait for him to figure some of that out. I don't think I can help him with that." Mattie spoke quietly.

"Joe picked up some good books and his best clothes from his house. I know he is looking better, dressing better, and much better at communicating. I guess he and Bear are going to be here another two or three weeks."

David and Joe were outside raring to go. After we got started, Joe told Mattie about the birthday party that she missed, about Kaylee and her tricycle and the kitten, named Shadrach. I told her that my childhood home was looking more like the old house I remembered and that I didn't know what it would be when we finished. David told her what he thought I was planning for Veeny. It would have a new 'old forties look' for the town, and businesses that would survive and thrive, according to my ideas.

We did find a place to have pizza in Frog Town. The food was good and we were laughing and having a good time even before we arrived at the appointed fun place. Joe wanted to pay for everything since this was his first date with Mattie. Before we left, Joe tried to explain to Mattie that he had left messages for his wife, with her family, asking her to call him. His message for her was that they needed to talk.

He said, "Maybe I should not be dating since I am a married man."

"Joe, we are all just friends now and having fun together. Let's go and check out this Hee-Haw show," I injected my feelings.

I called Maxine and got directions; they were already there and saving us seats. When we arrived, it was almost dark. There were lots of vehicles in the yard of an old building. It had no designated parking area, just a field. The building looked like it had been a shelter of some kind, maybe a small warehouse. I thought this was most likely a place where drugs were being sold. It was big and probably full of people from the looks of the parking area.

Maxine was ready to introduce us to the people they knew. I was looking at the place. The ceiling was low and the lights were not very bright. Tables were set up in long rows with chairs for everybody. I could smell popcorn. Music was playing through the speakers, but it was recorded not live. Most of the recorded songs were by Elvis Presley, our favorite son from this area. He was born just over the state line in Mississippi. His untimely death a few years ago had saddened us all. I still had a hard time believing he was dead.

David asked Maxine, "Who are our entertainers tonight?"

She said, "There seems to be something different tonight. Usually there are some men playing their instruments and we know what the show will be. There are a few people on stage getting ready for something."

"Okay, I'll try to be patient. Did you meet Mattie? She is our driver tonight. You remember Joe. His leg is much better and he is almost ready to start work again."

Anthony spoke to me, "Everybody knows everybody now. Jane, you need to say 'Hello'. What were you thinking about, you looked so serious?"

"Oh, just remembering and wondering what the show will be like."

The people up front asked for everybody to be quiet. Maxine whispered that the lady, sitting in the chair and her husband owned the place. Their daughter had the microphone and she explained everything.

"This is my Mom and it's her birthday today. We have a surprise for her and all of you. We'll serve you birthday cake later. Her favorite performer of all time is coming to sing tonight. I hope you enjoy the evening."

The small band on stage began to play and we all started talking. David bought us all coffee to go with the cake we were going to be served later.

Elizabeth Oliver Wooten

Suddenly the bright lights shone on the stage and the spotlight went to the door. The group played louder and the applause started. The guest of honor, the mother, was standing and looking very surprised as her idol came on stage. An Elvis impersonator, with guitar and white sequined jump suit, sang a love song to her."

"Hey, I might like this after all," I told our group. "He's not bad or at least if he sings Elvis's songs I will recognize them."

The guy continued to sing to the birthday lady. She was having a good time. Despite the terrible building and heat, we were enjoying it. The sound was too loud for David, but he did not complain.

Our Elvis impersonator disappeared for a while and we wondered if the show was over. Shortly the lights dimmed and the spotlight shone on the back door. Elvis appeared dressed more elaborately with lots of scarves hanging around his neck. He walked or pranced on top of the tables, singing and playing and dodging the rafters, giving out scarves, even stopping to kiss the ladies. I didn't get a scarf or get kissed which was fine with me. He really didn't look like Elvis and his singing wasn't that good. I would have preferred to hear recordings by the real Elvis Presley. But no one asked me for my opinion and I didn't give it. I did compliment the entertainer by taking his picture and shaking his sweaty hand.

The evening ended after cake and coffee. We said goodbye to Maxine and Anthony and the new people we had met.

I had sent Joe outside during the break, to sniff around to see if drugs or alcohol were being sold. I was waiting to hear what he found.

He said, "I didn't find anything suspicious. Maybe you should trust some people, Jane."

"Yes, I should, but the murders and illegal drugs are always in the back of my mind." I answered. "Let's go home and start over tomorrow. Maybe I can help on the house next week."

23

Betty Sue Sanderson called me on Sunday. She said they had been at an auction on Saturday and bought several pieces of furniture that were definitely used in the late forties. She wanted to know if there was a building in Veeny that was available now. She needed somewhere to unload them.

I told her about my visit with Mayor Finks and that I had an appointment with her the next day. "I think it will work out if you bring your truck of furniture and meet me tomorrow morning about eleven o'clock in Veeny. Just park near the large empty building. I'll pick you up and we'll look the town over. We can have lunch and you can meet the mayor. She will have the name and addresses of some of the owners of the buildings. The town owns some of them, so I think we'll find a place for you to put the furniture."

༄༅

On Monday, I had to explain to David and Joe that I couldn't work in the old house. I promised that I would begin that in a day or two. I really wanted them to get the water line finished and do the laundry for me. Butch had helped again on Friday and they got the faucet installed and had repaired the pipe connections. They covered most of the ditch. I thought it was almost ready to use.

Joe came to my rescue and offered to help remove old wallpaper. "I can easily walk around in the house and do that."

David didn't say much. He did ask, "Have we got any more work for Butch?" He only has a two day job which isn't enough to feed his family."

"I think we will have but not this week unless you have something. Sally is working for Preacher two days a week. I'm sure he is paying her. That will help their financial situation some."

"I will be in town. Betty Sue and I will be discussing our plans quietly, probably at Norman's. If you two would like to have lunch with us come there at twelve-thirty. David, I'd like you to know what we plan. This could mean work for Joe and Butch for months. Then I will be at the Mayor's office for a few hours, looking at old records of town meetings."

I printed copies of the history I had of Veeny and this area for Betty Sue. I quickly typed some ideas for consideration about re- making the town.

1. Our goal is to give it the feel of a bygone period, probably the early fifties.
2. We need to provide work, not only on repairs but also in shops.
3. Some of the buildings could be used for what they were. The old café could be a tearoom or ice cream parlor.
4. The small taxi building could sell old records, forty-fives etc. and have a jukebox and pool tables.
5. The bank building might be the museum.
6. The stores could sell antiques, flea market items, or yard sale things from that period. {I heard that yard sales are very popular around here.}

7. Signage and advertising are very important.
8. Finding the right person to be the manager. Someone that is creative and interested in saving this town is most important

After printing that list, I felt that I had a few things to talk to Betty about. This was sooner than I had planned to work on this project, but I was interested in talking to the Sandersons again. I wondered if Squire would be with her, I hoped not. I wanted to ask about Sally and Butch. She had seemed friendly enough at their house. If Butch had worked for his family, it must have involved Squire. What had happened? Squire seemed very prosperous and his brother wasn't.

☙❧

I met Betty Sue and we looked at how bad the buildings were, then we went to lunch. She was reading my information when David came in. She showed him the list and said, "These are great ideas. Do you think these building can be saved? We don't want them to look new or modern just make them safe. Surely, the owners won't ask for much. Maybe the repairs and paying the taxes would be enough for the first year."

"I am a pretty good fix-it fellow. I'll look at the ones you like when you get the owners permission and keys. I have two fellows that need work. Our old home place is waiting for decisions before we do much more to it." David replied.

We talked about the history and what we remembered about the area as we finished lunch. Betty Sue was not from this area. She said her husband was interested since he had lived here most of his life. She hoped to get him involved and talk to him about what he remembered. He had gone on a trip, and wouldn't be back before Saturday. They still needed to discuss the amount of funds they could put into this project.

She asked me. "What do you think about profits in the future? I'm thinking about a year from now."

"Well, I think we'll have to wait and consider that in perhaps ten months. You have more experience in antiques sales than I do."

We got to City Hall and met the mayor. I introduced Betty to Mayor Finks and left them in her office talking while I went in another room to start unpacking old file boxes. I could hear them talking about my ideas. The fact that Betty Sue needed a useable building was discussed. I heard the Mayor tell her which ones the city owned. Betty asked her for keys so she could look at them.

When the Mayor joined me, she asked what I knew about the Sandersons. She was wondering about letting her put furniture in one of the empty buildings.

"I don't really know anything for sure. Squire, her husband grew up here. They seem to have money. They live down near the Mississippi State line."

Mayor Finks said, "Oh! I know about that place. There is lots of talk about them. I hear it is amazing what they have done. I should get permission from the council to lease any building. We meet tomorrow evening. I think it will be all right to let her unload here. Did she drive the truck?"

"No, she didn't. She wants some men to bring it and unload the furniture. Maybe they can wait until Wednesday, if that is better for you," I said. "Let's get started on these boxes of papers. I am stacking everything that looks like minutes of town meetings here. I'll go back and put them in order of dates after I finish all these boxes. You can take care of the rest of this stuff. It looks like a lot of duplicates; maybe you only need to keep one copy of each. Forgive me for telling you what to do. I tend to be an organizer."

I kept talking while she looked at the papers. "I think I will be here a few days reading about the town. You will need to remind me not to be too bossy. One of my previous jobs was running David's office."

When Betty returned she was excited about the size of one of the buildings. "I can buy more antiques and things from the fifties, if the town will let us use that big building," she said. "Jane, did you ask her about us repairing them and paying the taxes instead of a monthly fee?"

"I didn't yet. Mayor, can you take that thought to the councilmen? We want to have a plan for each building, then try to rework each one so it will be ready for that particular business. We don't know yet how many buildings we will need."

Betty Sue spoke up again, "I believe we can pay for the repairs; remember we are only fixing them not remodeling. We want them all to look like the originals. Do you have pictures of the way the town looked during the forties and fifties?"

Mayor Finks looked shocked; "You two are going too fast for me. Yes, I'll ask at our next meeting, which is Tuesday evening. Betty Sue, can you wait about putting your furniture in until I get approval from the council? It all sounds reasonable to me. I hope your plan will work out and then we'll have some jobs for our people."

"Sure I'll wait. I think that's all I have time for today. Jane, be sure to contact the other owners. I'll see you in a few days."

"Isn't this marvelous." I said to the Mayor after Betty left. "I was hoping they would invest some money in this project. Honestly, Mayor Finks do you think this is a good idea?"

"It's the best one I've heard, or maybe I should say the only one. I'm sure the town people will work with you every way we can."

I still had not learned much about the Sandersons' business. I would meet Betty in town again on Wednesday or whenever she was bringing her furniture. I didn't finish unpacking the boxes in city hall, but I did borrow some minutes to read at home.

24

We had not heard from Sheriff Moore in over a week. David decided to call him and ask for an update. David also wanted to know why we were being asked to stay here. He wanted to a take a trip back to Georgia to see our family.

The Sheriff answered quickly. The number David had on his cell phone was probably the Sheriff's cell number. Sheriff Moore didn't directly answer David's question about our going out of state. He wanted to set up a time when the state detectives could come and talk to us. He said they wanted to look over our place and the area around the little cemetery.

They agreed on the next day about one. David agreed that the three of us would be waiting to talk to them and that he would show them around.

Detectives Hugo P. Thistle and Robert Smith arrived with Sheriff Moore on Wednesday. They were all dressed casual, with boots that would protect them from snakes. Detective Thistle asked that we call him Paul and refer to Detective Smith as Bob. They didn't want the local people to know what they were doing here.

Paul said, "We'll be back in a few days to talk to other people."

Detective Paul was the older of the two men and seemed to be in charge of this investigation. The information he gave us about the two bodies was very brief. The only thing I got from it was that they were killed from a high powered gun. Probably the same gun killed them both at different times. He would not say if they had identified either one.

"We are still working through fingerprints and other clues. When we do know their names, we'll contact the families, if we can locate them." Paul told us.

We found chairs for everybody and sat in a circle under our tree. Paul wanted to tape record our conversation. Bob explained that they only wanted the recording, so they could remember everything we told them. The information would not be used in any other way.

Sheriff Moore said. "I think their request is reasonable. Jane, David, and Joe, I know what you are going to tell us is true, so if you have to repeat it you will say the same thing."

I felt that the Sheriff was warning us to tell them everything as it happened. I could do that so I said, "Yes, you may record what I tell you. What do you want to know."

David and Joe nodded and said, "Okay."

Paul began the questions. "When did you arrive here and the bones were discovered on what date?"

I had to get my records from the motor home and then I was able to give him exact dates.

Next Paul asked, "Who retrieved the bones from the well? I understand they were at the bottom of the well and under water."

Since I had been talking I again answered, "Firemen from Blue Pond and volunteers from Veeny were here. After the firemen retrieved Joe from the well, someone went down and cleared the bottom of all the debris and bones. I think it was a fireman but I don't know his name."

Sheriff Moore explained, "When I came later that evening to pick up the bones, they were all in a bucket and had been washed clean."

"Mrs. Cotton, I understand you saw someone in the woods, before the well accident."

"Yes, they were at the back, over there where the bigger trees begin. I saw what I first thought was a tree, but it moved so it couldn't have been a tree. They didn't come out in the open, I can't describe them."

Next, the detectives asked about how we found the graves. David gave a brief description of the day after we got Joe home from the hospital. I noted that they had not asked about the accident or about how Joe was doing now. These two were dedicated to getting the facts and nothing but the facts.

"Mr. Cotton, who owns the land where the bodies were found?"

"My brother, Rory Cotton. He gave permission for Sheriff Moore and the deputies to dig there. He was present, so was my other brother, George and myself when the bodies were found."

"The Sheriff has told me about what happened that day. We need to know about any access roads to this cemetery."

David explained, "The road we used begins near my home place, right behind the house. It was used when the timber was cut several years ago. George's son lives in the house now and I doubt if anyone could use that road without them or George or the dogs knowing it.

"The other way in would be from Thaxton Road. About a half-mile back, there is a way off this road. It is more deserted and my guess is that is the way somebody took those bodies there. Jane and I walked for a short way on that road but didn't notice any vehicle tracks."

"All right, let's go back and talk about the buckets with dead plants in them. Why had you not found those before? They must have been there even before you bought the place."

"We had no reason to go into the barn loft. Jane wanted to that day because it was something she did as a child. You do know this was her grandparents home and she and her siblings lived here most of the time when they were kids."

"Yes, and I do know someone else owned it after their death, before you bought it. We are watching the son of the people who lived here last. His stepdad is being very cooperative. We know where the guy lives now and know that in the past he has been involved with drugs. My guess is that he put the marijuana plants in the loft; probably after the family moved away."

When the conversation between Paul and David seemed finished, I asked if they would stop recording. Bob turned off the recorder and asked if I had anything more to tell them.

"This is possibly only my suspicion but I want to tell you about the Sandersons. I hope I'm not talking about innocent people, but there is talk about them dealing in drugs. They live in a very expensive house. They have pastures, with beautiful fences surrounding them, and only a few cattle. They deal in antiques, and have refurbished a place in Jarmore, Alabama, for an antique store. We don't know where their money is coming from. Could you find out where they get financing for all that?

"I have met Squire Sanderson and his wife, Betty Sue. They live in that elegant estate. I am planning a project with her, hoping to learn more about them. We also are friends with Squire's brother, Butch, and his family. Butch did work with his family but not anymore. He is not speaking to Squire now and I don't know why." I told the Detectives that was all I knew right now.

"That's interesting. We'll see what we can find out about them. Did you say his wife's name is Betty Sue? The brother, Butch, do you know his name?" Bob, the other detective, asked.

"Yes, Squire's wife is Betty Sue Sanderson. I don't know Butch's full name. His wife is Sally. They have a son and a two year old daughter."

"One more incident that I haven't asked about is the pickup that came here. Joe, I believe you were here and recognized one of the men." Paul questioned Joe.

"Bear, my dog, tried to attack the truck and they didn't stop. They must have thought nobody was here. David's truck was gone and they couldn't see mine until they went past our campers. I have told the Sheriff that one of them was that stepson, Perry. I have bought drugs from him. They did not see me that day, they may have had time to recognize my pickup."

David spoke up again, "Detectives and Sheriff, I get the feeling you may not trust us since we don't really live here. If you will contact Detective Blaze of the Rowley, Georgia police department he can fill you in about me. A few years back a fire in my shop building caused him to investigate everybody involved. It was arson, but they convicted the people who did it and that cleared us. He will be able to tell you all about us. I hope the Sheriff will allow us to visit our family in Georgia."

"Joe will be able to watch this place in a couple of weeks, and we want to go home, just for a visit," I added.

Sheriff Moore looked at the detectives. They all agreed we were permitted to go.

"I think you all have been very cooperative; we just need to know where to contact you." Paul said. "Sheriff Moore will keep you informed if we need you and also update you on what we learn about the dead men."

They did want to talk to George and his son that lived near the road to the cemetery. David gave them their phone numbers and suggested they call first. Detectives Paul and Bob, and the Sheriff left one hour after they arrived.

David and I made plans to go to our real home. We checked the date for six weeks after Joe's leg was broken. He should have the last cast off by then and we could go. I called our daughter and told her the approximate date we would be there. That was another two weeks from now.

25

We were finally having a quiet day at home with no visitors. It was a beautiful early fall day, not too hot, the right temperature for working. We now had water and I had finished all of our laundry before noon. David, Joe, and I had been working inside the old house most of the afternoon, when the phone call from Sally Sanderson came.

"Mr. Cotton, is Butch there?" She sounded excited.

"No he isn't here. Sally is something wrong?" David answered.

"Yes, I'm at Preacher Fredericks. There is a house on fire, just past his house. He wants to walk over there to see about the family. I don't think he can walk that far. I'm afraid he will fall. I have our phone so I can't call Butch. Butch dropped Kayee and me off here, so I don't have a car." Sally told David.

"Tell him to wait we'll be there in five minutes." David told her.

All three of us were in the pickup and on our way in less than a minute. I called the Blue Pond Fire Department to make sure they had been called about the fire. They were on the way; she asked directions to make sure they could find the fire. The person who called was so excited that the directions weren't very clear. I listened to what she had and confirmed that was the correct way to get there.

"I'm Jane Cotton. We are on our way to the fire. I'll call you back if we need the emergency people." I told her.

"Thank you for responding to our well accident so quickly. I think Mattie has told you what happened that day."

Sally, Kaylee, and Preacher were standing by his driveway. We got everybody in the truck and went less than a quarter mile to the fire. The fire trucks arrived right behind us, and a few minutes later volunteers from Veeny got there.

It was a large old frame home and was completely engulfed in flames. There was no way to save any part of it. The firemen and volunteers used their water to prevent it from burning the out buildings. They kept the fire from spreading into the nearby woods and pasture.

The people who lived there were in a group, sitting and lying under a tree. Some were crying; the man was so mad he could hardly talk. Their van was nearby. We all tried to talk at once. The man answered Preacher's question about what happened.

"When we got here the house was burning from the inside. It was so bad we couldn't get anything out of it. What would have happened if my family had been inside? I know who set the fire!" The man exclaimed.

Preacher tried to get him to calm down. He told us the family was the Pierces and tried to introduce us to Jason Pierce, but Jason was still talking. "I'll find out which one did it and I'll kill him! They have threatened me too many times. Maybe I do owe them money, but I don't have it. What could I do?"

Joe put his arm around Jason Pierce and asked him to sit down in his van. Joe then told him, "I think I know what you are talking about. We'll discuss that later. The people here are friends of mine. They are good people; you can trust everybody here, and they will help you and your family. Let's talk about what you need right now."

Mrs. Pierce stopped crying to ask, "Where will we go, what can we do? We have nothing left no money, no clothes, and no friends. Thank the Lord our kids are safe and no one was hurt."

"What about your family?" David asked.

"They live five hundred miles from here. We can't go there, Jason is still on probation." She said.

Preacher Fredericks spoke up, "There isn't anything you can do here. Let's all go to my house and talk about this."

The fire chief was listening. He wanted to ask Jason about the fire but quickly said, "You all go to the Preacher's house and I'll stop there when we've finished with the fire. Don't go anywhere else. Joe and Mr. Cotton, you keep him at Frederick's house until I get there."

The Pierces had two boys. Those four, the three of us, Sally, Kaylee, and the Preacher all crowded onto the front porch at his house. Sally got drinks and everybody got quiet.

Jason spoke very quietly, "It's all my fault. I should have never started selling drugs. The money isn't worth it. After I was arrested I tried to stop, but they threatened my family. I didn't name any of them when I was caught. I've had to sell some drugs to get money for my probation officer. They did this thinking I would be too scared to talk. I'm ready to name every drug dealer I know! I should have before and this wouldn't have happened. My family wouldn't be in danger. What are we going to do now?"

We were all shocked. I immediately thought of Oliver and the Alabama Drug Agents who had arrested people in this area. Maybe I should call him to come talk to Jason

Pierce, or would that put Oliver in danger. I knew Jason had to be protected from the people he was willing to name.

Preacher Fredericks interrupted my thoughts. "God has said in his word that he will take care of those He loves. That is all of us. Now, first my friends and neighbors need a place to sleep and food to eat. I have two extra bedrooms right here. I am asking them to please use them. Sally has cleaned everything. We will need more food, but I think my other friends that are right here will help and so will the church."

David quickly said, "What a wonderful thought, that God will protect all of us. Jason, you must not tell anyone what you plan to tell the authorities. I will get in touch with the Sheriff for you. After they provide some protection for you and your family, you can tell them names of drug dealers you have dealt with."

The fire chief broke up our meeting. He began to question everybody. "What are you Cotton's doing here? Who is the lady with a little girl? Preacher, I know you live here. Jason Pierce, I think that's the name you gave me, tell me who started the fire that demolished your house."

Butch Sanderson arrived and joined the group. He didn't know anything about what had happened so the chief couldn't think of a question for him. Except the chief said, "Who are you?'

Jason began by explaining that he only rented the house that it wasn't his. "I sure hope the owner had it insured. We don't have any insurance on our belongings. Somebody needs to call Mr. Bill."

I remembered an appointment I had in Veeny. I asked Butch if he would take Joe and David home and I asked permission from the chief to leave. He agreed if David stayed.

☙❧

Betty Sue Sanderson and her helpers were just about finished unloading her antiques off of their truck, when I got to Veeny. The big building was sound but she asked, "Would you have your husband come tomorrow and check the roof and the doors. I don't want these pieces to get wet or anyone to be able to steal them."

"Yes, I'll ask David and Joe to check on that in the morning. If the building needs work, what should I offer to pay them? This will be our first expense on this project."

"If they are good at what they do, offer them $8.50 an hour. Maybe we can wait on any other repairs. I have to go out of town for a few days."

She seemed in a hurry to leave. As soon as the furniture was unloaded she said, "Goodbye, Jane, here is the key to this building"

The men left; Betty Sue went in the other direction, and I went home. "What a day! Not so peaceful after all."

26

The morning after the fire David told me what happened after I left Preacher's house. He and Joe had been ready to go to bed by the time they finished there the night before and they had not told me what happened.

"The fire chief had lots of questions for Jason Pierce, who had been living in the house that burned. Jason said he was renting and told him who owned it. The other questions seemed to indicate that he thought someone had set the fire. Jason then explained that it was burning when he and his family returned. Jason said he called the Blue Pond Fire Department and Veeny volunteers, but knew that it was too far-gone to save anything. He wouldn't let his wife or boys go in to try to save their favorite things."

Jason told the chief, "Everything we had is gone and we didn't have insurance on our stuff."

"I had warned Jason not to mention anything about who he suspected. After the chief left, we had to plan how to protect the Pierces. This all could be very dangerous." Joe told me.

"We did go get food supplies for Sally to feed everybody. She and Jason's wife were getting the bedrooms ready and they cooked for all of us. Butch and Sally's two kids and the Pierce boys were playing like nothing bad had happened. I think they will be good for each other. Butch and Sally will realize that they have so much more than some people. I think Preacher will be sharing Christ with all of them as soon as we get some things settled."

David waited until the morning after the fire to contact Sheriff Moore about Jason Pierce. The sheriff was thrilled to hear some news that might help their investigation. He wanted to come that day. He didn't know what time since he had to be in court; it would be the middle of the afternoon before he could get to Veeny. Joe and David had planned to bring Jason to our place and let him talk to the sheriff here. I asked him if the detectives were coming.

"No, they are not. The sheriff wants to get all the information he can. He does know Jason Pierce and that he is on probation. He thinks he will talk more without others listening." Joe told me.

David and Joe had it all planned.

Joe explained to me, "Yesterday, before we left Preacher's house, we took Jason's van and hid it behind the church. We did not want the men, he is afraid of, to know where they are staying. I will go pick up Jason and bring him here."

David said, "We don't want Jason to tell anybody but the sheriff who those people are. We could all be in danger if we heard names. Since they are probably looking for Jason, and since his family is there we don't want them to connect Preacher's house with him."

"So you two volunteered to put us in danger." I added

"Maybe not, Jane." David answered. "We agreed to help these people. If those men who burned their house see the sheriff here, they'll probably think it's related to the bones."

"David, do you think those people that Jason was dealing with are connected to these murders?" I asked. " I think they are."

"Yes, it's pretty likely that it all is connected to the drug ring that Oliver told you about."

"I think I'll call Oliver and tell him what we know. Then if the Alabama Drug people get involved we would probably be dealing with him. He can decide whether to report this, about Jason Pierce, to his superior."

"I don't always agree with your plans but that seems like a good one," David answered me.

David and Joe were working inside the old house when I went to report on my call. "Oliver said he would pass the information about Jason Pierce to his boss. He thinks some of the drug agents will be here next week."

Joe left to go pick up Jason to have him here when the sheriff arrived.

I had time to take a good look at what they had accomplished in the old house. The first thing I saw was a hole in the ceiling and I wanted to know what was in the attic. The hole was in a corner behind the door between the two large rooms.

"That's the corner Memaw had her quilt cabinet in," I told David. "I want to see what's up there."

David got a light and a ladder and helped me look.

"There's something up here, in a bag. David, get it down for me!" I was excited.

David yelled. "Do you think it's another body?"

27

When Joe returned with Jason and Preacher Fredericks, we were sitting outside looking at our latest discovery. It was not a body, not anything bad at all. I had found one of Memaw's quilts. It was her 'Odd Fellow' pattern that she had worked so long on. Then she must have hid it for safekeeping. I remember that she took all the different scraps from the materials she had made dresses from and cut one piece of the quilt top from each. Since it was the 'Odd Fellow' pattern every piece had to be different. She then traded scraps with other quilters until she had a different color, or pattern, or stripe for each of the many pieces in the quilt. It was very pretty and in good shape. I could remember that I had dresses like some of the floral pieces.

The men were not too interested in my discovery so they sat under the tree in the chairs we had used for our report to the detectives, and started their own discussion. I learned later how Preacher got Joe and Jason interested in his life.

I decided to go inside our motor home and plan what to do with Memaw's quilt. I located some poems I had saved. They would describe how I felt about this antique. I sure needed something to think about besides drugs and murders.

My mind continued to think about Memaw's quilts. A lot of the women made quilts just for the warmth. We all used handmade quilts instead of blankets, which had to be store bought. Memaw made most of her quilts pretty as well as useable. I didn't know if her grandchildren had any of them. I had a few. I decided this one was so special that I would share pieces of it with all of her family.

> "Lives pieced together
> Stitched with smiles and tears
> Sewn with memories
> Bound by love to last throughout
> The years."
>
> "You are not now forgotten
> Nor will you ever be,
> As long as a piece of your quilt remains,
> We will remember thee!"
>
> "A quilt is more than pieces
> Of cloth stitched together.
> It is a labor of love
> That honors its maker
> Forever."

These poems were perfect for what I decided I would do with the quilt. I'll print each one of them on a card with Memaw's name, date of birth, date of her marriage to Papaw, and date of death. Maybe I'll include a picture of her as I remember her when I lived here many years ago.

I planned to make beautiful pillows using pieces of the quilt for the top. I would have enough to give to each grandchild, and every great-grandchild of Memaw's. With the poems and picture, they would make a special gift at Christmas. *"Take time to do that this year"* was the note I attached to my work area. I just hoped that I could remember what it meant.

28

Sheriff Fred J. Moore got to our place at three o'clock, which was about two hours after Jason, Joe and Preacher arrived. I knew they had a long serious talk under our tree while waiting for the sheriff. I wanted Preacher to tell me about it later.

After introducing Jason Pierce and Preacher Fredericks to the Sheriff, the sheriff immediately asked if he and Jason could use our motor home. He knew about Jason's arrest and wanted to record some of their talk if Jason didn't mind.

The only thing they told us when they finished their talk was that Jason was being arrested for violating his probation. Sheriff Moore explained that he found him carrying a gun. "The arrest is for his own protection. Will you people see that his wife and children are cared for and protected? I will try to get some people picked up very soon. If they are charged and held, Jason can be released."

Joe was the one to answer directly to Jason "We will do our very best to keep your family safe. I know we can, so don't worry. I'll be in touch to keep you informed about them."

After the Sheriff and Jason left we all wondered and I spoke quietly asking, "Are we in danger? What else can happen? Will I ever get to the end of this mystery?"

Nobody answered me. I agreed to go with Joe to take Preacher home. I wanted to talk to Jason's wife and Sally if she was there.

As Joe drove he said, "I'm glad we had that chat while waiting for the sheriff. The things David and Preacher said will make Jason think about his life. I needed to hear more about how God helps in out lives if we let Him."

"Preacher, I want you to tell me more about your life as soon as we get these people settled. Right now, we need a plan that will keep Jason's family safe. Do you think the men that burned their house intended to hurt them or scare Jason into paying what he owes?" I added.

Joe answered me quickly, "I think they will do more if they don't get the money. These drug people are dangerous. Jane, can you come up with a plan to hide Sue and the boys?"

"I've been thinking and praying about that. I think we all might be in danger, but I know they are." I admitted. I stopped to pray again while Joe and Preacher were going in the house.

Sally and Kaylee were there with Sue, Jason's wife. We let Preacher tell what had happened to Jason. Sue was quiet for several minutes before she muttered.

"Jason does carry a pistol, even though it's not allowed on probation. He wanted to protect us. I'm glad he is in a safe jail. That sounds awful, to be glad he's in jail. Who are these people trying to hurt us? I've seen two different men talking to Jason, but don't know who they are."

I hugged Sue and asked. "Sue, where are your boys?"

"Sally took then to school with her son."

"I think you will be safe here. Those men probably will think all of you left this area. If they can't find or see your vehicle here, I believe they will look other places. Since they don't know Jason is talking to the law, maybe they will stop looking for now."

"Preacher, can you let Sue and her boys stay here for awhile?"

"Sure, Sally, Kaylee and I can take care of them with God's help."

Sally responded with. "Okay, I cook and clean, Sue can help. I'm glad to help them anyway I can. We do need to find clothes for them. I've brought a few of Matthew's thing for the boys, but Sue isn't my size."

Joe spoke up, "I think Sue and Mattie, my friend, are about the same size. I'm planning on going to Blue Pond tomorrow; I'll ask her to buy clothes and things that women need. She might share some of her clothes. I'll bring them here.

"Jane, do you think it's safe for us all to attend church Sunday?"

"Yes, I think that is a good idea. We can all go and praise God for his blessings." I was so glad to hear Joe was ready to go to church.

"Now, let's think of something pleasant. Where's Kaylee and the kittens? She's always smiling."

☙❧

On the way home I told Joe, "We have a 'Wild Boar Roast' to attend on Saturday at the Squire Sandersons estate. I wonder what we can learn about them. It should be interesting if not fun."

29

Squire Sanderson had invited us to his annual 'Wild Boar Roast' when he was here asking about Betty Sue. After I told him all I could about the last day I saw her in Veeny; he had calmed down and was very friendly. He, Joe, and David talked for a long time. He went into the house and made suggestions for restoring our piece of history. He thought our location would make a great place for a restaurant, or perhaps a private hunting club, a place for guys to hang out together. David didn't like either suggestion. He and Joe did want to attend the Roast and it was this evening. I had to decide if I wanted to go with them or stay home alone. They assured me that I was invited and that other women always attended.

"Do I have to eat the wild boar?" I asked

"Well, you should if you go. I think there will be other food, Squire said it was all provided and his cook would be in the kitchen. She'll make you something else. It must be a special event," David told me.

I decided to go and went to find what I could wear. I decided on jeans for us all and the prettiest top I had. David and Joe could pick their shirts. I had asked about Mattie and Joe said she had to work.

The guys didn't remember the time so we decided to get there before dark. They knew where we were going. 'The Roast' was at the Sandersons' private club. David said the road turned where the Sandersons' home place had been. We soon found the road and a small sign that said 'Members Only'.

There was no name for the club and no rules posted. I thought, if asked we could claim we were friends of Squire and Betty Sue.

The driveway was gravel and wound through trees and up a hill. Two men with dangerous looking guns were walking near the drive. Their vehicle was parked along the road.

When I voiced my fears, Joe assured me. "Those are deer rifles. They are only checking for signs of deer or maybe wild boars."

We suddenly arrived at the lodge. It was at the top of the hill in the middle of a large cleared area. Cars and trucks were parked all around, lots of them. The lodge was a restored barn. The land had once been a field and farmed by Squires' parents. As time passed it had been planted in pine timber, and was now hidden from the road. Outside it still looked like an old barn that had only been used for storage of hay.

Inside was very different. The designers had worked their magic and it must have cost the Sandersons a lot of money. Some of the original gray lumber was used on one wall. A huge stupendous rock fireplace was the focal point and filled an end wall. The other end was devoted to a kitchen, lots of mis-matched tables and chairs were in that end of the room. Windows lined the back wall. The fireplace area had country style sofas and chairs. The chandeliers and lamps matched. The total look was prodigious and eclectic. I could see Betty Sue's antiques had been used to furnish the eating area.

People were everywhere. Squire came to us the minute we entered. He introduced us to several couples and I tried to at least remember the ladies names. The one person we already knew was Rex, the Veeny councilman. We were offered something to drink. David and Joe asked for a coke. Squire insisted that I try their special pink lemonade. I soon learned it was special because of the alcohol that was in it. I sipped slowly and went to look at the food in the kitchen. The men went outside to see the roasting wild boar. There were plenty of other snacks and a wonderful looking dinner buffet. The cook was a woman of questionable age, possibly around fifty. She wore a chef's hat so I knew she was in charge of the kitchen. As I talked with her I noticed her Hispanic accent, but I could understand her. I learned that she lived about twelve miles away and had not worked for the Sandersons very long. She told me that, "Yes, Betty Sue is home and will be here soon."

I avoided Rex by going outside to see what was happening. The boar was being removed from the pit. It seems that it had been put in the ground, after it had been gutted and washed, on large sheets of foil. Large sheets of foil had then covered it. Then it was covered with dirt and a hot fire had been kept burning over and around it for twenty-six hours. Various seasonings had been added before cooking. The whole cooked hog was now on an outside table. They were trimming the skin off each leg and slicing it for the table. Bar-B-Que sauce of various kinds would be on the buffet table. It actually looked good and seemed to be free of the dirt; I still didn't want to eat it. But I now knew how to cook and serve a wild boar.

David and Joe were enjoying all this. Joe was talking to a guy he seemed to know. I thought, that must be one of the buddies who wouldn't come to help him.

One of the men we saw walking on the road wanted to teach me how to shoot his gun. They had a practice target set-up with a deer picture on it. He said it was important to hit the buck at the right spot. I told him I had a thirty-eight pistol and could hit pretty well with it. In case a buck came by I might try it out, but no thanks to shooting his gun.

The dinner gong sounded and we all went to the kitchen end for food and drinks. Betty Sue joined us at our table Squire was somewhere else. I asked if she enjoyed her trip.

She answered "Yes."

She wanted to talk about what we needed to do first in Veeny. She was happy that the building she was using was free of leaks. I explained we were going to be gone the next week.

"I'll have more plans when I return. You and Squire need to come up with some ideas since you are paying for the repairs. I'll try to have a layout so we can decide what we want in each building. If we know what might be in the building, our workers can fix them for that business. I have found very few photos of how they looked in the fifties, but several people can remember and will advise us."

Betty Sue commented, "This is going to be so much fun."

"And lots of work," I added "I have been asking around for ladies that would like to have a shop there. Let's plan to begin work in two weeks."

Rex and his wife joined us. He didn't remember meeting Joe at the auction and wanted to know who he was. I explained that he was our friend that had been helping restore my home.

"I want to know what you are planning to have out there. You know you are in the city limits and you must get permission for any enterprise out there." Rex told us.

"Yes Mr. Arnold, we know that. When we decide what the house will be used for, you'll be one of the first to hear about it. Maybe you'd like to make a suggestion. You may come see what we are doing if you like." David answered Rex.

"Thanks for the invite." Rex replied and remained quiet after that.

We stayed at the party until late, met, and talked to most everybody there. Squire had one other brother there. He remembered us from school. He was in the same grade as David. He told us their parents had died years ago and the land had passed to the children. Nothing was said about Butch.

On the way home I remarked that I certainly didn't learn anything new and interesting about the Sanderson family.

Joe said he did, "The guy I was talking to outside sold me some marijuana on the credit. I knew I needed to contact him again so I didn't pay for it."

"Joe, you told me that you quit using drugs!" I raised my voice and almost yelled at Joe.

"Wait, I don't plan to use it. You are jumping to conclusion again. It's for the Sheriff. I figured I could help by leading the law to him." Joe explained.

"Oh, that's different. Maybe our wild boar roast did tell us something, but can you connect that to Squire Sanderson?"

30

Monday morning after the 'Wild Boar Roast' we were all guessing what had happened with Jason and Sheriff Moore. David said he thought the sheriff would call today and let us know. Joe said he was going to visit the jail and report to Jason about his family. He had permission to give him Preacher Frederick's phone number; then Jason could call Sue if he was allowed to make calls.

We all had attended church the day before. Pastor Parke and all the members were willing to help the Pierces. Pastor Parke understood the danger and said their van was out of sight and could stay behind the church. He told Sue that she could call on him or other church members if she wanted to go somewhere. The church had an emergency fund and he could give them up to three hundred dollars for what they needed immediately. Then later he would find a house they could rent. The church family would help furnish it.

Joe told us, "After I see Jason I want to tell the sheriff about my drug buy. Maybe he or the drug agents can set up something to catch this guy selling marijuana. I know his first name and I've got his phone number. I have to meet him somewhere in order to pay him and I'll tell him to bring more of the good stuff."

I asked, "David, do you know of any work that needs to be done right away on the old buildings in Veeny?"

"No, since you don't know which ones will be used. The one Betty Sue's antiques are in is in good shape. Do you two know what is going in the others?"

"Not yet, I am going to see Beth and ask her opinion. I think she would be the perfect person to be charge of finding people to have shops in our new town. I bet she will have some great ideas."

"Joe, don't you see the doctor this week?"

"I do, on Wednesday afternoon. I bet you want to plan on leaving the next day to see your family. I'll be glad to live here longer and watch the place while you and David are in Georgia. Do you have anything that Butch and I can work on while you're gone?"

"I'll talk to the owners of those old stores and Mayor Finks tomorrow. You two can work on some of the things that need repairs. Fix the roofs that leak, the porches, the steps, and anything that's about to fall, but don't change the old look. Remember we saved some of the old wood from this house. You can use that for repairs. Betty Sue has agreed to pay $8.50 an hour. Is that agreeable with you?"

Joe nodded, smiling, "It is with me and I know Butch wants to work, I think he'll agree. Will somebody, Betty Sue or the mayor, be around to advise us?"

"Yes, I'll talk to them before I leave. We'll be back in a week or two. I've been invited to a high school reunion here. I think it's only a week away."

Joe left going to Trussellville and the Benjamin County Jail. David and I had lunch. Again David asked, "What are we fixing your old home for? Are we going to live here in two rooms? Are we ready to sell the house and little farm? I bet you want to have an antique shop here."

"That's it, David, we can do that! Then we can travel all over the world buying things and taking our trips as a business expense. Of course, it may not be big enough for all we'll be buying. Can we fix the barn for storage?"

"Oh Jane, I love you, you're my best friend, and you're pretty smart. Please don't say that an antique shop is my idea. We'll talk about what this place will be later." David begged.

"I'm off to talk to Beth about her ideas on our 'New-Old-Town'. Oh, by the way, I checked the date and we have to be back in time for my class reunion. It's a week from Friday. If we leave Thursday we'll have a week at home."

31

David does not like to talk very much when he is driving. Our visit home had gone well. We visited our family, saw our friends at church, and cleaned our home. I packed some warmer clothes just in case we had to stay in Alabama longer than planned. Now we were going back to Veeny, first to attend my school reunion and then to solve the murders we were not involved in.

The three-hour drive gave me time to plan for the 'new old Veeny.' Betty Sue Sanderson had agreed to put some cash in our project. Mayor Finks and most of the councilmen of Veeny were supportive of our plan. Beth Cotton had agreed with me and had great ideas on what type of businesses we needed. She planned to talk to others and find out how many women, and maybe men too, would be interested in setting up a shop or booth in Veeny.

I started a list of the kind of entrepreneurs we needed.

    An Antique Store

    The Auction House

    A 'food of the fifties' building

    A rest area—with bathrooms

    A Shoppe of needlework—old and new

    A Shoppe of kitchenware used in the fifties, could be combined with food

    Museum—Any item used from 1900 through 1950. These items could be given or loaned from past or present residents.

Elizabeth Oliver Wooten

One building with booths to be set-up by different people. Their choice of things to sell. One section could be antiques; another section could be flea market type items.

A tearoom—An attractive place for meetings, parties, showers, etc. Could serve as office for person in charge.

Anything else suggested.

I planned to draw to scale, the streets, and buildings as they were now. I also prepared a sketch of locations of all the places I remembered. I recalled at least twenty-five businesses that I could describe.

The minutes of town meetings that I picked up from the mayor's office had been helpful. The problems of the town were in almost every set of minutes. Conflicts, elections, and people were discussed, but we really didn't need those details for this project.

The date of incorporation on March 9, 1909 with thirty-one votes for and none against was interesting. I wondered if that meant there were thirty-one voting citizens in the area. Businesses in the town at that time were the White Oak Hub Company, Blue Creek Land and Lumber Company, and Veeny Banking Company. I added forty years to that date and recalled the town as I remembered it. Now, another forty years later it had almost disappeared.

"Why don't we plan an "Eightieth Birthday Party?" I was talking to myself again. "Hey, that's a marvelous idea, Jane."

ॐ∞ॐ

I had shared my thoughts with David after I got them on paper. He was interested and approved most of them, after lots of questions about how are you going to do that. He asked about my visit with his brother's wife.

"Did Beth agree to help on this project?"

"David, you won't believe how much help George and Beth were. Beth was excited and called Rory and Joy to come hear what we were planning. George, Rory, and Joy all lived here in the fifties and recalled so many things I had forgotten. But Beth is the one who loves antiques. She could fill a shop with what she has collected."

"Well, tell me about that afternoon you spent with them."

"You should have gone with me. They talked about your Dad and the home place too. I'll tell you about that after I fill in some new facts about the town that the Cottons told me. My notes from that day are pretty good."

George told me, " Hob Black was chief of police for the town of Veeny. I think the bank was robbed four times during the forties and fifties. Some crooks were passing through town; decided it would be easy to rob the bank. They only got pennies and were caught. Another bank robbery was foiled by two ladies that came into the bank; the robbers looked at them and fled."

Joy told us about the fun people she remembered. "Mrs. Dave Chambers was one of them. She loved to tell about her bloomers falling down to her ankles while in the post office. She just stepped out of them, picked them up, and put them under her arm, hoping nobody saw them."

" I had heard that and other fun stories from her. Mrs. Chambers and Memaw were friends. I think she came to our wedding dinner Memaw cooked for us. You should remember that. Memaw went to spend the night with Mrs. Chambers and we spent our first night together in the house we are remodeling."

Rory told us, "Dell Mahan was said to have worn his overalls two weeks at a time. He stood them up, got on the bed, and jumped in. If he shaved, he was sober."

Rory talked about the school principals and teachers. "Mr. Carney Hughes was principal for a very long time. You could get sent to the principal's office to be paddled if you misbehaved." Rory said, "Oh yes, you remember we were paddled by teachers back them." Most all of the teachers were females. We had Mr. W. O. McTune for Science and John Morrow taught shop. I learned a lot of things in shop and the girls learned how to cook and keep house in their home economics class. That stuff should be taught today. I don't believe the parents are teaching it to their kids at home."

"George, your older brother talked a lot about family. He was in the Army from 1947 to 1949, then went away to college. After meeting Beth, from Kentucky, and marrying her they lived in Tennessee for many years. He and Beth moved back to the home place a few years before your Dad died. You probably know all this but I didn't. His stories about Papa as we called him were very interesting. One thing I didn't know about him was about his being called on to stop bleeding. That is almost unbelievable, unless you know our God."

George told us, "People would come to him or others would come if the injured person couldn't. Dad would silently repeat a text he had committed to memory from the Bible. I believe the scripture was Ezekial 16:6. The bleeding would stop although Dad had not seen the person. Later he received phone calls asking him to stop bleeding and he did. Dad gave the credit to God. Mama's mother had the gift to heal babies mouths of thrash, and she could stop the pain of a burn by blowing on the burned spot of skin."

"David, did you know that? Did George tell me the truth?"

"Yes Jane, I think you must have heard that and forgot it because you didn't believe it."

"Well, I'm older and wiser now and I do believe it."

George also talked about the farm you all lived on as teenagers, the same one they live on now. Their son bought the house you all built for your parents. This is his story about that home place.

" In 1947 or 1948, Dad purchased two-hundred-ten acres from Dr. Underwood of Blue Pond. The bank loaned most of the twenty-five hundred dollars for the land. There was no house, barn, or buildings of any kind on the acreage. There was a good spring of water and six hundred feet of frontage on the road. Five acres of the land was on the opposite side of the road, which made it very inconvenient to use. That spot was later sold and Mama had some neighbors nearby."

Beth and I asked some questions and then let George finish.

"Only a small part of the land was ready to plant. We needed a house and a garden nearby to feed our family of eight, we also needed a barn to house the cows and horses, and a pen for the pigs."

"The biggest part of the acreage was in timber. Dad and the boys cut the trees and trimmed them ready to be sawed. We killed up to twelve snakes a day while clearing the bottomland. Some of the logs were sold for pulpwood. The willow timber had to have the bark removed, by hand, before they would buy it. A sawmill was moved on the tract to saw the logs into lumber. We then used the lumber to build a five room house. When we were ready to build the barn, neighbors came for the barn raising."

"All of the kids, except Lee, were married and not living at home when that house burned in 1958. Again Dad, the sons, and sons-in-law built another five room house with two porches and a bathroom. Electricity had been installed in the first house when it was available for this area. The wiring was the cause of the fire. The family got out safely, but the pine lumber burned so quickly nothing was saved.

"Back to the time we bought the land. Our family lived in a rental house nearby for one year. We farmed the hill land and worked on clearing the rich bottomland. After cutting the trees for lumber, we had to remove the stumps and brush. The horses could pull out the younger growth after we dug around each stump or small tree. We used dynamite to blow up the big stumps. Some of the sticks of dynamite were still in a shed forty years later. We called the authorities that knew how to handle old dynamite, to come get rid of it"

"That's most of my notes from that afternoon. Do you have some memories to add?" I asked David who was still driving.

"Yeah, I do. Didn't George tell about Dad witching for water? People from all around the area would come get him to witch for water before they would have a well dug. I remember one time I walked behind him and held onto his forked stick. He always cut it fresh and preferred peach tree limbs because they were forked the way he needed. When we walked over water the straight end of the stick turned down. It twisted with so much force, we held onto the bark and the stick still pointed down. Our four hands couldn't stop it. When the well was dug, they found water at the depth he said. The way he found the depth was by finding another place on the same underground stream, that would make the stick point down. Then by walking back toward the spot where the stick turned down the first time, he could estimate the depth. He was always correct to within one foot about how deep the water was. That made a believer out of me. I walked all around with that forked stick and it didn't move in my hands. Dad had the gift; I didn't."

"Another thing George didn't tell about Dad was that he liked to have fun. I remember one time late in his life that he tricked George into cutting the grass. George had retired from teaching and coaching; he and Beth were living in the little house we built for Grandpa. That's the house you call 'Beth's bed and breakfast'. That was before they finished the house they live in now. The grass had grown pretty tall around the area where the spring was located. Although the water was now pumped to the house, Dad liked to stop at the spring for a fresh drink. One day as he and George sat on the porch, he didn't remind George to cut the grass. Instead he went to the peach tree and cut a branch. Then he proceeded to cut it just so for witching. George asked who had called for him to come witch for water. Dad said, "Oh, no one, I'm just going to see if I can find our spring. That got the grass cut around the spring."

That was all the time we had for reminiscing. We had arrived back at our little farm and motor home. Joe had lots to tell us.

32

Bear and Joe seemed happy that we were back. Joe told us what had taken place while we were in Georgia.

"I have been to the jail twice to see Jason Pierce. I took his wife and boys to visit him one day. The sheriff allowed him to visit with us in a separate area. Jason seems to be fine but still worried about something happening to his family. Butch and I are watching the roads around Preacher's house, where his family is staying. We have not seen any unknown vehicles around there. The boys are going to school with Butch's son. Butch or Sally usually takes them to school and they ride the bus back to Preacher's where Sally is still helping. She tries to keep the old Preacher eating well. She says he sometimes forgets about eating, but at his age I guess other things are more important."

"Jason wanted me to bring Preacher Fredericks to see him, so I did the next time I went to the jail. The day Jason was arrested, when we were all sitting outside waiting for the sheriff, the talk got around to the most important day of our lives and what happiness is. Jason said then that he had his life in such a mess that he couldn't talk about happiness, but he has been thinking about it since.

"The deputy in charge of the jail learned that Preacher Fredericks was a reverend and let the three of us talk in a room. I am learning so much about life listening to Preacher and you two. Things that Jason and I have not considered, how our actions not only affect us but also all the people around us.

"The day David, Preacher, Jason, and I sat under that tree and talked really started me to thinking about what was wrong in my life. David had said we had to think of the others that might be in danger and help in any way we could. Jason was afraid that the people who set fire to his home would be looking for him, and might try to get even by harming us. David was very quick to assure him we all would support him although he admitted to being involved in illegal drugs. That made me wonder why, when it could put you both in danger.

"When Preacher asked, "What do you feel is the most important thing that ever happened to you?" We all had different answers. I thought the war had affected me more than anything else. David had the best answer, he said, "I know marrying Jane was very important, so was the birth of our girls, but I guess being born was the most important or none of that would have happened. Jason's answer was, "I don't know, maybe nothing really important ever happened to me. I remember exactly the words Preacher used, "The most important thing that happens to any of us is our birth. We don't have much to do with it, don't recall the event, and may not have been told any details about that day, but we celebrate it once every year. From day one we grow and change. It's up to us to control most of the circumstances that affect our destiny."

"Preacher Fredericks gave us a mini sermon that day under the tree on what makes a Christian want to help his fellowman. Then he talked about being happy and how God can help us. The one thing that stuck in my mind was what he said about being happy. Jason said he didn't know what happiness was. That's why he wrote all those things about happiness and had that paper ready when Jason asked him to visit. I had not really considered what it meant either. I guess most of us are too busy trying to live day to day and don't think of the people around us.

"The day we talked at the jail, Preacher was ready to explain his thoughts on being content with what we have and how believing in God can help us find happiness. He even had some things written out for us to think about. I have a copy of that and it sent me to my house to get our Bible. Preacher had one to give Jason, hoping he would read it while he was in jail. We told him his wife and boys were going to church and how the church family planned to help them."

Joe kept talking and telling us what he had been working on while we were gone. I thought how different he is from the first day he came here looking for work. I wondered if God was getting through to him. Was Mattie making a difference, or maybe we had helped to make the change.

Next Joe told us, "Butch and I have worked on the old store buildings in Veeny. Squire's wife has been there telling us what to do and she works too. That building, with her stuff in it, is beginning to look like an antique store. She plans to advertise the next auction in Veeny and have lots of stuff to sell.

"The Mayor, Rex Arnold, and others watched us work and gave their suggestions. They had lots to say. Mrs. C, you should have been there, maybe you could use their suggestions.

Elizabeth Oliver Wooten

"Mattie came by one day when we all there working. The Mayor, Mrs. Sanderson, and Mattie had lunch together at Norman's café, after Mattie had mentioned her marketing experience. Mattie may be willing to help you all with this town project after this drug, murders, and house burning thing stops. If all that gets solved, she said she would be willing to help with publicity and a brochure about 'Ye Old New Town'.

"Mattie did come here one day and helped me clean the trailer and helped give Bear a bath. She took my laundry to the Laundromat at Blue Pond. We had a good time that day and Mrs. C, we didn't do anything you wouldn't approve of. My trailer smells better now. Mattie keeps reminding me to be careful with my leg that was broken. She says it's not completely healed. I try to do that, but it sure is good to be able to work again and drive my truck.

"I have one more thing to tell you. I've talked to my wife twice. She doesn't want me to come see her but I plan to go this weekend. She is working and living with her parents."

I thought I shouldn't ask Joe any questions about that so I changed the subject.

"We have returned to go to my high school reunion on Saturday. David is not real excited but has agreed to go with me."

33

A class reunion was not something David usually wanted to do with a free evening, but I had convinced him this one was important. I would have graduated with this class, if I had not moved away. I just knew the people attending would remember a lot about Veeny. I needed all the information I could find and we needed their support on our project.

"What do we wear to a class reunion in the dead town of Veeny, Alabama?" David remarked the day of the party.

I had attended a picnic the evening before at the little park in Veeny. Many of my classmates, most of whom I didn't remember, were there with their spouses. I told them I needed their help and would explain after dinner the following night. The dress was casual at the picnic and when I asked about the dinner the organizer said, "Nothing fancy."

"I think we can be dressy, comfortable, or casual, but not fancy." I assured David I would plan his attire. He agreed to go, just to see what I had in mind. For some reason, he didn't always trust my ideas.

We arrived late at the dinner. I had not heard about the change of time, which was told at the picnic. I probably was talking instead of listening, so David said. The meal was a typical southern Bar-B-Que with all the trimming and there was plenty left for us.

And would you believe Rex Arnold was there. He was married to a former classmate. I recalled later that he didn't say much. I think he was tired of us showing up at so many places.

Mrs. Dee Finney, the former class president, began the after dinner activities. Classmates told things that had happened in high school, some were fun, others sad. She reported deaths of classmates and spouses. A moment of silence or prayer was in memory of them. When she asked me to tell them what I wanted them to do, I began with questions.

"How many of you have lived here most of your lives, or at least all of high school?" About half of the thirty people said they had.

"Do you remember what Veeny was like when you graduated?" I asked.

One classmate answered, "It sure was different then from what it is now. It was a busy small town. It had everything we needed. It was almost as big as Blue Pond. They were the football team we always wanted to beat. Most of the time they won."

Another person said. "Veeny looks so bad now, it's almost deserted. What happened?"

"Who knows when the first train came through here? The town was incorporated the next year."

Dee answered, "I think Veeny was formed in early 1909."

"That's right. The town was incorporated on March 9, 1909. The first passenger train ran through Veeny over the Illinois Central tracks on February 10, 1908. Several of the businesses we remember were formed before that date. We are in a town that is about eighty years old and it's about to die.

"A friend and I have a new vision for this town. I need your help in recalling everything we can about what was here in the 1950's. We plan to reopen shops and hope to have them all resemble the stores and businesses that were here in the past.

"I don't have any details yet. If any of you want to help. contact Dee or me. I will keep you posted on what's happening. We do plan an eightieth-birthday party for the town next March; you will all get an invitation. Now, I want to hear your memories."

One person said, "I remember Moomaw's Café. I think he came from up North somewhere. He was a 'character'—called everybody 'Hon'. I think he was usually half drunk, but he had fun. His café was right in the middle of town. He had two sons, younger than us."

Another man said, "J. W. Rogers was the banker. He had a black driver named 'Shorty'. I think his name was Shorty Black. He was short and black. The bank clerk was Evelyn Reid. I think she is still living." He also said, "Julius Reid and wife Eva Dell were the Postmasters. I know she is still living here in their old home."

"That's good to know; we will talk to both of those ladies."

"Flossie Deadman was the telephone switch-board operator. She knew everything that happened in this part of the county. Their house was right downtown and the switchboard was in a front room. Later the Deadmans ran a café across the road from the Bank.

Elizabeth Oliver Wooten

"Right in front of their house was the taxi stand. Jim Shotts was the driver and Pud Ray was his assistant. They sold liquor and cigarettes at their little place. The liquor sales were illegal." This came from a spouse of a classmate that had lived here most of her life.

"The oldest stores were owned by the Weatherfords. Harve Weatherford had the large store on the corner. Ross, his son continued to run the store. We all remember his wife, Mary Bliss. She was one of our teachers. Mary Weatherford taught school, I think she was married to Tom Weatherford. He was president of the bank. Miss Evie Weatherford, an aunt taught second grade. She never married, but she was a sweet person and a good teacher. The huge building that held their business for many years, was on the corner and the building is still there." Another person told us.

I was taking notes but wished I had asked to record their memories. I would have much more information for Betty Sue.

"Speaking of stores, I remember Ed Osborne's hardware and everything store. Cleve Shotts and his wife, Madge, owned a general merchandise store. That building is still standing, so is the one E. L Davis built for his grocery store. Mrs. Wright had a ladies type store right beside those other two. Oh, I have to tell you about Mr. John Holland. He was the clock and watch repairman and had a clubfoot. That is a badly deformed foot. One young girl was said to have laughed at him. Her baby was born with a clubfoot. She did ask Mr. Holland for forgiveness." Someone else informed me.

"Do you remember Brother Bill Burns. He was our street corner preacher, except he sat on the doorsteps of businesses. If you passed him he always asked, "How's your commandments? Are you living up to them?" One time he was asked to go to Mississippi and pray for rain. He did, and they say it rained a flood.

"The town also had its share of bootleggers and drunkards, but I won't name them." Those facts came from another person.

Dee was taking notes for me. Now she was ready to tell what she remembered about those years.

"J. C. Williams owned a saw mill, lumber yard and planer mill. Newt Massey owned and managed the hub mill. It was the only manufacturing business in town. I read that it was the last operating hub mill in the United States that made hubs for buggies and iron wheel wagons. Mrs. Belle Massey, his wife, taught school. No one has mentioned the drug store. Abe Martin started it and he served really good ice cream and fountain cokes."

Bud was waiting to talk. He had come back to Veeny after college and taught at our school for many years. He began with "Tom McKinney was the blacksmith. His business was in the middle of the sand bed, that's what the middle part, or lower level of town was called. There were three filling stations. They pumped gas and fixed the automobiles. The owners were, Stencil Reid, F. Albright, and Pony Nelson. One of the old stations is still standing. Jane, do you plan to hand pump gas again?"

"No, Bud, we wouldn't be allowed to do that, but maybe we can have an old pump for show. We hope to have a museum to show things like that. Our children have never seen many of these things we used just forty years ago. You know, one of my favorite places was the railroad station. The trains delivered the mail and everything else we ordered from Sears Roebucks or Montgomery Ward catalogs, including baby chickens. The passenger trains traveled from Birmingham to Chicago. They stopped at our station until the fifties. I know because David and I caught one the night after we married and went to Chicago. He had a job there."

One other memory from a lady, who had lived on a farm, "I recall all of the cotton gins. Bill Shotts owned one and Hosey Scott owned another one. Going to the gin was the highlight of my year. When the was cotton picked, we got to ride on top of it, going to the gin and watch while it was sucked into the gin. I was afraid I might get sucked in."

I thanked them. "This is great, You have told me so much I hate to stop. Thank you all and you'll be hearing from us. It is getting late, let's eat again and then go home. If some of you want to, we could walk around town. I bet we would remember more interesting things that happened here."

34

It was now time to consider what we had accomplished and what we could do next. David and I sat down at breakfast the next day to make a list of what we had done, the events that were happening here, and what we might be able to do about them.

I talked first and wrote down the highlights. "We came here to rebuild this old house and make something of this little farm that I grew up on. So many other things have kept us busy we haven't had time to do that."

I begin to name things; "We arrived here only six weeks ago and look how much better this place looks. We have new friends. We found human bones in the well. Joe Burns has become a changed man and has helped so much. He and Bear are watching this place so we can visit others and go home for a week. Joe is trying to help solve these three murders by connecting his drug buddies to some of these events.

"We are reacquainted with your brothers. I've seen some cousins. We've visited the church we attended in the past. I feel like we are helping Preacher Fredericks, who is a former pastor of that church. We've met Butch and Sally Sanderson, attended their daughter's birthday party. We attended an auction in town and met the mayor and a councilman. We attended a wild boar roast and met more Sandersons that I am still suspicious of. That's three Sanderson brothers, one of them doesn't speak to the others and I don't know why. I do like the wives of two of them. Betty Sue, wife of Squire the oldest one, and Sally, Butch's wife. Squire and Betty Sue are very interested in antiques and I admire that. She is trying to preserve some history by helping to restore the town. That reminds me, I plan to meet her tomorrow.

"Oh yes, we discovered two graves of murdered men hidden in a cemetery. Now the authorities are trying to connect us to all the murders. I think we have to help solve these crimes before they blame them on us. Maybe I can become another Jessica Fletcher. She was the fiction writer that solved all the murders in that television program. Don't forget the pots of marijuana in our barn loft. I really think that guy that lived here, Perry, is a part of all of this. He probably used this place for selling drugs. I bet he knows who killed those people. I hope the Sheriff arrests him soon."

I kept reviewing all the things we had done. "We attended a high school reunion and I have lots of information about the good things that went on here in the fifties and before. We even went to a Hew-Haw program and met Elvis. We have become friends with Mattie who wants to get married and start a family."

David interrupted, "So, I know all that! What next?"

"Whatever is next I hope it's something good. We didn't mention the fire, and Jason Pierce. I am worried about his family. He plans to tell the sheriff names of the people he thinks set fire to their house.

"We need to contact the sheriff to tell him we're back. I think Joe has talked to the sheriff about his drug purchase.

They are planning something to get evidence, the next time Joe meets his drug dealer."

"Jane, what should I do to the house next? I am not going to sit here and think about all that." David almost yelled at me.

"Okay, I have been thinking about the house. I see Joe has cleared more of the growth around the barn. You need to look the barn over and fix a few boards. Make sure the roof doesn't leak. That area is looking like it did when I lived here.

"I want the well to become a focal point in the yard. I think the well shed can be fixed. It used to have wood shingles on the top. Can you find enough to repair the side that's missing the shingles?"

"Why do you want the well shed fixed, it will never be used for water. We have city water here now."

"I know that, but it will be one more thing that I remember from the past. We'll fill in the well or cover it over and put an outside faucet or fountain under the shed.

I began telling David all the things I had thought of about the house. "The original house had wood shingles on the roof. I recall Papaw splitting shingles off logs and letting them season before replacing ones on the roof. The rooms that were added to the original house had tin roofs. Maybe you can use tin for the areas that need replacing. I doubt that wood shingles are available any more.

"The outside wood planks on the original parts of the house look fine now that the old siding, that had a fake brick look, has been removed.

"I have sketched the way the original porch looked and drew a plan for the size and where it was attached to the two rooms we have left. You will have to tell me if it can be replaced. Did you test the fireplace yet? I'd like to build a fire in it. Cold weather will be before long."

"Yes, to your last question. The fireplace is safe to have a fire in. The old chimney is good. Maybe, to your question about shingles on the well shed. Joe and I will work on the barn first then we'll talk about replacing the porch. What else have you dreamed up?"

"I have a few more ideas, but I need a little more time to decide about the inside. I'll tell you about those later.

"Next, I have to work on plans for restoring the town and getting the people involved in a worthwhile project. I won't be able to help you today."

35

Saturday began as a typical day for us. The sun was shining and the temperature was just perfect for a fall day. I tried to get David to relax and rest since Joe was busy and Butch was not coming to work that day. Joe told us he had a meeting in town and would explain later.

Bear, Joe's dog, was very friendly and happy with us. He seems to think we were all family. When we let him off his chain, he ran around and sniffed everything, I think he would have attacked anything or anybody that tried to come around our farm. He would mind us if we told him a person was a good guy. He made me feel safe, even with all that had happened. Nothing had been solved. I said a prayer that the sheriff, detectives, or drug agents had something to report. The report I got from Joe was something different and even funny.

When Joe returned from Veeny, he explained what had taken place at Norman's café.

"I had already planned with Sheriff Moore about my drug buy from Mac. The sheriff wanted to use a wire recorder and got one for me to wear when I met Mac. He showed me how to put it on when I was at the jail visiting Jason. He thought it would be best if I didn't meet with him the day I planned to get together with Mac to buy more drugs. Since the state drug agents are now working with the sheriff, they wanted to know all about our plans. A couple of days ago when I called to tell the sheriff that I was meeting Mac today at Norman's he told me the agents, whom nobody in Veeny knew, would be nearby and listening to what we said."

"Mac showed up right at noon as we had planned. He was driving a big pickup with all his hunting stuff, including guns in it. He was alone, which I thought was good. I tried to decide if he had a gun on him and couldn't tell, since he is a big heavyset man. You saw him when we went to Squire Sanderson's. I begin our visit by talking about hunting. I went hunting with him once; we drank too much and didn't see a thing to shoot."

Mac told me his latest hunting story.

"Joe, you gotta hear this about Po Boy, my coon dog. You are not going to believe this but I swear to God, it's the way it happened. Willie and me went out coon hunting the other night. Our dogs wus trailing a coon across a cornfield. That old coon ran to some trees near a creek and climbed one. Joe, don't you remember that creek near the Sandersons that had lots of water in it. Well, when that coon went up the tree, Po Boy went up right behind it; he climbed that tree just like the coon did. That dam coon jumped to the next tree and got away. Now, my dog is about fifty foot high in that tree, we could see his eyes shining when we shined our light up there. We called and called, and could see the limbs moving but he wouldn't or couldn't come down. It was after midnight so Willie and me went home.

"The next day, about noon, we went back to that tree and called and whistled for Po Boy and sure enough the limbs moved. He was still up there. I tried to climb that goddurn tree but I could only get about twelve feet up. My poor dog was in real trouble sitting in that tree. We decided to call for help, Squire has a ladder, but we knew it wasn't long enough, so we called this guy with a bigger, longer ladder. He wanted to help us and showed up pretty quick. When he got there and found out how high that dog wus he didn't even unload his stuff. He told us to call somebody else. We tried the fire department in Blue Pond but they wouldn't come, so we called the power company. They couldn't officially help us but gave us the name of one of their men who climbed poles and who was a hunter. We called him and he came right away, after Willie gave him directions about three times.

"Now, you understand this was getting to be quite a show. I bet there was forty people there. They were taking pictures trying to show that dog fifty-five foot high in a tree. One guy filmed the whole rescue effort."

"Mac had to stop to eat and drink, while everybody in Norman's was waiting to hear what happened." Joe told us. "I was afraid that wire thing I had on wouldn't last long enough to record what we needed. I wondered where those agents were and if they were listening."

Mac continued his story. "The pole climber had all his stuff and said he could climb that high with no problem. The next thing was to make sure the dog wanted help and wouldn't fight him or try to bite him. Po Boy never bit anything except his bread or an old bone. I told the fellow that my dog was tired and hungry and that he wouldn't hurt him. Then we had to figure out how to get Po Boy down. You see, this tree was so near the creek that he was up over the water. The climber guy wanted to tie ropes around him and let him down that way, but straight down he would be in the creek. So one of the men watching went and got his boat and got ready to catch Po Boy. That dog was so happy his tail wagged all the way down that fifty-foot drop.

"Now if any of you don't believe my dog can climb a tree, this guy has a video of him coming down. I tell you it was hard to believe how high up he went after that coon."

After Joe told us his 'coon and dog story', I was waiting to hear about the drugs. Joe said he waited until the lunch crowd left the café then he showed Mac his money and asked him.

"Mac, did you bring me more marijuana or that other drug?"

"I have both; which do you want?"

"I just need a little of both of them. I'm doing much better and don't use it very often. I'm working again and trying to find my wife. I don't know for sure but maybe she was my problem.

"I think I had told Mac all that to make it seem like a usual drug buy." Joe explained to us. "We exchanged money and drugs and Mac left. I waited for him to drive off and then looked for those drug agents. They were in a car over by the side of the café that didn't have windows. They said they had heard all of that and that it was recorded. They even took pictures of Mac and his truck, but didn't want to arrest him yet. They said I might have to testify at his trial."

"What trial? They have to arrest somebody first." I injected.

Joe didn't seem concerned about any of it. I decided we were safe for now.

After hearing that wild story about Mac's dog, we had a fun evening at home. Mattie came and the guys grilled hamburgers. We played cards until late. Joe didn't mention that he was going to see his wife the next day.

The other thing that seemed worse than the accident, the murders, or the house burning happened the following Monday morning.

36

We had just finished a late breakfast when we got a call from Butch Sanderson. He was so upset David had a hard time understanding him.

"David, I called the county law! Did I call the right one? They took Kaylee about ten minutes ago!"

"Butch, what's wrong? Yes, that's the only law enforcement we have here."

"A man grabbed Kaylee and put her in a pickup. Sally saw what happened but she couldn't see the man or truck very well. They were too far away. Sally screamed for me and they were gone before I could see anything. Someone else must have been in the truck or they couldn't have left so quickly, it was parked on the old logging road."

"We'll be there in a few minutes. Don't try to follow them. It may be dangerous"

David, Joe, and I jumped in the truck and were on our way to Butch and Sally's house. David explained that something happened to Kaylee

"David, tell us what happened! Did you lock our doors?"

"I did. Some man took Kaylee. Butch called the law and doesn't know what to do. I don't either but we can be there for them. Maybe the sheriff or law can track them. Their pickup was on the logging road but they don't even know which direction they went."

Elizabeth Oliver Wooten

When we got to the Sanderson's home, Sally's mother was there with them. We tried to calm Sally by telling her they wouldn't hurt Kaylee and that we would find her. She was finally able to tell us more about what happened.

"I was watching her." Sally held tight to her Mother's hand as she talked. "She was outside with Shaddie, her kitten. When Shaddie went towards the woods over there she ran after him. She had just picked him up when a man ran out of the woods and grabbed her. At least she has her beloved Shadrack with her. I saw the whole thing; Kaylee screamed, but he was running so fast. I got off the porch and ran after them but the pickup left so quickly I couldn't do a thing. I don't know what color it was, it was a dark color, maybe black, I couldn't see the tag."

Butch said, "I had just got home and was changing a bad tire. I couldn't follow them. We aren't sure where they went, through the woods or back to the road. I'd been to take the boys to school. Sally and I both screamed and cried a bit before I thought to call the law. Then I called David; I knew David knows the sheriff. He was in the office when I called and said they would come talk to us."

David got everybody together, and asked that we all hold hands and pray. He led the prayer and asked God to protect Kaylee and her kitten, to comfort her and let her feel safe wherever she was. David also prayed for the men who took her, that they would let us know where she is and why they kidnapped her. Then he asked God to be near her family and all of us as we wait.

Sally's mother, Mama as we called her, fixed coffee and brought over her homemade doughnuts. We all had relaxed a little by the time Sheriff Moore and two deputies arrived.

The sheriff's first question was to David. "What are you doing here? You two seem to be involved in everything that happens around here. Joe Burns shows up at the jail about every day and now he's here."

David explained, "Butch and Sally Sanderson are friends of ours and we came to help. We're waiting for you to tell us how to start looking for Kaylee."

After the Sheriff had all the details he could get from Sally, he and the deputies went to search the woods. He did not want us helping.

The Sheriff was back in a few minutes and said there was no tracks to follow. It had not rained in over a week.

The Sheriff told us, "We feel sure the truck got back on the highway less that a quarter mile from here and headed west, away from here. My deputies are checking with residents to see if anyone noticed the pickup. We hope to have a description of the vehicle soon. What time did this happen?"

Butch put his arm around his wife; "It was just before nine. Are you sure there is nothing we can do?"

"I want you and the others to tell me everything you can think of that might cause somebody to steal this little girl."

I was the first to answer and ask, "Could this be connected to the fire and Jason Pierce being willing to talk? Kaylee's mother helps Preacher Fredericks at his house and Kaylee goes there with her. Jason's wife and boys are staying there. Butch picked the two boys up this morning to take them to school with his son, Matthew."

"Jane, you talked to me weeks ago about some Sandersons. Are these Sandersons the same ones?"

"Different brother, Butch is the younger brother who doesn't talk to that brother." Squire is the brother I wanted you to check out."

"Mr. Sanderson, or Butch if I may be friendlier, you need to explain. Would your brother do something like this?"

"I don't think he would. I don't know what reason he could have to scare Kaylee and us. Betty Sue, his wife, really likes our kids; she came to Kaylee's birthday party a few weeks ago. I haven't wanted to talk to him since I moved back here and he hasn't contacted me."

David asked the sheriff, "Have you learned anything since you arrested Jason Pierce? You haven't given us any more information about the dead men."

"I can't answer you right now. We have some information from Pierce and are working on that. I need to know more about this situation. Who can tell me anything else?" Mrs. Sanderson have you ever seen any men around here that you don't know or anybody around where you and Kaylee go that could have been watching her?"

Sally had been crying again but she answered, "No, I haven't noticed anybody. I can't think of any reason those men would grab her, or why they would be out there in those woods."

Joe had been listening and decided to ask, "Butch, since we have no logical explanation for this, maybe you or the sheriff should go see your brother. I know you don't want to talk about what has happened between you two, but this is important."

I asked Sally and Butch. "I'll call Betty Sue and at least tell her what happened, I have her cell number. Is that all right with you?

"Yes, do that and ask if her husband is home." Sally answered for her and Butch.

"David, you do have our phone don't you?"

There was no answer but I left a message for her to call me saying it was urgent. None of us knew their home number and Butch didn't want to go there. He didn't think his brother would do this.

The sheriff said he was going to work with the deputies to check on some other things. He asked to be notified immediately if the Sandersons received a ransom note. If Kaylee wasn't returned in twenty-four hours he would report a kidnapping and get more help for the search. He got Butch's cell number and promised to let them know of anything he learned.

ೂೊ

We talked Sally into going with us to the Preacher's house since he was expecting her. Butch wanted to stay home in case they brought Kaylee back. Sally's mother would also be there. I asked Butch to call Sally or me at the Preacher's house if he learned anything. I planned to stay with Sally and bring her back when the boys got out of school. Matthew would be so upset about his sister and we really needed to keep a watch on him. Those men might try to harm him.

We made room for Sally in our pick-up to go to the Preacher's house. I wanted her busy with something. Preacher and Jason's wife would let her talk and pray with her.

Elizabeth Oliver Wooten

I went back to the Preacher's house after I had taken David and Joe home and stayed until the bus brought Matthew and the Pierce boys home. On the way to their house, Sally told Matthew what had happened. He was very upset and asked questions that we couldn't answer.

Butch was home and very mad. I told him I had not heard from Betty Sue, I did have our phone with me. He had not heard from anybody. Mama, Sally's mother had a big meal cooked and insisted that we all sit down and eat. We had prayer again and I stayed and ate with them. The food was very good. Mama was doing what she did best, trying to comfort her family and staying busy, while praying for them all. She wanted me to take the leftovers to David and Joe. I did and arrived home before dark.

The day was not over yet. I received an urgent call before bedtime.

37

"Jane, this is Betty Sue, I have to tell somebody. Will you listen?"

"Of course, what's wrong?" I knew from her voice something had happened. It can't be anything worse—please God let it be good!

"When I was getting things ready to meet you tomorrow, I went to the lodge to get a table set to put in my Veeny store. I didn't know anyone was there and unlocked the door and went in just before dark. I first heard a child's voice, then realized somebody was in the kitchen. I walked in and found Kaylee with Mrs. Sanchez. You may remember her, our cook, from the roast party. She and Kaylee, and the kitten were talking and eating. I was so surprised. Kaylee was glad to see me. She hugged me and asked me to take her home. Mrs. Sanchez got so excited and scared. She said,. "No! You can't do that! I have to keep her here for a few days. Mr. Sanderson knows about us. You can't take her or tell him you saw us here."

"I had to leave them there. I know Mrs. Sanchez will take good care of Kaylee. Jane, I don't know what is going on. Squire isn't home and I'm afraid of him. I won't even ask, or let him know that I saw Kaylee. Please call Sally and Butch and tell them she is safe. But promise me you won't tell them who told you or where she is. I know this could be very dangerous for Butch."

Elizabeth Oliver Wooten

I took a few moments to think about what Betty Sue had said. When I realized she was just asking me not to tell Sally and Butch where this came from, I agreed. "Betty, Kaylee was snatched from her yard this morning by a man. We all have been so worried. I promise I won't tell them how I got the information but I must call them right now. I'll say she is well and being cared for by a woman. Will you be all right?"

"Yes, I'll be fine, I won't talk to Squire about this, I think he will be home late tonight. He knows I plan to work at Veeny tomorrow. I'll leave early and would you meet me at Norman's for breakfast?"

"Yes, I'll see you there about nine in the morning. Thank you so much for calling."

I looked for Butch's phone number the second we ended our conservation. I quickly told David what I was doing and what Betty Sue had asked me to promise: not telling where I got the information about Kaylee.

"David, I didn't promise I wouldn't tell the sheriff. She only asked that I not tell Sally and Butch. She thought it would be dangerous if Butch tried to come after Kaylee."

When Butch answered I told him I could only talk a minute "Butch, I had a phone call that said Kaylee was well and being cared for by a woman. I think you will hear more about it tomorrow. I know who called but I had to promise not to tell you who it was. I am calling the sheriff with the information I have. We'll talk to you tomorrow, now tell Sally that Kaylee is safe."

"David will you call the sheriff; if you get him, I'll tell him what I know."

38

Sheriff Moore showed up at eight-thirty the next morning. He assured us they had a plan.

"What you told me last evening is pushing us to act now. I really need to know how I can verify that the Sanderson girl is being held at this place owned by Squire Sanderson. Mrs. Cotton, how can we do that? You talked to somebody; tell me about it."

"The person who called me is afraid of the people who took Kaylee. That person found Kaylee, by accident and wanted Kaylee's parents to know that she was safe and wouldn't be harmed. The people who abducted her don't know about the call I received. You know where she is being held. Now tell us what you can do."

Sheriff Moore hesitated, "We do know more about Squire Sanderson. Jason Pierce has given us some information about him. The Alabama drug agents have been watching the Preston Perry that you told us about for weeks. Perry has had contact with Squire and his people. The agents are out now looking for Perry. After they arrest him and we get search warrants for Squire Sanderson's home and other buildings we plan to go there. We know that Joe's contact, Mac, is connected to those people.

"My deputies and I, the drug agents, and the state detectives are planning on raiding the Sanderson place. We had hoped to go in there very early one morning when most of his people would be there. This information about the little girl possibly being held there has changed our plans. The drug people are delaying this until they find Perry. They want all of them arrested about the same time. We have tried very hard to keep word from getting out that we have arrested Jason Pierce. He is so sure the Sanderson people set fire to his house and has given us names of who he thinks did it."

It was time for me to go meet Betty Sue Sanderson but I didn't want to tell the Sheriff that. I was just about to interrupt him when David's phone rang. We all listened after he said it was Butch.

David repeated each sentence that Butch said; he knew it was important that we hear it.

"David, I know you and Jane want to know this so I called the minute I got off the phone."

"Who called you, Butch?"

"My brother, Squire."

"What did he tell you?"

"He said Kaylee would be brought back within the hour. His men took her to scare me. He made me promise not to talk to the law about that ranch in Texas and not to report this as a kidnapping. I offered to swear on my Bible that I would never talk about that if he would just leave my kids alone."

"Butch, I'm so glad Kaylee will be home soon."

"David, I promised Squire and he believes me. I think he's satisfied and won't bother us again. I really believe the Lord was watching over Kaylee. We can't wait to see her."

David ended the call with. "We'll come see her soon, but Jane is busy this morning. Thanks for letting us know."

Memories and Murders

"David and Sheriff Moore, I have to go. That's great news."

ം൙

I knew I could tell Betty Sue about Squire's call to Butch and that Kaylee was being returned home. I could also tell her that I didn't reveal that she was the one who called me last night.

On my way to Veeny to meet Betty Sue for breakfast at Norman's I had a lot to think about. I wondered what she wanted to talk to me about. I didn't think it had anything to do with our plans for Veeny. She sounded very upset when she called last evening. Finding Kaylee was good; I'm so glad she called and told us. She had no idea why she was at their lodge. Now that I know her husband had the little girl snatched, should I tell her? I guess I need to listen to what she has to say first.

Betty was already having coffee and I needed some badly. "I'm so sorry that I'm late but things have been happening again this morning. I need some coffee. Betty, how are you today?"

"I'm alright, didn't sleep much. Squire came home at one o'clock. I didn't talk to him. He was still asleep when I left this morning. After we have breakfast, I want to tell you something. I hope it won't upset our friendship or working together. I just need to talk and don't have anyone else I trust." Betty Sue replied.

Then she asked. "Do you think Kaylee is alright?"

"Yes, I think she is fine. Her parents were told last evening that she was okay and being cared for.

"The sheriff was at our house this morning asking questions. He was planning to start a search for Kaylee and had questions for me about where I got the information. Luckily, Butch called before I answered him.

"Butch had a call from Squire this morning. He said Kaylee was being returned in an hour and that everything was fine. He didn't want to treat it as a kidnapping. He needed to get that information to the sheriff."

Our food came and we both were quiet while we ate. We finished and found that we were the only customers left in the café.

I asked her, "What is wrong? I'll be glad to listen."

Betty Sue began. "I am afraid of Squire. A few weeks ago, I asked him some questions about our finances. He became furious immediately and yelled at me. I thought he was going to knock me down just for that one question. I was wondering why he always had cash. He has always had me pay for antiques and stuff with cash rather than checks or credit card. That was the day we brought antiques to put in the building here.

"I left that day after we unloaded the furniture. I soon realized I didn't have anywhere to go. I stayed in a motel a few days and came back. Squire was glad to see me and didn't ask me anything. He's been awfully quiet since. He never answered my question. I have not asked him anything since, but I still would like to know about the cash.

"I also want to know why he had Kaylee at the lodge."

"Betty, where is your family? How long have you and Squire been married?"

"My parents are dead. I don't have any brothers or sisters. I lived in California after college. The friends I had there were not very special. I met Squire in Texas about five years ago; we've been married three years. He is divorced.

His ex-wife has their two children. I think they live in Texas. He goes there a lot. I went with him when Butch and Sally lived on his ranch. I really like their kids but I don't get to see them very often. Butch and Squire are not talking to each other since they came back here."

"There is something I don't understand. Your home here is very nice and you all have cattle. Does your money come from the sale of cattle, do the antiques sell at a good profit, or does Squire have another job? Forgive me if I'm too inquisitive. Your question about money seems to have set him off."

"I guess the cattle bring in some money. He pays his helpers to take care of them and go to auctions. They bring some cows from Texas. I think some of them may come from Mexico. I heard them talking about a shipment from there. The antiques are more my hobby; they do show a profit but not much."

Betty continued. "I have to ask him about Kaylee and what is going on. I think he will be mad and he gets so violent. What do you think I should do?"

"I do know a little about this. I'll tell you what happened with Squire and Butch this morning. Squire called Butch and Sally's house and agreed to bring Kaylee home if Butch would swear to never tell about the ranch in Texas. Butch agreed and Kaylee should be home by now. Butch must know something your husband is afraid of. They don't know you were the one who called me. He can't blame you for that if he doesn't know about that call.

"I'll tell you something else. Squire came to our house and asked me where you were the day you left from here recently. So, it won't do for you to come to our place to hide. I do think you might need to disappear for a while, or at least don't ask questions about money."

Betty Sue then said. "I've involved you in my problem and I shouldn't have. I just don't know what to do."

"Betty, I'm glad you told me, if something did happen to you, I would know who to blame and ask if you don't show for our next meeting. I'm trying to think of something to help you. Let's go see the mayor and talk about our 'New-Old Town' for a while. You can tell Squire we've been working on that project."

"All right, I feel a little better but I'm still afraid of him. We can work here most of the day. Work is what I like, especially creating something."

"Did you know that I have a degree in interior design? I did that for twenty years. It became too much work so I turned my business into a gift shop in Rowley, Georgia."

"No, Jane, I didn't know that. Then you do have experience in shops and hiring people. We may not exactly need to hire employees but we need more good people to help sell this town idea. I met your friend, Mattie, while you were gone. She is a little interested in what we're doing here and she has a degree in marketing. Wouldn't that be nice if she would help us?"

"Betty Sue, you go on over to the mayor's office. I need to go home with food for David and Joe's lunch. I'll come back in about an hour."

"That's okay, I'll be fine here. Call if you can't get back today."

I really had to know what the sheriff's plan was about arresting those people. If he planned to raid Squire and Betty Sue's place, I wanted to keep her away. I really didn't think she was a part of any illegal drugs.

39

I returned to our temporary home as quickly as I could. When I had their lunch of sandwiches and iced tea ready, I called for David and Joe to come eat. I needed to talk to David and find out what the sheriff was planning. Since Joe was with us at our table, I had to discuss Betty Sue's problem in front of him. Before I told them what was wrong, I asked, "David, what is the sheriff going to do about arresting those people?"

"He was not sure. I don't think his plans changed very much. He thought the drug agents had already arrested Preston Perry. Since Perry lives near Mississippi, he didn't reach them this morning. He wanted to tell them the situation with Kaylee was resolved and they could wait about arresting Perry."

Joe told us, "Sheriff Moore didn't want you two to know when they planned to conduct the raid on the Sanderson's place. He thinks you might tell them or mention it to his wife or brother."

"Oh my gosh, that makes me so mad! I'm going to give him a piece of my mind when I see him again. After all we have done to find these people. Joe, you helped a lot. Did he think about that? I guess he trusts you more than us. Can you tell me what his plans are? I have to protect Betty Sue."

David immediately asked. "What do you mean by protect her?"

"Well, I got you two together to tell you what I heard from her this morning. I met her for breakfast at Norman's like she asked. After I told her that Kaylee was being returned home she tried to calm down, but she asked if I would listen to her problem. Of course I did. She is afraid of Squire. She had asked him about his cash money a few weeks ago and he became furious. She left for a few days but didn't have anywhere to go, so she went back home. He hasn't talked to her since. Now with him involved in taking Kaylee and threatening his brother she is scared of what he might do next. I didn't mention anything about drugs or what the sheriff might do.

"She is waiting for me to work with her in Veeny today. Squire knows she will be there all day. If she goes home and the law goes in to arrest Squire, they would probably arrest her too. Squire may be so upset that he will hurt her even before that happens. I'm sure she does not know what he has been doing. She talked about going to Texas with him. She thinks he gets some of the cattle from Mexico."

"Jane, how do you get so involved with everybody?" David asked.

"I only try to help, I only want to help. I only want to solve these murders," I yelled. "I am so mad at that sheriff; he must think we have something to hide. I may want to hide Betty Sue from him and her husband. What should we do now?"

"Don't ask me what we should do." David spoke quietly. "You get us involved in other people's problems. You figure it out."

No one spoke for at least five minutes. I knew that if David was mad at me, I should not say any more. I think we all decided to pray and think about the problem. "What could I do to keep Betty safe? I really feel that she could be in danger." Instead of talking to myself I finally spoke and asked, "Joe do you think Mattie could meet me in Veeny? Do you know if she is working today?"

"She isn't scheduled to work today. We plan to get together later today and have dinner together tonight. You can call and ask if she would meet you."

"I think I'll do that. If she has time, we can plan our first announcement about our restoration of Veeny. I think I can get her to help. I'll let you explain to her about what's happening with Kaylee and the sheriff and drug dealers."

"That's not all I have to explain to her. I want to tell you first and see how it sounds. Do you two have time to listen?"

David finally said, "Yeah, we'll listen. Jane can take time to listen before she goes off again."

"I never did tell you what happened when I went to see my wife. She was nice enough to me. We talked for a long time. I tried to make her understand that I had changed since she left. I apologized over and over about the way I acted when we were together. I really was sick then and those drugs just made things worse. I told her I wanted to start work on our old house. She listened but didn't really consider coming back."

"Joe, do you still love her? Do you think she loves you?"

Joe spoke softly, "That's not a question I can answer. I don't know. Anyway, she said she did not want to come back to that house and live with me. She told me that she had met somebody else and wanted a divorce."

David had questions. "Joe, what can you do? Is she sure the divorce is what she wants?"

"I don't think there is anything I can do. I wanted your advice. I think I want to tell Mattie. She needs to know what I plan to do or I should stop seeing her. My problem is I don't know what to do."

" Joe, your problem is as bad as mine. Yours is a life changing decision. Of course, if something happened to Betty Sue I would always feel guilty. If Squire thinks she knows about the drugs and murders, she might disappear like those other men."

"David, can you tell us what you think about our problems?"

"Not now, I need to pray about it. Jane, you do whatever you can to protect her. Joe, I think you should tell Mattie what you told us." David answered.

40

Mayor Fink and Betty Sue were standing in front of the small block building that had for many years been the taxi stand when I returned from lunch at home.

"Hey ladies, are you planning on opening that business as it was in the fifties?" I tried to sound ready to get to work planning. I joined them and we talked about the two men who had operated the two vehicles for hire back in the fifties. I told them they also sold cigarettes and probably whiskey from this small store.

Mayor Fink answered me. "We have looked at each building and talked about what type of shop could be put in them. Let's get some lunch and then go to my office. We need you to put our ideas on paper and tell us what you think."

"Yes, we need to do that. I have been thinking of people that might want to own some of the shops. I had lunch with David and Joe. I'll look at the old buildings and meet you in about thirty minutes. We have lots to do."

Mattie arrived before the others got finished with lunch and found me in front of the mayor's office.

"What is wrong? You sounded upset and you didn't tell me anything. I came as soon as I could. Joe called right after you did and told me part of what's happened."

"First we are working on our plans for Veeny this afternoon. Betty Sue is here. She and the mayor are having lunch and will be here soon. My real problem is how can we keep Betty Sue from going home after we finish. She is afraid of Squire and doesn't know about the drugs or possible raid. If she is there he may think she talked and do something to harm her. They are not on speaking terms right now.

"Did Joe tell you about Kaylee? That she is safe now. That Betty saw her at their lodge and called me last evening."

"Yes, I was so glad that nothing bad happened to her. I'm sure that brother won't talk. Joe told me what the sheriff is planning."

"We don't know when he will arrest Squire and his helpers. I think he wants to arrest them all together or about the same time. He didn't tell Joe when that would be, or Joe didn't tell us.

"I am so mad at Sheriff Moore! I have to calm down before I see him again."

"I heard about that from Joe. He didn't say what you were planning about protecting Betty."

"You and I have to think of something. Here they come. We'll talk about our town plan for a while and forget this for now. Maybe something will pop up in my mind. Let's be as cheerful as we can.

"Look who came to help! Mattie is off work today and I begged her to come. With four smart females pondering all the possibilities we should have lots of ideas and a perfect plan before we leave today."

We all sat at the planning table inside City Hall and the Mayor begin telling us what she had learned. "I've talked to the city council and they all approve of your plans. The owners of the buildings are excited and agreed to the plan of not charging rent for six months. They want to look at things after that. They may want some money for the taxes."

Betty asked, "They do know that our plans are to repair the buildings, not totally remodel them, don't they?"

"Yes, I explained that. That you are just making them useable and keeping the old character of the town."

"Did Rex Arnold really agree to this? Maybe you kept my name out of it." I asked Mayor Finks.

"Rex wants to help. I told the town councilmen that you and Mrs. Sanderson were working on this together."

"This smart female forgot to bring her file. Give me some paper and a pen and I'll make a new one here today. First, that's a big help to know the town council is for the plan. Next, we have permission of the owners. We have some financial help promised from the Sandersons. We have two people ready to do the repairs. I'll write up a draft of our agreement so everybody will know who has agreed to do each of these things. What we need now are entrepreneurs, people that are willing to work here and invest some of their time and money."

Mattie added her thoughts. "You are really going great! I'm getting excited too. What can I do? I can't run a business here since I work full time."

Betty Sue spoke up. "Mattie, after we met here and talked that day, I knew we needed you to get the word out. If you can write an article about what we're doing and get it in the Blue Pond weekly paper and maybe other papers as well. Any 'Antique Publications' would probably like to have the news, since we are aiming for sales to that crowd. I have some of their newspapers I'll bring you."

"I can do that. I'll need photos, maybe one from the time Veeny was a busy town and how it looks now. You need to give me a list of the businesses you hope to have opened here."

"That sounds terrific, Mattie. I have two pictures from the past. One has my grandfather's 1935 Ford pickup in it. That will certainly date it. Who can get a new picture?" I asked getting excited.

Mayor Finks said. "Rex Arnold's hobby is photography, I'll ask him to take a few. Do you want photos of Betty Sue and Jane?"

"I might later but for now I'll name you two and the Mayor, as the planning committee. Who will be the contact person? I need a name and phone number for people to call for more information."

"I think I can do that after we have planned everything. I'll need to know the answers before they call. What and who we want? The expense they will have to get started? When we plan to open the shops and so on?" Mayor Finks told us.

Betty Sue responded with, "Opening on the first of the month is best. If the shops are open only three or four days a week that will help us convince ladies to start a part time business. Right now I can't open my antique store every day. Thursday, Friday, and Saturday all day and maybe Sunday afternoons if everybody is willing, sounds good to me."

"The first of next month is only two weeks away. I think we need at least six weeks to get ready. We want everybody on board and ready to open at the same time.

Can we plan for the first weekend in October?" I asked our smart females.

We were interrupted by Mattie's phone ringing. I wondered if she might be needed for an emergency. She answered quietly and listened for a few minutes then said, "It's Joe, I'll call him back later."

"Good, we'll talk about him later unless you have something to tell us." I hinted.

"Jane, you promised to tell me more about him." Mattie said.

"I haven't learned much more about him, except I see a big change from when we first met him. He does have something to tell you when you see him again. I'll leave that for him to tell. Mattie, what can you share with us? Or, not, if you don't want to."

"I was just thinking about when I first saw you and David, and Joe. If you want to hear about that night I'll entertain you three for a few minutes."

"We need a little fun, go ahead. This planning is a lot of work."

"It was hilarious that night after we rescued Joe from the well and got him to the hospital. He had taken medicine for pain and drank whiskey so he was pretty drunk and looked awful. We couldn't do anything until the doctor got there. The x-ray tech knew his leg bone was broken. Since he wasn't feeling the pain, we decided to clean him up. He agreed so the nurse and I rolled his wheel chair into a shower and turned the water on him. He thought it was funny. We got his dirty clothes off and washed his head too. After he was dried and wrapped in a blanket, I asked him if we could cut his whiskers. He said, "Sure why don't you shave my face and cut my hair, too."

Betty Sue had not heard about the well incident. She was confused and asked. "Why was Joe in a well? I knew he had been hurt but nobody told me how if happened."

"I'll tell you about it later. He was in our well trying to clean it out. Let's hear more about how he and Mattie got acquainted."

Mattie continued. "I found that a good way to get acquainted with a man is having him down with a broken leg and injured hand. Well, the nurse got a razor and a pair of scissors and we began. I cut his hair and she shaved him. We couldn't help but laugh and he did too. Then he started to cry, saying nobody loved him, and what was he going to do if he really was hurt bad.

"By the time the doctor got there I felt like Joe and I were friends. I had to reassure him and tell him we would help him. He was looking much younger without his whiskers and long hair. I had no idea who he was or if he was married. I think I assumed he wasn't married because he said nobody loved him.

"Jane knows the rest of the story. I showed up the next day and the next week to help him because I had promised I would. Now we are best friends and I still don't know much about his marriage." Mattie sat quietly; it seemed she had finished her story.

"We all think Joe is a really nice person. He has helped us a lot and is behind us all the way on this project. He knows it means some work for him and Butch, also some jobs for other people." I finished the discussion about Joe.

"Let's see what we can get down on my paper. We are going to need to run a want ad for people who are interested in having a shop here or maybe just a booth in our flea market-antique building. I have talked to Beth Cotton. She is really happy about this and I think she might be our manager. I also met a lady who is a very good cook. I plan to find out if she would be interested in the tearoom."

"Jane, I will write the story and have it for you three to approve next week. I will need dates and a drawing of what you have to rent or at least the square footage of each space. If you will do the want ad, we'll put it in the paper the same week." Mattie was all business again.

Betty Sue said. "We really are progressing on this. I am glad to be involved and have friends like you all. I have the list of suggested shops Jane did earlier. Let's try to find people for all of those. Food is a big draw so we need to plan for a hamburger joint and a tearoom. We'll need more equipment for those than anything else. If we have somebody apply who has the stuff from a prior business that would help."

"Let's plan for another session next week. I'll bring my file and you all bring some new ideas. Rex should have us some pictures by then. Mattie will have a rough draft of her story. We'll assign space for what we want in the old stores. After the story and ads are in the paper we can decide if people will support this project." I was about to end our planning session and still did not know what to tell Betty Sue.

Mattie got my attention and asked to tell me something in pirate. I excused myself and said I'd be back in few minutes. Mattie and I went outside.

Elizabeth Oliver Wooten

"Joe called to tell us that the raid is on for early tomorrow. The sheriff called him." Mattie said.

"Oh dear me, what do I tell Betty Sue? If she is home, they will probably arrest her too.

"Mattie, can she stay at your house tonight? I'm going to ask her to call Squire and decide how he is feeling about her. If he is not nice to her, she should not go home. I can't tell her what may happen tomorrow."

"Yes, I think it will be all right for her to stay with me. She isn't wanted by the law is she?"

"No. I just want her safe and not at home tomorrow morning."

Mattie and I joined the others, and set a day and time to meet the next week.

೭ಎ

I talked to Betty Sue about her problem while Mattie waited in her car. "Betty, I'm worried about your going home. Would you call Squire and try to decide how mad he is. If he has heard about you seeing Kaylee at the lodge, he'll let you know. Pretend you have some business to attend to and might not come home until tomorrow."

"I'll do that but I don't have any place to go except home. I feel awful about this. I think I will be fine. If he answers, I'll pretend to be mad at him for being gone last night. He will let me know real quick if he has decided to talk to me or not."

I went to talk to Mattie while she phoned home. We knew she was talking to Squire and waited. After one minute Betty Sue screamed in the phone. "I will not tell you where I am. We have planned all day and I have to take care of this other problem today. I may be home tomorrow or I'll call you!"

She came over to the car and told us. "I think you know already that Squire was mad. He may start looking for me. I have to get away from here."

"Yes you do, Betty. Calm Down. Mattie says you can go to her house for the night. You both need to leave now. Put your car in her garage and since Squire doesn't know Mattie I'm sure you'll be fine at her house,"

"If Mattie really means it I'll follow her there. I didn't bring anything with me. I'll have to go home tomorrow. Maybe Squire will be reasonable by then."

41

The last few days had been so stressful that I needed to retreat to a more comforting place. David and Joe were busy so I planned to hide away somewhere. I wanted to think about my childhood here on this old home place that belonged to my grandparents. Recalling the pleasant times we had as children and visualizing the way it looked then should help calm me.

I found my file of photographs from that time and some notes I had written earlier. Taking those and my notebook, I went to the hill overlooking the house and land. I asked David to take any calls and tell them I would call back later. This was to be my day.

One picture of us with Memaw and Papaw, showed my sister, and me standing on the running board of Papaw's 1935 Ford pickup. I looked to be about four years old, May would have been eight. We did have some happy times riding in the back of that pickup. I recalled falling out the back once while Papaw was driving on a gravel road. I only had a skinned arm and bruised leg. That proved that I should have listened to instructions. They always told us not to sit near the back end of the pickup bed. I remembered only a few times when I was in the cab with Memaw. When Papaw took us to school, we did ride in the front with him.

The truck was used most often for our veterinarian Papaw to go see sick cows, mules, pigs, and any animal that needed him. Rarely was it used for vacations. I didn't re-

Elizabeth Oliver Wooten

member ever going on a vacation as a child. We sometimes went to visit relatives for the day, but not often. Papaw took us to the Church of Christ in Veeny a few times. That was the belief of his family. I don't know that he was ever a member of a church. I do believe he was a Christian. He is buried in the cemetery of a Church of Christ, where his parents are buried. I guess his family were members of that church.

Memaw believed as the Baptist did and we attended the Baptist church most often. Since Papaw was the only one who drove the truck, we didn't go every Sunday. That day was always a day of rest. None of us were allowed to do any work on Sunday. Of course, Memaw had to cook and clean up the kitchen. I remembered walks in the pasture looking for wildflowers, playing by the branch under the willow trees, and most enjoyable for me was reading. My grades in school were always good so I did not have much homework to do. My fourth grade teacher taught me how to check out books from the high school library. I discovered a whole new world, through reading. Some of the books were fiction and entertaining, which Memaw didn't think I should waste my time on. Others helped my understanding of the world outside of Alabama. Papaw loved to hang large maps on the wall above the beds. There was one of the world, another of the United States that had all the presidents pictures around the border. I learned all the states, their capitals, and a lot about our past presidents. Too bad that I can't remember all that now.

This little farm, we had bought a year ago, looks so different now from the vision I have from my early childhood here. Farming then was growing cotton to sell for cash, corn as food for the animals and us, and vegetables. The boll weevils damaged the cotton crop so badly that it was not profitable to try to grow cotton anymore. We were paid ten-cent a can, if we would pick up the fallen cotton buds which had the egg of the weevil in them. It was hot, dirty work and we didn't make much money at that. That taught me what working for money meant. That lesson continued when as a teenager I picked cotton for other people.

Once during those years, Papaw had the cotton fields sprayed with a poison to kill the boll weevils. It was done with an airplane. I was so scared that it would crash. Memaw had us stay inside because of the poison fumes. The odor was awful. Later it was proven that the stuff used was a danger to our health and was banned for spraying on cotton.

After Papaw quit farming because of the boll weevils, his health and other work, the land just began growing up in weeds and bushes. Now these same fields were in a terrible mess. At one time most of them had been planted in pine trees. Twenty years later and only recently the pines had been harvested and nothing has been done to preserve the land. We needed to address that problem soon.

A few other things were more pressing. The long driveway needed some work. The plan for my remodeled old house showing what it would be like when finished and what it was going to be used for needed to be put on paper.

Today I was relaxing. More photos of my ancestors brought back more memories.

My thoughts went to the book I planned to write about my family. I did have several beginnings, if I print them out and consider how to begin, that will mean I have actually started my book. I still need to research some of the dates. I hope to visit the cemeteries in the area soon to check my dates. I decided to get started on that project. I thought it surely would be more comforting than the things that are happening these days.

I returned to have a late lunch with the guys and learned that I had not had a call all day. That was very good, but I did wonder what had happened at the Sanderson's place and how Betty Sue was.

Joe told me something else. "Jane, I forgot to tell you that Preacher Fredericks wants you to come see him when you can. He has something to talk to you about. He did say he wasn't rushing you and just come when you have time."

42

Six Men Arrested in Drug Raid

Authorities arrested six men last Tuesday at a home in Northwest Alabama. Local law enforcement, Alabama drug agents, and federal authorities searched the estate of Squire Sanderson in an early morning raid. Illegal drugs, cash, vehicles, records, a cow, and other related items were taken from the home and surrounding properties. The men were identified as Squire Sanderson, Leon Sanderson, Mac Davis, Jose Hernandez, Vince Patterson, and Noe Sanchez. Charges range from importing illegal drugs to possession of illegal drugs and distribution of illegal drugs. They are being held in the Benjamin County jail pending hearings for bail.
Late Wednesday Preston Perry was arrested in nearby Mississippi. Authorities are charging him with distributing illegal drugs in Alabama and Mississippi.

Benjamin County Times
August 23, 1995

The article from the *Benjamin County News* was the first news we learned of the actual raid on the Sanderson place. Sheriff Moore was not keeping us informed. We had not had a call from him about the arrests.

An early morning call from Maxine in Trussellville alerted us to the newspaper item. She wanted to know what we knew about the raid. I don't know what made her think of us. Maybe because we lived in the area or because people seem to be suspicious of us. I told her truthfully that we hadn't heard about it.

David went to the Stop-N-Go in Veeny and got the newspaper. He didn't stop to talk to anyone at Norman's café. David, Joe, and I discussed what was in the paper and decided all we could do was wait to learn more. We needed to know if there were others, not arrested, that could link us to the information Sheriff Moore had learned. He really should tell us what to expect. Are we in danger are not? I was still mad at the sheriff and getting more upset every day.

I called Betty Sue. I had to know if she was all right. She answered on the first ring.

"Hi Jane, I just couldn't call you with more bad news. I didn't get an answer on our home phone or on Squire's phone the next morning so I came home."

"I wanted to make sure you were safe. You can tell me about this later if you don't want to talk about it now. We read the paper this morning and that's all we have heard."

"I don't know much more. Squire called about noon yesterday and I went to see if he could get out on bail. There hasn't been a hearing; we don't know if any of them will be allowed out on bail. He was calm. I think I will be safe here, at least for now. The authorities don't have any charges to arrest me on since I wasn't here. Mrs. Sanchez is the only one they left here."

That information made me think that we were safe for now, unless there were others not arrested.

43

Two Million Dollars worth of Drugs Taken in Raid

The men arrested near Veeny, Alabama on August 22, 1995 have been identified as Charles 'Squire' Sanderson, Leon R. Sanderson, Michael 'Mac' Davis, Jose Hernandez, Vince Patterson, and Noe Sanchez. These arrests came after a long investigation tracing the source of illegal drugs in this area.

Charles Sanderson has one prior arrest on possession of marijuana in 1976 in Texas. Leon R. Sanderson has prior arrest for driving under the influence of drugs and speeding. Michael Davis has been convicted of possession of marijuana with the intent to distribute. He served eighteen months in prison. Davis was released in 1986. Jose Hernandez has no arrest under that name. Vince Patterson, a former rodeo champion, has no former arrest that we have found. Noe Sanchez has no criminal record here.

The illegal drugs seized are reported to have a street value of over two million dollars. Cash and other possessions were taken in the raid of Charles Sanderson property.

Benjamin County Times
August 24, 1995

David went to Veeny each morning to pick up the Trussellville paper. All we learned about the raid came from those reports. We didn't know anything else to do but wait for the Sheriff to contact us.

Joe and David still wanted my help on the house. I was ready and willing to work beside them for a few days.

My good morning greeting was, "Here I am with sketch in hand to help you guys. Where do we begin?

"What is this house going to be used for?" David was insisting that I tell them my plans.

"I have two ideas of what it will be. We will continue restoring the two rooms, building a kitchen and bath addition and replacing the porch."

"What will it be after we do that?"

"After we install a bathroom and kitchen it will be ready to be used for a restaurant or a home."

"Jane that will cost too much. We'll have to put in a septic system."

"Hold it—we budgeted an amount for this project and haven't used very much of that. I'll estimate the cost of these items and you guess at the labor cost. I am usually pretty good at staying on the projected cost."

"You usually do that. You must be planning for a restaurant because nobody will want to live here, not even us."

"Hey, this could be our summer place. Let's get to work on it."

David and Joe started asking questions about my plans. I explained. "The addition will be on the opposite side from where the kitchen was before. The addition will be large enough for a big kitchen and the new bathroom. The bathroom will have two separate parts, the public could use one area if it becomes a restaurant, and the other area would be for anyone living here. I have all the measurements on the drawing.

"The entrance will be from the new porch, where the front door is now. If we decide to open an eating establishment, that porch could become outside setting. You both know there isn't a nice restaurant in this area. I bet it would be a popular place. If nothing else because of the bones found in the well."

David said, "Sure and we could name it 'Bones'. I wouldn't eat at a place like that."

"Don't be smart. We would get a chef and serve excellent cuisine. The name would be 'The Homestead.' We'll talk about that later.

"The addition and porch will keep you two busy for a few weeks. I'll have the plans for finishing the inside ready by then and I promise to help you on that. I am excited that so far the house is looking like I remember it, or at least part of it is.

"I plan to work with Mayor Finks and Mattie a few days this week. We don't want to put our plans for Veeny on hold because of the problems the Sandersons have."

44

David and I were going to church on a Wednesday evening when we passed a house that I remembered from my days in grammar school. The house had been changed; it was no longer white. It now had brick on the outside and a new wing had been added. I wondered if any of the family I knew many years ago still lived there. I really didn't want to talk to any of them today.

"David, I bet the people that live there are dealing in illegal drugs."

"Jane, you seem to think everybody is messing with drugs. You shouldn't be that suspicious. They are probably nice people."

The house did stir up some memories that I had never told David. I decided I would talk about those memories because I did learn a valuable lesson from one childhood incident that happened there.

"David, do you have ten minutes to listen to my story. It's not very important, but it will let you know that we told a lie a long time ago and how it has affected my life. What I want to tell you also makes me wonder why God puts some people in our lives."

"Sure, Jane, I always listen to you. Sometimes I learn something important!"

"Many years ago that house I just pointed to was white. Our house was unpainted and not nearly as pretty as that house. Every afternoon when I rode the school bus home from school we passed it. I thought about it often. Who lived there, how much did it cost, would I ever live in a pretty house with a big front yard?

"One day, much later, Papaw said he was going fishing with Sam Louis. We didn't know him or his family but Papaw said that Memaw, my sister, and I, were invited to stay with Mrs. Louis and her girls until they returned that night. We agreed and he took us to that very house I had admired and wondered about. The Louis family that lived there were just regular people, not rich or conceited. We became friends with them and many of their relatives. In fact my first boyfriend was one of their relatives."

David interrupted, "Who was that boyfriend that you never told me about?"

"David, we were only in the sixth grade. You were in high school and probably didn't know him.

"The incident I want to tell you about happened when I was about nine or ten years old, a year or two after we first met the Louis family. My sister and I went to the Louis's house to spend the afternoon and planned to sleepover. About six of us kids went to their pasture to play in some trees. We had climbed over the fence and everybody except me had climbed a tree and swung off a limb. I was scared to do it. They all kept telling me how easy and how much fun it was, so I tried. Instead of landing on my feet, I fell on the back of my head and was knocked out for a few minutes. That frightened the whole group. The story they agreed to tell our parents was that I fell climbing over the fence.

"I learned a lesson from that. The lesson that it is never wise to change the facts has stayed with me all these years. I never admitted to climbing that tree because the others told me not to. Since I was the youngest one of the group, I went along with whatever they said and did. Well, that night my right arm hurt. I knew I had not fallen on that arm but it hurt real bad. They took me home during the night since I didn't stop crying after they had applied a leaf pack on my arm. I don't recall if I went to the doctor the next day or not. If I did, they didn't do x-rays back then. I think I just took aspirin for a few days and then forgot about it.

"Years later when my right arm began hurting and I didn't have good use of my hand, a doctor did x-rays. The doctor explained that two of my neck vertebras were fused together, either from an accident or were always that way, and were affecting the nerves going to my right hand. I immediately remembered falling from that tree and landing on my head. It had made my arm hurt then and was still affecting me. I believe if we had told the truth and I had received treatment, I would be much better today.

"Now, I bet you are thinking that falling on my head effected me in other ways too. My question to you is, did telling a lie make things much worse for me? I can't think of any reason why God put those people in my life. They were not a good influence on me. Or, did God have anything to do with it?"

David had listened and was thinking about my questions. When we arrived at the church he parked a distance from the other cars and tried to answer.

"Jane, did that really happen or do you just want to hear my opinion on stretching the truth and how God uses people in our lives?"

"All of it happened. I couldn't just make that up or stretch the truth with you."

" I did learn something else about you so I'll try to answer your questions. I think it was wrong for you all to not tell what happened. It has caused you to remember the incident and to think less of your playmates. Whether if has affected your arm is not the question. The fall itself caused that. The fact that you remember telling a lie that many years ago, has helped you to not tell untruths without thinking of the consequences."

David was still thinking or praying about my other question. He began slowly.

"The question about God putting people in our lives for a purpose is hard to answer. I've met many people that I know I could have lived a happy life without ever knowing them. Maybe God put them there for me to influence; maybe they learned something from me, or perhaps I did learn something from them. God works in mysterious ways; the Bible tells us that. My answer is yes; God did have something to do with your meeting those people. I'm sure they learned something from knowing you and your family. You learned to change the truth, but knew it was wrong to do that. Don't you feel that has been good for you?"

"Thanks David, that answers something I've wondered about for years. I guess every person we meet does affect our life in some way. I'll try to think of other real life incidents to tell you about. Living here these few weeks have brought back lots of memories that I have tried to forget. As I have told you before my childhood was different from yours. With us not living with Mother and Daddy I felt cheated out of a normal loving home."

45

Sheriff Fred J Moore still had not called David or Joe. Of course, he did not say when he would. He only promised to keep us informed if there were any developments that involved the murders. Maybe he thinks the arrests we have been reading about don't tie-in with those men that were killed. I certainly do.

"I am going to Trussellville today." Joe sounded as mad as David and I.

"If you see the Sheriff, would you please kick him for me. Then after you get his attention ask him if they are keeping those men in jail. If you can get him to say they will not be out on bail, I feel we will be safe. I'm sure Squire thinks we had something to do with their arrest. And, Joe, you know that Mac probably thinks you turned him in."

David sounded so calm. "Are you going to visit Jason? Maybe he will be released soon like the Sheriff promised."

"Yes. You can go with and get your stuff for the house while I'm at the jail."

"That's a good idea, your truck will carry more than mine."

"I will be at Veeny most of the day. Call the mayor if you need me. If you have good news call me there."

ಶ್ಽ

Mattie had called earlier about our meeting that was planned for today. I told her that we would meet without Betty Sue. I got my files, photos, and plans and headed for Veeny.

Elizabeth Oliver Wooten

The Mayor was in her office with Rex Arnold when I arrived. Mattie got there at nine like we had agreed last week. We didn't expect Betty Sue to come. I agreed to tell her what we accomplished today.

"I did bring my file today. I have a draft of a simple one-page contract that I want you all to read. It is for the people who want to join in this effort. They all need to know what to expect and we need to have them agree to all work together, same hours, opening date, and stuff like that. The last paragraph explains that rent may be charged after the first six months."

Rex was interested, he said, "I have some pictures of the way the town looks now. Did anybody find some of the way it looked in the fifties?"

Mayor Finks answered, "There are not any photographs in the files. Jane said she had one and it may be possible to get some from the Benjamin County newspaper. I believe it is the same newspaper that was published during the forties and fifties. Mattie, can you check on that?"

"I will. Showing the way it looks now and telling what we plan to do is probably more important. I brought copies of the draft of my article. I need to do some research on the facts and dates. We should have it in the paper at least four weeks before we plan to open. Jane, did you do a want-ad?"

"It's here in this stuff somewhere. I have a drawing of where the buildings we plan to use are located and the size of each one. It's for allocating space. When people inquire, we want to give the same information. I'll be glad to interview them and explain our contract before we tell them they can be a part of this exciting project."

We were passing out copies of Mattie's article, the contract I had written, and the sketch of buildings when Betty Sue came in.

"I'm sorry I'm late. I hope you all want me here. I've been to Trussellville this morning. There is no news to report. I think they all go before the judge tomorrow and he may set bail." Betty informed us she took a seat at the table.

"It's good to see you and of course we want you here. Here are copies of what we agreed to write. I think we're going to read them at lunch and then work on them this afternoon. I think it's very important to have this committee agree on space and the type of business we want in each space so we can begin talking to prospects."

Mayor Finks asked if everybody agreed to meet again after lunch.

I'm staying here so come back when you finish. We all agreed. Rex said he would be back. Mattie, Betty Sue, and I left for lunch at Norman's taking our paper copies with us.

I began the afternoon session. "We have set our target date as October; the first Thursday is October 5th. Can we have the businesses ready to open by then?"

"Let's tell people that's our date. If everything isn't ready, we can change it to the first of November. That means Mattie's article should be in the papers September 10th or the latest 17th. Did everybody read it and are there any changes? I think it's good just like it is." Mayor Finks said.

"I approve what she has written. I think she needs at least one picture. If she doesn't find an old one of Veeny I say use one that Rex has taken of the way it looks now. She can write about the changes that we hope to make. What about the contract?"

The Mayor answered. "I understand it. It's simple enough but will make the people think about cooperating with everybody. It states the times they agree to be open. And has a time limit that they will try this for. I think a year is a reasonable commitment for them to make. We need to explain that they are responsible for the equipment they will need and that they are expected to keep their area clean and attractive. I certainly think everybody needs to sign one and keep a copy in their shop."

Betty Sue calmly told us, "I think those two things are good. We need to look at the spaces and decide what we want in them. I mean look at the sketch Jane has drawn. We're all seen the actual buildings.

"I have been thinking about the cost. We agreed to help and I will. I have some money in my business account Squire doesn't know about. It should be enough for now."

"Beth Cotton wants to have an antique shop, mostly smaller items with some furniture that will help her display them. If we want her to, she agreed to be the on-site manager the days that the businesses are open. She has a phone and will answer questions during that time and will try keeping everybody doing what he or she agreed to. If you all think that's a good idea, she will come talk to Mayor Finks and read our contract.

"I hope to use a part of her space for my antique glassware and crystal. I think our other sister-in-law will share that space also. We would have three people to alternate keeping it open." I told the group what we had planned. "It may be that others can combine their efforts. I plan to talk to Mama's family about using that idea for the tearoom

"Let's finish assigning names and spaces. I think Mattie should go ahead and put the want ad in next week's Blue Pond weekly and the Benjamin County News daily paper.

"Mayor, do you have all the information you need to answer the calls?"

"I do if all of this is approved. I'll take a quick vote from the committee on the contract, the article by Mattie that will be in the papers later, and the space allocations for a shop or a booth. I approve each of these proposals."

"I approve all of it," I quickly answered.

Betty Sue, Mattie, and Rex each agreed with, "I approve"

Mayor Finks said. "This meeting is adjourned. We'll meet again next week same time.

46

It was a rainy day and since I had not agreed to meet anyone, I decided to visit Preacher Fredericks. I found him sitting on his porch. He was alone and we could talk about what he wanted me to do.

"Jane, I know that you are a writer. Maybe I should say I heard that you are planning to write a book about your family. I have notes written about my eighty years and want to know if you could organize and type them for me?"

"Preacher, it would be an honor to help you organize your life story. I'm still learning about writing. We'll need to work together on it. I'll take your notes and type some pages and then you can edit them. That will be a beginning. Maybe that will help me begin my ancestors' story."

"That sounds great. Let me get what I have. This is for my family and I want it to be a surprise so let's not talk about it to others."

"Please don't rush me; it will take some time. It's our secret for now."

I visited for a short time and went home with a box full of handwritten notes.

ବ୍ଧ

We didn't find any news about the drug arrest in that morning's paper. The rain had stopped and David and Joe were working on the porch addition. They thought the porch would give them experience on building onto the old house. Then they would attempt the larger addition of a kitchen and bath. They didn't want my help.

I decided this was the perfect time to work on Preacher's story and then I would be ready to begin my book. What little he had told me was still fresh in my mind. I set up everything at the computer and spread out the notes from his collection. The handwriting was unusual but I could decipher most of it. There were lots of Bible verses, but since he had been a preacher most of his life, I felt it was all right to use them.

Notes as written by Preacher Fredericks

The past is history; the future is a gift we have to enjoy.

Turn right at the next corner of life. Do the things that you enjoy; enjoy the things you do!

Are we too busy with everyday things to enjoy the present? Time waits for no one, one day our time will suddenly end.

> The Holy Bible says -
> "The world and its desires pass away, but the man who does the will of God lives forever." I John 2:17 (New International Version-NIV)
> "So we fix our eyes not on what is seen. For what is seen is temporary, but what is unseen is eternal." II Corinthians 4:18 (NIV)

We need to take the Bible as our guidebook. If we live in harmony with the purpose that God has assigned us, we can experience life as it is supposed to be. We need to understand He wants us all to live a full and meaningful life here on earth. We are promised eternal life, if we accept Jesus as our Savior, and that we will live beyond the time element. Regardless of what you believe about what happens to us after death, one thing is certain, our time in this life is very short. A lifetime is like a flash of lightning in the sky. We should make the most of our days by living in loving, helpful, and compassionate ways every moment. To live that life we need Jesus and the Holy Spirit to guide us.

> *"For God so loved the world that He gave his one and only son that whoever believes in him should not perish, but have eternal life." John 3:16 (NIV)*

According to the Bible, all we need to do is believe that Jesus is the Son of God and that he gave his life for us. If we ask him to forgive our sins and turn from our sinful ways we become his children and receive eternal life.

> *"...I am going there to prepare a place for you. And if I go and prepare a place for you, I will come back. And take you to be with me there that you may be where I am." John 14:1-3 (NIV)*

Christians are a spiritual city set on a hill. We are called to be the light of the world so others can see God's glory through us. That is a privilege we should treat as an honor. The blessings God gives us are ours to share with others.

God has guided my life from the time I was thirty years old. For every situation, He had a plan. The highs and lows of my life affect everything I do. I would have no idea how those things would work out for my family and me, but God knew. Later I could look back and see how those bad times in my life helped me to learn a valuable lesson that I could pass on to someone else in need. We should strive to make our life fit the plan God has for us. We should ask, is this where God wants me at this particular time?

It is important to separate must-haves from don't-needs. Separating those two and letting go of some memories, like getting rid of clutter, helps us to live a purpose-driven life. Memories help us maintain family ties, values, and traditions. We can cherish these precious memories, but how important are they?

Nostalgia is different from loss—one is memory, the other is absence. Divesting is about freedom, and redefining ourself and dreaming new dreams. God has a purpose for our life on earth; we need to live up to it. Life is a test and a trust. God's plan for our life is for us to bring God glory by worshipping Him, by loving others, by serving others with our gifts, and by telling others about Him.

People of all nations, races, colors, creeds, economic situations, and political views recognize that Jesus' message of love is the answer to life's problems. The minds and hearts of mankind must understand this basic truth. The first and greatest commandment "to love God with all one's being" and the second "to love your neighbor as yourself" are the basis for all of life's relationships. The love of which Jesus spoke is for all people, including one's enemies. The past two thousand years of human history have proven beyond a shadow of a doubt that Jesus Christ was right. If there is to be any changed lives, any sharing of the love of Jesus in this world, it will only be as people like you reach out to others with the 'Good News of Jesus Christ'.

> *"This is love: not that we loved God, but that he loved us and sent his Son as an atoning sacrifice for our sins. Dear friends, since God so loved us, we also ought to love one another. I John 4:10-11 (NIV)*

We learn about life, not only from the good times alone, but also from the bad times. Some heartache is caused by the world, but many of our problems are caused by what we do. Many of us wait for something big to happen to us. One definition of wait is—'Remaining inactive or in a state of repose, as until something expected happens.' We waste much of our life waiting—inactive. Time is definitely NOT infinite; we can totally miss the present time by waiting. During the time we spend mourning over losses—the world is still spinning and we're missing everything else. Don't let life pass you by. Have expectations and look forward to the exciting experiences to come in life. Life is short so, forgive quickly, love truly, laugh uncontrollably, prepare for any disappointments, and enjoy the present.

> *Keep smiling—it is the best advertisement for God at work in your life.*
> *Work like you don't need the money*
> *Love like nobody has ever hurt you.*
> *Dance like nobody is watching,*
> *Sing like nobody is listening.*
> *Live as if this was paradise on earth.*
> *Copied*

Elizabeth Oliver Wooten

I know God has a special purpose for each of us, this Poem by Grace E. Easley echoes what each of us should strive for.

A PLACE FOR ME
There is a special place in life,
That needs my humble skill,
A certain job I'm meant to do
Nobody else can fill
The hours are demanding,
And the pay is not too good,
And yet I wouldn't change it
For a moment, if I could.

There is a special place in life,
A goal I must attain,
A dream that I must follow,
For I won't be back again.
There is a mark that I must leave
However small it be,
A legacy of love for those
Who follow after me.

There is a special place in life
That only I may share.
A little path that bears my name,
Awaiting me somewhere.
There is a hand that I must hold
A word that I must say,
A smile that I must give, for there
Are tears to blot away.

There is a special place in life
That I was meant to fill,

A sunny spot where flowers grow
Upon a windy hill.
There's always a tomorrow,
And the best is yet to be,
And somewhere in this world I know
There is a place for me.

୭ଈ

Typing that had been a real test of my ability. Preacher's handwritten notes seemed to have been written when he thought out a profound truth. I had arranged them in a rough draft for him to edit. I really need more of his real life. He has some dates of events but not in any order. I need to interview him with specific questions. I think we will have a good story after I do that and spend more time including those facts. I wonder how many pages it will take to tell his eighty-year story?

47

Five days after Squire Sanderson and his crew had been arrested, we were still waiting to hear from Sheriff Moore. When Joe had visited Jason Pierce at the jail on Thursday, the Sheriff was not there. Jason told him all he knew and that wasn't much. Jason confided to Joe that the men arrested were the ones he had told the Sheriff about. He thought he might be released soon, but not until a hearing was held and they knew that those men would not be out on bail.

I wasn't quite so mad at Sheriff Moore now. I realized that by not telling us about the raid and not following up on reports to us was his way of not putting us in danger. David, Joe, and I wanted to know more about the bones and bodies. We wanted to know when Jason might be released, since we had really caused his arrest after the fire at his house. I still felt that we all, including Jason, had done the best thing to protect him and his family.

"David, I'm going back to interview the Preacher today. Sally, Kaylee, and Sue will not be there this morning. I hope to get him to talk about his life. I've started what he asked me to type but I need more information to finish his story."

"Joe isn't working with me today. He had a doctor's appointment and probably having lunch with Mattie."

"I'm letting Mayor Finks and Betty Sue do the planning for Veeny this week. After the story by Mattie and the ads go in the paper, we will need to decide about getting our places set up for the opening next month. I think we'll need Joe and Butch for a few days next week. Betty Sue is still planning to pay for some repairs and for their labor."

☙☙

Preacher Fredericks was pleased that I was back so soon. He wanted to read what I had for him.

"No, I want to talk first then I'll leave you copies. I used a bigger font so you could see all of it. You write in your changes and I'll get them later. I have questions for you to answer this morning."

"What kind of questions? I don't remember everything and I have a good reason. I'm eighty-two years young. That's a good excuse for anything that I don't want to do." Preacher was smiling.

"These are simple questions, I think you will know the answers. Your notes didn't tell me anything about your personal life. We can't write a life story without those details. Now, tell me, what do you remember about your childhood? Begin with your grandparents, then your parents, your school, and so on. I'll need you to write down their names, birth dates and date of marriages and deaths. Do the same thing for you, your wife, and your children. Today, I want to hear you talk about your childhood."

"I've thought about those early years. Most of them were happy times. We were dirt poor but didn't know it; we always had food to eat. Most of it was what we grew in the garden and on the farm. My Momma canned or dried and preserved it for winter eating.

"My parents farmed on part of his daddy's land. That's all my folks did was farm. We were mule farmers—work from sunrise til sunset, plow the fields with a mule, hoe the cotton and corn, pick the cotton, pull the fodder, and shuck the corn. I remember working in the fields before I was old enough for school. I had two sisters and three brothers. I was born last of the six kids, but I didn't get spoiled, I had to work like everybody else. I mean it was hard work too. Besides the crops, we had to cut trees, saw them into logs for the fireplace, and split some for the cook stove. Then there were the animals to feed and cows to milk everyday. I was glad to go to school in the fall after the cotton was all picked. I liked school and made good grades. I didn't ever get to college. I did attend Bible school when I could. Is this the stuff you want to hear, Ms. Jane?"

"Yes, tell me more. You can write down other facts and stories as you think of them. When did you meet your wife?"

"At school, I picked her out when we were in the seventh grade. She didn't know that until we were old enough to date. Her family lived in town, but I found out where they went to church and I started going there. The young people had a group that did picnics and stuff together. So, we got acquainted there. On our first real date, I told her I wanted to marry her."

"Whoa, that was being brave. Did she agree?"

"Not then, it took a year of really dating her before she agreed. I had an old car by then. We had a good time with the group from her church and I did see her everyday at school. We graduated in June and got married the first of September that year.

"We had to live with my folks until all the cotton was gathered and sold. Then I had enough money to buy some furniture and rent our own place. I'll have to write about our life during those years. We didn't have much money but we were happy. Then our three boys arrived, the last child, a girl, died when she was three days old.

"The years after that were hard, the great depression, the war, and I was not a Christian. My Maggie sure went through some bad times with me, but she never changed. I'll try to write some of that. I still believe life is what a person makes it."

"Sure, that will be great. Just divide your time into sections, like years one through twelve and so on. Think about what you remember and write down some events. You talked some about teen years. What about age twenty to thirty. I know you have been preaching for about the last fifty years. I need stories and highlights about those years. What do you enjoy most about retirement?

"One more question, Preacher. I know you wrote some things about happiness after your talk with Jason and Joe that day under our tree. Joe was impressed with them. He got his Bible and started reading after he got a copy of that. Could I include that paper in your story?"

"Sure, but I don't have it. Ask Joe for it and type it. Tell him I said you could."

The girls getting back from grocery shopping interrupted us. Preacher was happy to see Kaylee, so was I and I stayed and talked for another hour. Kaylee was the same happy child, playing with the kittens. She had brought Shadrach, her kitten, to see his brothers. Sally said she didn't worry about being grabbed by that man. She seemed to think the kidnapping was a game. She had told her mother that Mrs. Sanchez was a punky dunk. That she told her a story about a duck.

"Goodbye, it was great seeing all of you. Sue, I sure hope we have good news about Jason very soon. Preacher, I'll see you next week." I needed to get home and type the things he had told me before I forgot any of it.

☙❧

I got a copy of his Happiness Paper from Joe and immediately put it in his story.

Preacher's thoughts on happiness prepared for Jason when he was arrested.

What happiness is I don't know, but I know it when it comes. I think it is taken from many things, people of all kinds, and from many different places. I believe happiness is many things put together:

Love of God and love from God.

A companion (mellowed from years together), and happy, lovable, bright, children.

Work we enjoy.

Friends, and the ability to trust others.

Food for the body and food for the soul

Something precious is gained from all these things and we should hold onto it.

We may search far and wide for happiness, but when one has lost hope it is not found. You must search diligently for the purpose and meaning of your life. No one ever promised us that life would be easy.

Benjamin Franklin said,
"All the constitution guarantees is the pursuit of happiness. You have to catch up with it yourself."

Elizabeth Oliver Wooten

God has provided us the strength to endure and at the end of our journey, a mansion not made with hands. Death is a part of our destiny; it is not a destination, but one important step in our destiny. I advise everybody to stay alive as long as they live. By that I mean, be a self worth living with, have a work worth doing, and have a faith strong enough to carry you through bad times. It is important to our happiness to be able and willing to help others. Our Christian creed is, what I have is yours if you need it, and I'll gladly share it with you when you need it.

A person's life can be incredibly rich when he has God leading it. It can be even richer if he has family, friends, and food. If a person can look, listen, think, and feel, and if he will trust God, everything else will come including happiness.

The Bible is a book of faith. It is also the inspired work of God, given to us as a guidebook. I use it every day. I trust you are ready to read some passages that I have marked. The Table of Contents at the front of your bible will help you find these in your Bible.

The Bible says God loves you. He has a wonderful plan for your life—purpose-peace-happiness.

I'll give you a few samples but you must read the Book.

When you say- I'm worried and scared, God says-Cast your cares on Me. I Peter 5:7

When you say- I feel all alone, God says-I will never leave you or forsake you. Heb. 12:5

When you say- I can't figure things out, God says- I will direct your steps. Proverbs 3:5-6

When you say- I can't manage, God says- I will supply all your needs. Philippians 4:13

When you say- I am afraid, God says- I have not given you a spirit of fear. II Timothy 1:7

When you say- I am not able, God says- I am able. II Corinthians 9:8

When you say- I can't do it, God says- You can do all things. Philippians 4:13

When you say- I don't understand, God says- I will direct your steps. Proverbs 3:5-6

When you say- It's impossible, God says- All things are possible. Luke 18:27

When you say- Nobody loves me, God says- I love you. John 3:16 and John 3:34

When you say- I don't have enough faith, God says- I've given everyone a measure of faith. Rom.12:3

When reading the Bible always consider:

The writer and who he is writing to.

The date of the writing.

The usage of words at the time it was written.

Possible change in the meaning of a word or how it is used now versus what it meant then.

Jason, I believe you will read some of the scriptures, but I want to give you two that you will need in the coming weeks.

> *"For God did not give us a spirit of timidity, but a spirit of power, of love and self discipline."* II Timothy 1:7 (NIV)
> *"Be thankful always; pray continually, give thanks in all circumstances, for this is God's will for you in Christ Jesus.* I Thessalonians 5:15-18 (NIV)

One more scripture from the Old Testament may give you courage. This promise is made to Jacob but it applies to all of us, and especially for you in your present situation.

> *"...do not fear, for I am with you; do not be dismayed, for I am your God. I will strengthen you and help you: I will uphold you with my righteous right hand. Isaiah 41:10 (NIV)*

Faith teaches us that God will not lead us into trouble that He will not lead us out of. Paul wrote in Hebrews what Jesus said; *"I will never leave you nor forsake you."*

I found that so uplifting that I shared it with David.

48

"Jane and Joe come sit down, I have something to tell you. This is so funny and it really happened. I went to Beth and George's for lunch today and George told me this story. I have the letter to prove that it happened. I had mentioned to them that we tried to find a stream to dam up for a pond here." David sounded happy and involved again. Joe and I were glad to have a reason to sit down and do nothing for an hour or two.

"I knew we had always had problems with beavers damming up the creek back when I lived at home. Well, George has had the same problem. Since their house is nearer the water he tried to do something about those pesky animals. He tried destroying their dams but they would build them back overnight. Then he got some dynamite and blew one up. Somebody reported his activity to the Department of Environmental Quality Control. So he received a letter from them. I knew I couldn't remember it all so I brought the letter and his response to it. Here Jane would you read them both." David smiling asked.

"Sure, I'll read it to us."

March 21, 1987

Mr. George Cotton
Route one, 9 Hollow Dr
Veeny, Alabama

Elizabeth Oliver Wooten

Subject: DEQ File 72-79-0033; T22N; R 12W, Sec. 30; Benjamin County Alabama

Dear Mr. Cotton,

It has come to the attention of the Department of Environmental Quality that there has been recent unauthorized activity on the above referenced parcel of property. You have been certified as the legal landowner and/or contractor who did the following unauthorized activity:

Construction and maintenance of two wood debris dams across the outlet stream of water flowing across your property. A permit must be issued by the state prior to this type of activity. A review of the Department's files shows that no permits have been issued. Therefore, the Department has determined that this activity is in violation of Part 201, Inland Lakes and Streams, of the Natural Resource and Environmental Protection Act, Act 451 of the Public Acts of 1972, being sections 324.30101 to 324.30113 of the Alabama Compiled Laws, annotated.

The Department has been informed that one or both of the dams partially failed during a recent rain event, causing debris and flooding at downstream locations. We find that dams of this nature are inherently hazardous and cannot be permitted. The Department herefore orders you to cease and desist all activities at this location, and to restore the stream to a free-flow condition by removing all wood and brush forming the dams from the stream channel. All restoration work shall be completed no later than November 30, 1987.

Please notify this office when the restoration has been completed so that a follow up site inspection may be scheduled by our staff. Failure to comply with this request or any further unauthorized activity on the site may result in this case being referred for elevated enforcement action. We anticipate and would appreciate your full cooperation in this matter. Please feel free to contact me at this office if you have any questions.

Sincerely,

*William Z. Hardegree, District Representative
Land and Water Management Division*

"George said this letter amused him at first, then because he was mad at the beavers for building the dam he decided to answer Mr. Hardegree." David explained. "Jane, read George's letter."

April 2, 1987

*Mr. William Z. Hardegree, District Representative
Land and Water Management Division*

Subject: DEQ File 72-79-0033; T22N; R 12W, Sec. 30; Benjamin County Alabama

Dear William,

I am the legal landowner but not the Contractor at 9 Hollow Dr, Veeny, Alabama. A couple of beavers are in the process of construction and maintaining two wood "debris" dams across the outlet stream on my property. While I did not pay for, authorize, nor supervise their dam project, I think they would be highly offended that you call their skillful use of natures building materials "debris."

I would like to challenge your department to attempt to emulate their dam project any time and/or any place you choose. I believe I can safely state there is no way you could ever match their dam skills, their dam resourcefulness, their dam ingenuity, their dam persistence, their dam determination and/or their dam work ethic.

As to your request, I do not think the beavers are aware that they must first fill out a dam permit prior to the start of this type of dam activity. My first dam question to you is: (1) Are you trying to discriminate against my Stream Beavers, or (2) do you require all beavers throughout this State to conform to said dam request?

If you are not discriminating against these particular beavers, through the Freedom of Information Act, I request completed copies of all those other applicable beaver dam permits that have been issued. Perhaps we will see if there really is a dam violation of Part 201, Inland Lakes and Streams, of the Natural Resource and Environmental Protection Act, Act 451 of the Public Acts of 1972, being sections 324.3001 to 324.30112 of the Alabama Complied Laws, annotated.

I have several concerns. My First concern is; aren't the beavers entitled to legal representation? The Stream Beavers are financially destitute and are unable to pay for said representation-

so the State will have to provide them with a dam lawyer. The Department's dam concern that either one or both of the dams failed during a recent rain event, causing flooding, is proof that this is a natural occurrence, which the Department is required to protect. In other words, we should leave the Stream Beavers alone rather than harassing them and calling their dam names.

If you want the stream "restored" to a dam free-flow condition please contact the beavers—but if you are going to arrest them—please be aware they are unable to read English and therefore did not pay any attention to your dam letter. In my humble opinion, the Stream Beavers have a right to build their unauthorized dams as long as the sky is blue, the grass is green, and water flows downstream. They have more dam rights than I do to live and enjoy The Stream.

If the Department of Natural Resources and Environmental Protection lives up to its name, it should protect the natural resources (Beavers) and the environment (Beaver' Dams). So, as far as the beavers and I are concerned, this dam case can be referred for more elevated enforcement action right now. Why wait until November 30, 1987. The Stream Beavers may be under the dam ice then and there will be no way for you or your staff to contact/harass them then.

In conclusion, I would like to bring to your attention to a real environmental quality (health) problem in the area. It is the deer! The deer are actually defecating in our woods. I definitely believe you should be persecuting the defecating deer and leave the beavers alone. If you are going to investigate the beaver dam, watch your step!

Elizabeth Oliver Wooten

Finally, being unable to comply with your dam request, and being unable to contact you on your answering machine, I am mailing this response to your office.

Sincerely,

George C. Cotton
Property Owner,
State of Alabama, County of Benjamin, Town of Veeny
August 28, 1995

ଚ∽ଚ

"David, did George do that?"

"Yeah, He did, He mailed a copy of what you just read but never got an answer."

Joe laughably said. "I love it, that's great."

My reply was, "I have heard George tell stories before. They are usually about something that has happened and he makes them so funny. Maybe we need him to sit on the porch in Veeny and spin yarns."

49

No Bail for Men Arrested

Seven men arrested by Alabama Drug Agents and local authorities were arraigned before Judge Nolan Bradford on Friday, August 25, 1995. Charles "Squire" Sanderson is charged with importing and distribution of illegal drugs, racketeering, attempted murder, assault, and arson. Leon Sanderson is charged with distribution and selling marijuana. Michael Davis is charged with distribution of illegal drugs and carrying a firearm while on probation. Jose Hernandez and Vince Patterson are both charged as a part of a violent drug enterprise in Northwest Alabama. Noe Sanchez is charged with illegal firearm possession. No bail was allowed for any of the six men.

Preston Perry arrested in nearby Mississippi is charged with murder and distribution of illegal drugs in Alabama and Mississippi. No bail was set for Perry.

Law enforcement officials in Benjamin County, and special agents from Alabama Drug Enforcement, FBI, U.S. Immigration, and Customs Enforcement and the local Fire Marshal's arson unit are investigating these charges. Three homicides in the area are possibly tied to these charges. Drug trafficking and related charges were made in Benjamin County last September and could be a part of this alleged distribution ring. A house fire, in nearby Veeny, is believed to be related to the sale of illegal drugs.

Benjamin County Times
August 28, 1995

Elizabeth Oliver Wooten

The story in Saturday's paper was the news we were waiting to hear. Finally, I felt we were not suspects in the deaths of three men. Those murders could have been committed on our property but surely, the Sheriff didn't think we did them or even knew who did.

David immediately went to Preacher's house to tell him and Sue, Jason's wife, and Sally, Butch Sanderson's wife, the good news.

David returned with more notes and written pages of names and dates from the Preacher. He had made a few changes on the pages I had typed. Maybe I can finish his story and begin mine now that some arrests have been made and we all feel safer.

Joe, Mattie, David, and I went to dinner in Trussellville on Saturday evening to celebrate. We also attended church together on Sunday. Mattie came from Blue Pond to go with us, since Joe was going. I was surprised to see Jason Pierce there with his family. It was nice to see so many of our friends together. Some family, the Pastor and church family, the Sandersons—Butch, Sally, Kaylee, and Matthew, and the Pierce family. David and I were beginning to believe that maybe we belonged here.

❦

Monday morning about eleven, we finally had a visit from Sheriff Moore, Detective Robert Smith, and FBI Agent Skyler Sims. After introducing us to the FBI Agent, the Sheriff explained about the raid.

"We had everything in place and after we knew the little girl was back home safe we followed our plan the next day. Jason Pierce gave me information about the men who worked with Squire. We knew about how many were probably staying there. He said the gate to the club would be locked and told my men how to find a key in a nearby tree. Some of our men went to the clubhouse at the same time we went to the home. We had no trouble arresting and handcuffing the six men. One man was out early tending to the cattle. The wife of that man was not arrested and was left there. Squire's wife was not at home or else she knew where to hide. Squire said she had not come home, the evening before.

"We found plenty of evidence, drugs, guns, money, and other stuff related to hauling and distributing drugs. I didn't think they would be released on bail, but I waited for their arraignment before coming to talk to you. We have watched the Sanderson compound since the arrest for any others that might show up there. Mrs. Sanderson returned the next day. Since she has visited her husband at the jail, we feel she will be available if we find evidence that she aided them in any illegal activities. No others have been seen near the place. I bet she and the other lady are doing a lot of work, taking care of the cattle and horses."

David asked, "What have you learned about the murders? Are these people responsible for killing those men?"

Agent Sims answered, "We are investigating each of those homicides. Two of the bodies have been identified. No identification yet on the bones from your well. Another cemetery just south of here has some suspicious graves. We are getting things in place to investigate those."

"Oh, my gosh. Not more bodies." I injected and couldn't say anything else.

Joe asked about Jason being released, "Is Jason Pierce out on probation now?"

"Yes, he still has to finish the time he has left on his probation. We didn't add anything related to the gun I found on him. In fact it hasn't been mentioned." Sheriff Moore said.

"Let me say, 'Thank You', for your assistance with the drug arrest and for finding those two graves in the cemetery, and for reporting the human bones in your well." Agent Sims continued. "We need all the help we can get, and it will still be difficult to solve all three crimes. There aren't enough clues on the bodies. One man was fifty miles from his home and had been reported missing almost a year ago. His family has identified his clothing and tests are being done to match DNA. We have some information about the other body, but nobody has positively identified it."

"We hope more evidence will be coming from the men that have been arrested." The Sheriff told us. "The District Attorney and Judge Bradford have promised to try for a trial in about six months. Of course, they will have to be ready with as much evidence as they can find and the attorneys for the men will have to agree."

Detective Bob told us, "The information we got from you three has helped bring murder charges against Preston Perry. Since he was seen here and had lived here, he is the most likely suspect at this time. We think at least one of those men arrested will talk and give solid information about what happened here.

"Jason Pierce gave us some information and we're working on that. My partner is checking on a few leads right now. We appreciate your cooperating with us."

"Sheriff Moore, does this mean we are not suspects now? Can we come and go anytime? I still had some anger in my voice.

I didn't get an answer. I recalled something Preacher Fredericks had said about we should look for opportunities to be a blessing to someone. Maybe I should look for that opportunity and forget my irritation about the Sheriff not keeping us informed.

50

The sky is a clear blue, white fluffy clouds drift by. I watch through the tall Georgia pines as I lie on my chaise lounge near the water. This is truly relaxing, warm spring sunshine; a few early shrubs are blooming and give off a spring fragrance. David and I are the only people at the lake club. It's still early for the other residents to arrive for the summer season. . The water is so still; I see perfect reflections of the trees across our part of Lake Altoona. The tall trees are five colors of green; this would be a real challenge to paint in watercolor. I have almost found time to start sketching again. My watercolors, brushes, and paper are all laid out in front of our big windows at home. But the cabin at the lake needs a good spring cleaning to be ready for our family to use while we're gone.

The few months we have spent at home has helped me to put aside all the events that took place at our Alabama farm. Now David and I are both ready to go back and finish repairing the house, see our friends there, and wait for the trials to begin.

I have heard how well the rebirth of Veeny is progressing. I must take more old items for our booth. Checking out flea markets and yard sales had been something we had enjoyed during the winter months. David insists that I never run out of something for him to do. We both would be bored to death if I did.

Elizabeth Oliver Wooten

My two sisters-in-law have kept me informed about the 'Old New Town'. All the people with little businesses seemed pleased with their efforts and sales. The advertising by Mattie had people coming from all different parts of Alabama and Mississippi. The mayor and all the councilmen, except Rex, had been very involved.

Betty Sue Sanderson had worked just about every day the shops were open. She was always bringing more antiques and people bought them, even the expensive ones. The Auction House stayed open every day. The owners had cleaned it up and installed a sandwich bar. They still had the auction once a month.

We had calls regularly from Joe. The work on my childhood home was almost finished, he needed me to be there and supervise the inside decorating. Jason Pierce had worked on it with Joe after Butch had to quit. Butch felt he needed to help Betty Sue with their cattle. He had done that before on his brother's Texas ranch. The job here was much harder with no other help so Sally, Matthew, and Kayee stayed with Betty Sue much of the time. Mattie and Joe were still best friends, which didn't tell us anything about their romance.

We planned to leave in one week. I had finished Preacher Frederick's story and wanted him to approve everything before I had the copies made for his family and friends. It was very interesting, or I thought so. I have learned how hard it is to write about the eighty plus years of one man's life. I believe it will please the Preacher, since I have included so many of his religious thoughts. I think that will be a blessing to his descendants in years to come. Joe said he was not well, that he was barely able to get to his chair on the porch. I'm so glad that it has worked for the Pierce family to live with him. Sue took over what Sally and Kaylee did before. The Preacher's sons were happy for them to take care of their Dad.

I had even written a first chapter about my ancestors. It may or may not be a part of my book.

What else would we find at my grandparents old home? Joe and Bear had been taking care of our motor home and watching the place while we were gone, David still wants to know what it will be used for. Who knows, but I am still optimistic and happy to be saving it.

51

Fourteen long neck geese are swimming by. All look exactly alike; brown feathers on their backs, small white tails turned up, black slender necks and heads that turn to gaze at me. They form a long line and all are the same distance apart except the last one. He varies his distance and then gets out of line—that's why he is last. Their honk-honk-honks resound loudly as they leave our part of the lake. The sound is like kinfolk at a family reunion, all talking at the same time.

I'm thinking about my life story as I watch the geese. Maybe that one leading is the ancestor that first arrived in America many years ago. I would certainly be the last one in line that doesn't comply with family traditions. I can't write about all of them but maybe I can begin a tradition of writing about our life while we are still alive and able. I know most of my ancestors could write but I don't have anything written by any of them, except a few things written by my mother.

I know nothing about the personal lives of most of these ancestors. Dates of birth, marriage date and date of death are recorded if I know where to look. Census records give me some information about where they lived. I'm sure their real life stories would be different; not alike as the geese; but to me they are the same, unknown to me as a living person. Taking into consideration how each family multiplies through the years the fourteen geese may or may not represent the families in my legacy. Including the ancestors of those added by marriage, all family trees branch out in different directions like a real tree. I think those geese will have different families also.

Another set of geese is flowing by. The male is about two feet ahead and to the side of the mother, and three young ones. I'm sure this represents that he is the leader and protector of this family. I can visualize them as my father and mother's family. I would be the one in the middle of the three young geese. My sister is older and my brother is younger. My brother has also broken some tradition in the last half of the twentieth century. How can I record all the things that have happened to the families that I remember? I have decided to limit my story to the lives of seven people that I remember. I will write about one paternal great grandmother, one maternal grandmother, two paternal grandparents, one father, one mother, and myself. Each of those people had other persons that made a difference in their lives and I'll have to write about them also.

I have many memories of my parents, grandparents, and a faint memory of my great grandmother. I was eight years old when she died. I want to write a story about each of those ancestors before I record the events of my life. I plan to write things I remember and the statistics about each one. I'll include a limited number of charts to help follow my story.

'THE DASH'
by
Jane E. Cotton

PART ONE

Jasper Alexander Wheat (1860—1931) and Susan Virginia Smith (1860—1943)

She moved into the house with us when she was almost eighty years old. She was not unattractive, just old. All of her dresses seemed to be black, or that's the way I remember her. My grandfather, with whom we were living, was her oldest son. He wanted to help care for his Mother although there was not an extra bedroom in the house. She came with a large trunk and a single bed. The bed was put in the end of the dining room and her trunk nearby. There were a few things other than her clothes in that trunk. She liked to show them to us but we were not allowed to touch them, since most were breakable. The fragile pieces of china were beautiful and indicated that her home at one time, maybe only her childhood home, had been furnished with nice things.

The year was 1941. Old Folks Homes or Retirement Centers were not available for parents who were unable to live alone and maintain their home. Her husband, my great grandfather, had died on January 18, 1931, years before I was born. At this time Granny needed care and my grandparents, sister and I were chosen for this. I don't recall many things about her. Most of her teeth were missing and she didn't see well or hear very well. I remember her for one event that happened in relation to her having the 'gift'. I learned that the 'gift' was something she never talked about. Some people thought she could read tea leaves and tell the future or the past. Perhaps in her younger years she was a fortuneteller; I just don't know.

Elizabeth Oliver Wooten

Susan Virginia Smith was born 5 May 1860 in Mulberry—Lincoln County, Tennessee. She was married in Madison County Alabama to Jasper Alexander Wheat. Their first child was my paternal grandfather, Henry Calvin Wheat. In the next twenty-five years nine more children were born to them.

The only photographs I have of Susan and Jasper were taken when he was at least sixty years old and one of her probably in her seventies. Those pictures of them were not taken as a couple, but I believe they lived together until his death. Their youngest child was married five years before Jasper's death at age sixty-nine. It seems Susan would have been left living alone. I hope to learn more information from some of their many grandchildren that are still living in all parts of the United States.

A descendants chart of Jasper Alexander Wheat (1860—18 Jan 1931) and Susan Virginia Smith (5 Jan 1860—18 Dec 1943) family will be found on page ___?

Ancestor Charts for both of the above will be found on page ___?

The events that I know of this couple are so few and most facts about their parents are unknown. The charts will give dates of births and deaths and will trace their ancestors back to the early 1700's. It seemed that the parents of Susan, Samuel Preston Smith (B 1827/32—D 1912) family came from Lincoln County, Tennessee to Madison County, Alabama, sometime after 1860. Henry Wheat (B 1814—D 1884), father of Jasper arrived in Alabama, sometime after 1834 from Lincoln County, Tennessee. Their children grew up in the aftermath of the War Between the States (1861-1865).

The historical events of the years after that war are well known. Many plantation farmers in the South owned slaves that were freed in 1865. The farmlands in Benjamin County were not suitable for large-scale cotton fields. More likely the Smith and Wheat families farmed on a small scale and grew food for their large families and had cows, mules, pigs, and chickens. I will continue to search the records for information and hope some of their descendants will have some personal stories about these people.

That's the most I can write about ancestors of that period. My book will have more stories and information about my grandparents and parents. Most of the stories will be about my family, my marriage, careers, children, grandchildren, pets, and a wonderful husband.

52

Everything is packed and it's a warm spring day perfect for driving, David and I are going back to Veeny, Alabama. Again, we have had our mail and newspaper sent there since we have no idea how long we'll be there. The trials for the men arrested last year for drugs and murder are set to begin next week but they could be changed or could last a month or two. It sure will be good to know what might have taken place on our little farm in the last few years. We planned to go sit in the courtroom and hear what the authorities have learned and what those men have to say.

We do plan to stop at my brother's house in Alabama. I have one question I forgot to ask him when we talked about the drug-related arrests. Oliver is still with the Alabama Drug Agency. He already explained that his boss didn't allow him to be a part of that raid because of another case he was working on. We had already told him what we knew about the raid and had the newspaper write-ups for him to read. At that time, he told us about how dealers get drugs in from Mexico, false bottoms in their cattle trailer and paying off some of the border agents work, especially, if Sanderson's people were coming across the border often with cattle.

We agreed to have a cup of coffee with them and hear about their family. Finally, their youngest daughter was expecting a boy. They all were happy to hear that news. Oliver and his wife have four girls, the oldest one now has three girls, another daughter has one girl, and this daughter has one little girl. This will be her second child and it is a boy according to the ultra sound. I thought to myself, he would be as spoiled as my brother was. Oliver got lots of attention when he came along seven years after me. I recalled the tricycle he got for Christmas one year. I never ever got a bicycle. Oh well, I loved him anyway and was not jealous of the attention he got. I'm sure this little boy will be a special one to his Granddad, Dad, and Uncles; also, to all the girls.

"Oliver, why did the law take a cow when they raided the Sanderson place? Nobody has been able to explain that. The newspaper said they did."

"Uh, that's a new way they are bringing in drugs from Mexico. They do surgery, cut them under their bellies, and put packs of cocaine in them. Then, after the cattle are at a ranch or somewhere in the United States they take it out and sew them up again."

"Oh my goodness, do the cows live after that?"

"Most of them do unless an infection starts. We had one instance of that happening. The crooks got greedy and sold some of them at auction and one of them died right away. We traced it back to the drug dealers and found out how they did it. We arrested all of them. We didn't arrest any cattle. I bet the cow they took was for evidence or maybe she still had a tummy full of drugs."

※

We arrived in Veeny about three o'clock on Saturday. There were lots of people, the ones running the shops and the customers or visitors. It was a changed town; nothing like it was when we had first returned last year. I felt so very proud that I had a small part in planning to restore the almost deserted town. It still had the atmosphere of the town I remembered. The old buildings looked much like they did in the 1950s. Almost half were missing, should we try to rebuilt them to look as old as the ones here? We will probably need more in a few months. The spaces that had been repaired were filled with some kind of business. "Hand Turned Ice Cream—Three Flavors" was the sign on the door of Miss Mary's Tearoom. A big sign announced, "AUCTION TONIGHT". We couldn't stop to see everybody now, we needed to see about our motor home and Joe was there expecting us. We planned to come back to the auction and visit with our friends.

"Look, a garden. Oh! David, can we plant flowers too?" I was excited and emotional again. Seeing the house and well made me feel like I was coming home again.

Joe and Bear were expecting us. They both looked healthy and were happy to see us. Bear remembered us although we had been gone almost six months. The place looked good—Joe had planted a garden just where Memaw's had been. I think he had the same vegetables planted and lots of them. He had heard me talk so much about Memaw's garden that he had duplicated it.

The well shed was restored. It looked like it did in the fifties. They had poured a new base of concrete that sealed the deep well. The same tall round concrete tile and top sat in the center of the shed. Water was piped to just above an old bucket lying tilted on the lid that used to open to draw water from the well. A chain attached to the bucket went up to a pulley above. Joe had even rebuilt the old windlass. The four old posts held up the square top and the wood shingles on the roof looked like the original ones. It was a perfect centerpiece for the yard.

My old home had a new porch, with a roof that sloped to the front like the old one did. All of the outside wood looked like it was aged, gray and rough. The house did have a new front door and a side entrance. The side of the house looked different than the original since we had torn off the old kitchen and dining room but the roof was the same wood shingles. I asked Joe.

"Did you split more shingles and make them look old?"

"No, I remembered a man that did restorations and he had some, we didn't need many so it didn't cost a lot. He also told me how to made the new wood look old. How do you like it?"

"I love it." I exclaimed. "Let's go inside I don't care what the back side of the house looks like. I know you added more rooms there."

Going up the three wood steps to the porch and in the front door was as I remembered it from many years ago. The front room looked bigger than I recalled since it didn't have any furniture. The fireplace was there on the same wall as a window. That was Papaw's place by the window near the fire. The next room was an original one, a bedroom that always had two full size beds and a green dresser. It was empty now. Where one window had been, a doorway went into the new addition. All the floors were covered with wood like I asked but still needed to be finished.

The new rooms were complete, the bath had fixtures placed where I had drawn them, and it had tile floors and the walls were finished. The new room also had a tile floor and the walls were painted a pastel green.

"Joe, is the septic tank in? Can we use the bathroom?"

"Yes, it's all done, you can use it."

"You're done a good job here. Was Jason as good a worker as Butch?" David declared.

"Jason knew more about building than we did and he worked hard. He has helped me on my farmhouse. I have stayed here in my camper every night to make sure everything was all right. I haven't seen any strange people around here."

I asked Joe. "What about you and Mattie. She called me a few times to say she missed us but didn't say much about you."

"Mattie and I are still best friends and maybe more. My wife divorced me; the papers were mailed to me and I signed them. She asked for half of the profit from the sale of our farmhouse and I agreed. She didn't want anything in it, said I could keep that, or sell it. I only talked to her one more time and we agreed this was best for both of us. The divorce was final last week. Our house is almost ready to sell. I hope to have some money after I pay off the mortgage. I have made some improvements, but still need to get the pump fixed.

"I guess it's too soon for you to know if you're happy about that."

"I've put that behind me and am really looking forward to a new beginning with Mattie if she will agree to marry me."

"That's sounds like you haven't asked her. She told me once that she wanted children. Be sure you discuss that with her," I reminded Joe.

"Enough questions for now, let's get ready to go to Veeny. We'll eat at Norman's café and then go to the auction. Call Mattie or I will, that's the first place she went with us."

Joe said. "I'll call her and tell her you are here and ask if she can meet us there."

53

By Monday, the news was out that we were back to attend the trail of Charles 'Squire' Sanderson. Joe and Jason, both scheduled as witnesses for the prosecution, had only heard that the Judge, district attorney, and attorneys for the defense were ready but they didn't know when the trials would begin.

David called the sheriff and asked that we be notified when the first trial was scheduled. The sheriff did tell David some of the things that had happened in the last few months. Preston Perry had pled guilty to distributing illegal drugs and was willing to testify for the prosecution in the trails of Charles and Leon Sanderson, Jose Hernandez and Vince Patterson. Mac Davis had pled guilty to selling drugs and agreed to give testimony against the others. Noe Sanchez who was charged with being a party to the sale of illegal drugs will not have a jury trial. Sanchez was out on bail. Charles Sanderson, Leon Sanderson, Vince Patterson, and Jose Hernandez will all have separate jury trials. Preston Perry will still face the murder charge at a later date. The sheriff didn't know which trial Jason Pierce would be called to testify in or whether Joe would need to testify about his meeting with "Mac" Davis.

Sheriff Moore said all of these trials would be held in U.S. District Court in Florence. The Drug Enforcement Administration, Alabama Drug Enforcement, and Internal Revenue Service-Criminal Investigation are all a part of the prosecution because of the amount of drugs and money confiscated from the Sanderson home. If the murder charges against Charles Sanderson and Preston Perry are related to drugs, those trials will be held in federal court also. The Sheriff did tell David that he would call as soon as either case was put on the docket.

☙❧

This gave us some time to evaluate the progress on the house. I totaled up what we had invested so far—all the materials, labor and utilities. We had spent almost all of what we budgeted for the house. We now had city water, a septic system, electricity from Tennessee Valley Authority, propane gas tank for cooking, and a central heat and air conditioning system. Before doing anything else David insisted we decide what this house was going to be used for.

I had thought a lot about that and prayed for guidance, but no direct answer had become clear yet. David and I had almost—definitely—decided we would not live here. He had said if I wanted an antique-gift shop or restaurant I would have to find a manager or a cook.

I had a plan for a combination restaurant and shop with antiques and souvenirs of the area. I knew of one restaurant that always had a pot of beans sitting on an old fashioned small stove. They were hot, soupy, and a favorite of all the patrons. We could do that here, in front of the fireplace. I did want more gourmet items on the menu, since no one could get a special meal in this area. All the tables and chairs would be old, some with lace tablecloths and all with real napkins and silverware. Other fixtures would be things found from the fifties and sixties such as phonograph players to furnish the music from old records. Those and other old items would be for sale. My other gift shoppe had sold lots of souvenirs. Things like a local cookbook, mugs, tee shirts, bags, and an afghan with scenes of the town had sold very well. I think all the shops in Veeny could sell those items. The location was two miles from Veeny, but since there was not a full-service food place anywhere around; I felt customers would come. I had not shared this plan with David because I was sure he probably wouldn't like it. I even had a name for the place, 'The Homestead'.

The kitchen appliances had not been installed and the inside walls and ceilings of the two old rooms were waiting for my instructions. I wanted them to have an authentic nineteen-fifty look, which meant I needed to find the wallpaper which would look spiffy, neat, pretty, and be just right for whatever the rooms would be used for.

A visitor, Betty Sue Sanderson, interrupted my thoughts. I had not seen her since we got back to Veeny. She looked so tired, exhausted, and five years older than when I last saw her six months ago. I knew she had been working hard, but she always enjoyed that. The stress of her husband being in jail must be terrible for her.

"Well, hello there, you haven't seen our place here, have you? I'm so glad you came by to see us."

"I heard you would be here today and I did want to see you before we open the shops Thursday. I didn't want to just see you at the trial either."

"I really do need you to help me decide what to make of this cute little house. I know it has possibilities but I can't decide what they are."

"Jane, you did so much the right way about the shops in Veeny, I know you can figure out the best use for this. It does look very unique and interesting. What's the garden for? Are you going to be here all summer?"

"We plan to be here a few months. Joe planted the garden, we should have lots of food from it later. I'll share with you."

"Let's sit down here under the tree; I want to tell you what's happened since you left. First, I need to say thanks for sending me to stay at Mattie's that night. The Lord must have told you to do that; it really saved me from being arrested along with Squire. I think you believed me when I told you I didn't know what Squire was doing and didn't know where the money came from. I have tried to tell that to the authorities, but I'm not sure if they believe me or not.

"Squire has insisted that I find him a good lawyer. I've tried to do that but had to retain him without much money. The cash that Squire had was taken in the raid; they found it all. Squire says there is more but I can't get to it now. He wanted me ask Rex Arnold to loan us ten thousand dollars, but he has left home and his wife says she doesn't know where he is.

"Jane, I'm sorry to be telling you all this. I heard you came back for the trial so I know you're interested. I think those murders are somehow connected to this and to your place. I guess I still need a friend to talk to. It's been a lifesaver to have Butch's family helping me. He knows how to handle the cattle and horses, and has been able to sell some of them for money for us to live on. The others cows are having babies and looking good. I even know how to feed them. Kaylee likes it at our place and Matthew is a big help. Butch and Sally are true Christians or they wouldn't have been willing to help me after the way Squire has treated them. I told Squire that Butch was helping me with the ranch. Noe and Mrs. Sanchez are back helping now but they know I can't pay them. I'm starting to feel like we can run the ranch without Squire and the others. I wouldn't trust any of them right now, not even my husband."

"You can come talk to me anytime. I may or may not help by listening, but it will help you to know that we're your friends. We'll have some time together this weekend. I plan to be in Veeny and talk to the committee about other things we can plan. They tell me that you are there working every weekend. If I can help you with anything let me know.

" By the way, Joe and Mattie may have some big news for us soon. Did you know he is divorced?" I informed Betty Sue.

"I'm happy for them. I like Mattie and Joe. They seem to be right for each other.

"Thank you for listening. I do worry about the charges and what the outcome will be.

"I'm not sure how I'll feel about Squire when and if he gets out. It seems I was awful dumb, or he was very smart to keep this from me, if he is guilty."

54

I had some time over the winter months to research more about drugs, substance abuse, substance dependency, and deaths from overdose. I learned that the use and abuse of illegal drugs affects us all, in one way or another and that we should talk about drugs to those who matter to us. I believe if our young people and others know the devastating effect of alcohol and illegal drugs, they would never start using them. When I read that substance abuse is directly related to many violent crimes, I immediately thought of the three dead men we knew about.

Alcohol addiction is something I can relate to. My Dad suffered from that for many, many years. It affected the lives of hundreds of people. Family, friends, co-workers on the many jobs he had and lost, and especially his kids and wife. Alcohol and other drugs not only become more important than people; but more important than the basic needs of food, clothing and shelter. These persons are searching for freedom from insecurities, fear, rules, problems, pain, and sometimes just from boredom. They become slaves to something so powerful that it can control their lives.

Tobacco is another addiction that affects the health of those who use it and yet, they can't quit smoking or chewing. It has been proven that cancer of the lungs and throat is much more prevalent in smokers. The incidences of heart disease and other serious ailments relate directly to tobacco use, yet people continue to smoke and young people begin smoking in their very early teen years.

Methamphetamine, or simply meth, is one of a group of stimulants used in World War II and other conflicts to keep soldiers and pilots awake through long battles. Amphetamines are sometimes used to treat nasal allergies and depression as well as to aid weight loss. Illegal production of meth became a problem in the 1960's, and led very quickly to abuse. It is considered by many to be the worst drug problem in America. There are several forms of these drugs and all can have the same effect. Long-term use can damage the brain, lead to psychoses such as paranoia and persecution mania. Addicts often behave in irrational, erratic and dangerous ways. Methamphetamine use affects the appetite. Addicts are often malnourished, look much older, and often have rotten teeth. Long-term use can lead to heart attacks or stroke. Meth addiction is very hard to recover from.

A statement by Kent Graham in an article in Texas Monthly magazine calls meth, "The most destructive thing I've ever seen."

> 'Now that you've met me, what will you do?
> Will you try me or not, it's all up to you.
> I can show you more misery than words can tell,
> Come hold my hand, let me lead you to Hell.'

The preceding words are taken from a poem by an anonymous author who is said to have been a jailed meth addict.

Marijuana is a dried mixture of shredded leaves, stems and flowers of the hemp plant, cannabis sativa. The mixture is usually green, brown or gray in color. The wild hemp

Memories and Murders

plant has a much lower concentration of this drug than the modern cultivated varieties. The hemp plant can grow up to twenty feet high and is grown in Mexico and the United States. It has a distinctive sweet-sour smell and can be detected on clothes or in a room. Marijuana comes in different forms, sinsemilla, hashish, hash oil; these have different percentages of THC, a mind-altering drug. It is the most commonly used illegal drug in the United States. Marijuana interferes with the ability to learn and retain information, and affects short-term memory. While not as addictive as other drugs, the high from THC can be psychologically addictive, especially to teens.

The leaves of the South American coca plant have been used as a stimulant since the time of the Incan Empire. When chewed or brewed into tea, they produce a mild euphoria and alleviate fatigue and hunger. An active ingredient in coca leaves, cocaine, was isolated in 1855. Far more powerful than coca leaves, it was used as an anesthesia. Cocaine became a fashionable illegal drug for the wealthy in the 1970's.

Cocaine is most commonly a fine white powder. It is usually snorted into the nose through a thin straw, where it is absorbed in the bloodstream through the mucous membranes. It can also be swallowed or injected. Cocaine triggers the release of dopamine in the brain, giving the user a feeling of excitement and pleasure. The user's energy level is increased and appetite is decreased. It also constricts blood vessels, and can cause heart attacks or seizures. Continued use can lead to depression, malnutrition and the body's ability to fight infections. Addicts have little ability to concentrate and can be paranoid and exhibit violent behavior. Many other serious problems of cocaine use are documented including frightening hallucinations. Recovery from any addiction is a long, difficult process.

I read about the frightening effects of other drugs like heroin, which can cause immediate death from an overdose and the difficulty of recovery from a heroin addiction without professional help. All drugs including prescription drugs and even caffeine can be abused, and are a determent to the mind and body. I felt like I could better understand the demand for illegal drugs after learning more about them. This can even explain some of the horrible actions caused by the use of mind-altering drugs. Most of these drugs are illegal and people caught importing and selling them are usually given a long prison term and a large fine.

The pending trials of the men arrested will possibly show some events caused by drug use. If they sold drugs, they probably used them as well. Could their paranoid and violent drug-induced behavior have caused them to kill three or more people?

55

Charles 'Squire' Sanderson Trial This Week

A jury has been selected and testimony is set to begin today in the trial of Veeny, Alabama resident Charles Sanderson. He is facing charges of importing and distributing illegal drugs, possession of drugs, arson, and money laundering. Murder charges against Sanderson have been postponed.

Sanderson appeared in court without his white hat. He had shed his jail issue clothes for a dark suit and tie. His attorney, Kenneth Tumlin from Birmingham, was by his side.

For six hours yesterday prosecutor Claude Simpson and defense attorney Tumlin questioned potential jurors with questions ranging from their occupation, to their views about the legality of marijuana use. Several jurors said they would have difficulty staying unbiased in a case involving alleged drug distributors.

Both defense and prosecution attorneys told the panel whom they will call as witnesses to see if any had business or personal relationships with those individuals. Named on the prosecutor's list were previous co-defendants, Preston J. Perry and Michael Davis, They would also call Jason Pierce; Real Estate Salesmen, Ronnie Barker and Ted Mixon, and Auctioneer Jim Edmonds. Defense attorney Simpson will call Sanderson's wife Betty Sue, his ex-wife Annie Mae Sanderson, Leon Sanderson and Veeny Alderman Rex Arnold.

Potential jurors had to discuss any dealings with businesses like cattle sales, antiques sales or the buying of real estate. They were asked what programs they watched on television. Some with yes responses to specific ques-

> *tions were asked to elaborate. Some stated they did not approve of drug or alcohol use. Once questioning was finished, several people were dismissed. Then the lawyers selected the jury of twelve and two alternates, eleven men and three women. The prosecution had six strikes while the defense is allowed to strike ten.*
>
> *The case will begin with opening statements today, with the trial expected to last two to three weeks. One of Sanderson's employees and Preston J. Perry, an admitted drug dealer, are to testify against him. Both accepted plea agreements from the government. They will be given credit for their testimony at sentencing,*
>
> *Benjamin County Times*
April 2, 1996

౿৵

If we had seen today's Times yesterday, we might not have spent our day sitting in court. The newspaper covered most everything that happened on Monday. Of course David and I were there, sitting with Betty Sue and Noe Sanchez. Joe Burns and Jason Pierce were also in the crowded courtroom. We all would be there today listening carefully for any indication of guilt of drug distribution and especially for news of the three murders.

We now knew that Mac Davis and Preston Perry were willing to testify against Squire and probably would give evidence against Leon Sanderson, Lance Patterson and Jose Hernandez—all of whom had worked for Squire. Where does that leave any murder charges? I still believed this was all tied together. Oh well, one day or one trial at a time.

56

Witnesses Tell Facts or Lies at Trial

In the opening day of testimony in the trial of Charles Sanderson, District Attorney Claude Simpson told the jury it would be its job to determine 'who Squire Sanderson is?' Is he a business man selling cattle, horses, and antiques from his ranch in Texas and his estate in Alabama or a 'drug lord' guilty as charged. The charges are arson, importing and distributing illegal drugs, possession of drugs and money laundering.

Simpson's opening statement and subsequent witnesses attempted to portray Sanderson as a ruthless thug heading a drug ring that engaged in threats and violence to make money.

Defense attorney Kenneth Tumlin told the jury his witnesses would prove that the charges are unfounded and he would show that the evidence produced did not belong to Charles Sanderson.

FBI special agent Skyler Sims identified dozens of exhibits taken from the Sanderson estate near Veeny in an early morning raid in 1995. These included cocaine, marijuana, guns, and $500,000 in cash. Photographs of a cattle trailer and a cow were entered as exhibits.

ABC Drug agents testified about a drug exchange, that took place in Veeny, between an informant and a man that worked for Mr. Sanderson. That man will verify that the drugs exchanged were from Mexico and brought into the United States through the Texas ranch owned by Sanderson and his brother.

Preston J Perry took the stand for the prosecution and testified that he has been buying drugs from Charles

Elizabeth Oliver Wooten

> Sanderson and his employees for three years. Perry was asked to identify the man he bought marijuana from. Perry pointed to Charles Sanderson and said he has known that man for years. Objections by the defense were overruled.
>
> Perry tried to speak about some bones and killings but that objection was upheld. The judge said this was not a murder trial.
>
> More witnesses for the prosecution will be on the stand tomorrow. It is not known if Charles Sanderson will testify in his own defense.
>
> Benjamin County Times
April 3, 1996

The Times report gave the details very well. We had been there listening to everything. The trial began after lunch, at twelve-thirty on the second day of Squire's trial. The morning session was delayed because of a problem. We did get to see Preston J. Perry and hear his testimony. Joe said that his appearance had improved drastically since he saw him last. He thought being in jail with no drugs had helped and it sounded like Perry knew something about the murders.

Betty Sue needed some consoling after hearing that testimony so I asked her to have dinner with us before we went home. David and Joe talked about the other defendants and wondered how long these trials would take.

"Will they really have a trial this long for each of them?" I inquired.

"It looks like they will. I should only be required to testify in Mac's trial. If he is giving state's evidence, maybe there won't be a trial for him. I'm glad he's doing that, since he's been convicted before on drug charges; this could mean a stiff fine for him and a long prison term." Joe said.

"I don't think I can get up there and talk about Squire and drugs. For one thing, I don't know anything. I don't know what they have been doing. I feel so stupid. Another thing, I am still afraid of Squire and the others. Will I be forced to take the stand?" Betty Sue was asking and wringing her hands instead of eating.

"The attorney you hired will talk to you before hand, but you must tell the truth." I tried to assure her but didn't know how.

David said, "Let's all pray about this now and for the next few days."

After we all held hands and prayed silently, Betty Sue said. "I'm not sure the Lord hears my prayer or I sure don't hear His answers lately."

"Sometimes we have to wait a long time to understand what the Lord has planned for us. I feel positive that He is going to take care of this. We just have to wait and pray." I added.

"Let's plan to be at the courthouse tomorrow at ten o'clock. Betty, I'd like to ride back to Veeny with you tonight."

57

The Benjamin County Times did not report on the trial in the April 4th edition. We knew we should attend every day. Today will be the second day of the District Attorney's witnesses. I was almost as tense and worried as Betty Sue. We arrived on time and waited.

After the jury entered and Judge Bradford was seated, he asked the prosecution to call their next witness. Squire and his attorney were seated and both were dressed in dark suits and ties, neither looked our way.

Michael Davis was called to the stand. He was dressed in casual clothes, as Perry was the day before. We weren't sure, but thought they were still being held in jail, although they had agreed to help the prosecution.

After the swearing in, the Federal District Attorney asked him, "Mr. Davis please tell the jury what you know about Charles Sanderson."

"I've known him for five or six years. I've worked for him for the last three years.

Most of that time I was here in this county. Sometimes I went to Texas and hauled cattle back here."

"Now tell us what you know about his business."

"Squire likes for us to say that he is a rancher, raising and selling cattle here and in Texas. He sells more than that. Illegal drugs from Mexico are what we all have been selling. Some of the stuff is sold to distributors and some to people that use them. I have done both but I did not kill anybody."

"Objection," from Defense Attorney Simpson.

"Sustained," from the Judge. "Strike that last statement, we don't have a murder trial here."

"Mr. Davis, you say you sold drugs but what do you know for a fact about Mr. Sanderson?"

"He was or is the boss, I worked for him. He told us when and what to do. Mostly, the others drove the truck and trailer. Squire went along part of the time. I worked at the Texas ranch sometimes after they brought the stuff in. The boys were supposed to be buying cows in Mexico, bringing them to Texas and fattening them for the people here. And we did, but that was a cover for the drugs. Some of those cows had packs of cocaine sewed in their bellies. We put them to sleep, took it out, and sewed them back up. Later when they were well and fat they went to the slaughterhouse. I think after making lots of trips bringing in cattle the drugs were put in a false bottom in the trailer. The border guards knew Jose and Vince and Squire by then."

"Did you ever go to Mexico to get these cattle and drugs?"

"No, I did not."

"Objection, how could he know this if he wasn't there"

"Over ruled."

"Did Charles Sanderson sell and distribute these drugs in Alabama?"

"He did, he's a good salesman. He delivered them to other states using the same trailer. They also used it to pick up furniture and stuff his wife had found and bought."

"Do you know any of the people these drugs were delivered to?"

"Yes, I know some of them and where we delivered them."

"Did Mr. Sanderson deliver to these same people?"

"I believe he did. He never went with me when I delivered to them."

"Objection, hearsay."

"Over ruled. Continue."

"That's all I have for the witness at this time."

The Judge asked the Defense Attorney if there were any questions for this witness.

Defense Attorney Mr. Tumlin approached the witness stand. "Mr. Davis I think you are lying to this jury. Do you know the penalty for perjury?"

"Objection, the witness does not have to answer."

"Sustained. Mr. Tumlin, what you think does not matter in this trial."

"Mr. Davis, You say you have worked for my client for three years. Does this mean you also lived on his property?"

"I did most of the time. I have a home but no family there."

"Can you identify the items here as definitely belonging to Mr. Sanderson?"

"I know the items in the pictures belong to the ranch. I've seen that trailer there and that cow.

"Most cows look a lot alike. How can you be sure that cow came from his ranch?"

"I guess because I was told it did."

"What about these items?"

"I have not seen Squire with any of those things; they could have come from his house."

"Then you really can't swear that any of this evidence belongs to Mr. Sanderson."

"I know the trailer in the picture is his."

"No further questions at this time."

The District Attorney called his next witness.

"State your name and your business."

"I'm Jim Edmonds from Tupelo, Mississippi and I own the Farm Auction there."

"Have you seen Charles Sanderson at your auctions?"

"I have, many times."

"What does he do there?"

"Most of the times he has cattle to sell, sometimes he comes and buys a horse or two."

"Is there anything different about his cattle, or anything unusual about his sales?"

"The cattle are not the best. The price they bring is low, but he doesn't seem to mind. Once when buying a horse I've seen him pay with cash."

"Mr. Edmonds have you or your help ever seen scars on the bellies of any of these cows?"

"No, I haven't and the buyers have never complained about that."

"How long has Mr. Sanderson been coming to your auctions and how many cattle has he sold there?

"I've known him for about six years. I can't say how many he has sold. He only comes every three or four months. Sometimes his workers bring them in."

"Thank you, that's all my questions."

"No direct, Your Honor," Mr. Tumlin said.

The next witness was also from Mississippi.

"Please tell the jury who you are and what you do."

"I'm Ronnie Barker and I'm a real estate salesman. I sell real estate in both Alabama and Mississippi."

"Are you acquainted with Charles Sanderson and have you sold him properties?"

"I've know him several years and sold him many pieces of land. Usually it's just acreage and no houses that I recall."

"Are these deals mortgages or cash?"

"Most of them are cash settlements, a few mortgages on the expensive sales but he pays a cash percentage on those. I've sometimes wondered about the cash money he uses."

"Can you provide the court the details and amounts paid by Mr. Sanderson on all those sales? Also whose name is on each deed as the owner?"

"My office staff can provide those for you."

"That's all the questions for now, thank you Mr. Barker.

Attorney Tumlin announced, "No direct, Your Honor.

"The prosecution has no other witnesses today. We reserve the right to recall these men at a later time."

"Meet back at ten o'clock tomorrow. Court is adjourned." Judge Bradford declared.

☙❧

Betty Sue was so upset, thinking that she might be called to the stand tomorrow by Squire's attorney; she wanted to go to the jail and try to get to talk to her husband. She refused my offer to go with her. She insisted that she would be able to drive home safely. Noe did not come with her today.

Jason and Joe were glad the district attorney did not call them to the stand.

Jason asked, "Can he get us up there later?"

"I don't think he needs any more evidence. Those men have told enough to convince the jury that he is guilty of all the charges." David remarked.

"I still want to know about the murder charges." I expressed my doubts.

58

The fourth day of Charles 'Squire' Sanderson's trial did not begin at ten or even at eleven. The spectators and reporters were in place. Betty Sue was not with us and I didn't know why. I wanted to call her but David said I shouldn't, so I waited hoping she would come in.

The jury had not been called in. The district attorney was not at his table, Squire and his attorney were not present, and of course, the judge had not come in.

Finally, at eleven-twenty the clerk informed everybody that the trial was over. The defendant had entered a guilty plea. The hearing before the judge will convene at one o'clock today.

The jury was brought in. The judge entered just long enough to thank them and dismiss the jury.

"Can we come back for the hearing? I want to know what happened."

"I think the next thing is for the judge to accept his guilty plea. I'll find the sheriff and ask if we can attend. I know they have to have it public in some way, maybe just the news reporters will be here." David told us.

I went out to call Betty Sue and tell her what had happened. This isn't what we expected. We wanted the jury to find him guilty as charged.

ಶ್ಠಿ

The Times told the details of Squire's plea.

Charles "Squire" Sanderson Guilty

After hearing the testimony of several witnesses, Charles 'Squire' Sanderson admitted his guilt. In an afternoon hearing, Sanderson formally changed his plea to guilty and accepted an agreement that should see him incarcerated for at least fifteen years and lose all his real estate holdings in three states to pay a one million dollar fine.

Sanderson pleaded guilty to three counts, importing drugs, distribution of illegal drugs, and money laundering. Charges of arson and murder were dismissed in the plea agreement.

"Regardless of his prior assertions of innocence, it is now undisputed that this once prominent local citizen was in fact for many years a drug dealing crook." District Attorney Simpson said.

The defendant will now cooperate with the government; he has agreed to divulge all he knows about his and other criminal activities to help in other investigations. At the hearing, Sanderson and his attorney entered the courtroom; still wearing the look alike dark suits and ties they had worn during the four days of trial. "Squire was somber, speaking politely but so softly Judge Bradford asked him to speak up.

"Guilty, Your Honor. This was repeated for each charge. He told the judge he would save any further comment for trials against two co-defendants. His sentencing hearing is set for July 1st. A fourth charge of murder against Sanderson will be dismissed.

Part of the agreements was that his wife Betty Sue Sanderson would not be charged in any criminal activity and that she would retain title to the property and home in Veeny. That is land inherited from his father. His two brothers own adjoining land. After the details were made public, Sanderson was led from the courtroom in handcuffs.

Memories and Murders

Trials for two co-defendants, Vance Patterson, and Jose Hernandez are scheduled to begin next week.
Benjamin County Times
April 4, 1996

59

"I know we have other things to do—stop telling me that," I yelled back at David.

"Today I'll do whatever you ask, but not right now."

We were all drained from four days of waiting in the courtroom. It will probably be a week or two before the trials of the other two begin and I still don't know who killed those men. Joe told us that both of the men found buried in the graves were identified and their families had funerals for them. Both were from small towns in Mississippi and both had a history of being involved with illegal drugs and arrests. The bones had not been identified and authorities had found no record of missing persons that fit the time and size of that man.

How many things did I need to do today? Check on Betty Sue, plan a fun outing for us, finish the interior of 'The Homestead', go see the Preacher, visit relatives, and go see Kaylee. Kaylee was now at Betty Sue's most of the time so I could do two of those things later today.

"David, I have decided to finish the house with décor suitable for a restaurant. First, you need to help Joe with putting a finish on the wood floor."

"Are you sure? I will not cook for you or have anything to do with serving food."

"That's all right, I promise to not ever ask you to do that, but maybe you could wash dishes. I think this part of the state needs a good restaurant and I know someone will lease it and make a great place out of it."

"The wood floors need a walnut stain and then two coats of finish. Don't make them shiny, I want a dull finish. You and Joe can clean them today, and maybe do a little sanding but it's best if they are a little rough. I'll go to Florence tomorrow and search for wallpaper for the front room. The next room will be the kitchen, so you can paint the walls the same green we have in the new room. I'll do a drawing of where to put the appliances. The center of the room needs an island and one corner needs to be a storage area. The storage area will be near the new room and could become a closet if this house becomes a home."

David continued for me, "And, you can shop all over for the right tables and chairs and stuff to decorate with. I'm not sure that's a good use for this, but finished like that it could be a sport club with different furnishings. Now we can finish it while we wait for the trials to end and you can pick the vegetables."

"I'll do that as soon as they are ready. Today, I need to visit the preacher. Do you want to go see him?"

"No, I want to work at something."

I had worried about Preacher Fredericks health. I knew he wasn't as well as last year but didn't know he was confined to bed most of the time. He was alert and smiling when I went in. I gave him a hug. Since writing his story I felt like he was family. He told me, "I've come to love the Pierces, they are good to me. You, David, and Joe sure livened up my life, along with Sally and her family. Kaylee is so sweet to me; the boys behave well. I get to tell them stories from the

Bible. They don't know they are from the Bible, but we talk about the moral of the story. Sally brings Kaylee to see me. She always brings Shadrach to see the other cats.

"This old body is worn out; guess I failed to take care of it through the years. I have to tell you something and then I want to see my book."

"What do you have to tell me?"

"I've talked with my three sons about some important things. They are all Christians and have raised their families with Christian principles. Did you know that both Jason and Joe have become Christians? I talked with Joe about his divorce and his past problems. Jason and I have had many talks about why having God leading your life is so important. Joe, Jason, and Sue have joined the church along with Butch and Sally's family. I sure wish I was able to go to church.

"The other thing that I haven't told anyone else is important because I need you to hurry and finish my book."

"It is ready for your last editing. If I don't need to change very much, I can take it to the printer this week. What else are you telling me?"

"The Lord spoke to me last week. Oh, it was very short, and, oh, so sweet. I had been praying for everybody and about my pain. Nobody else was in the room, so I know the words I heard were from God and just for me. He said, *'See you soon'*."

The tears were running down his cheeks as he finished and I tried not to cry. For him, it meant he was going home to heaven; to me it meant we would miss him. I knew he didn't want me to share that with others, or at least not now.

"Preacher, that will be a prologue to your story that I will write after you are in heaven with your beloved Maggie. Thank you for telling me, that will be our secret for now. Did you tell your family about the book?"

"No, I still want it to be a surprise. I'll write a little goodbye to them and you can include it in your next piece about me. I'll have Sue read me everything you have here and let her give it to you Sunday. Go ahead and print about thirty copies."

I left shortly afterwards, feeling very sad.

60

"Joe, you didn't you tell us you joined the church?"

"I was saving that for a surprise. I guess I have to tell you now, I bet Preacher Fredericks told you."

"Yes he did. We had a good talk the day I took him the text of his book for him to approve. The copies of his book should be ready this week. I plan to pick them up and take them to him real soon."

"That's great. The church has a welcoming event planned for this coming Sunday. They want to introduce the new members to everybody. Some of us will be baptized. Did Preacher tell you that Jason and his family joined the church?"

"Yes he did. He also said Butch and Sally and Matthew joined."

"Sally and Butch were already members of a church, so they won't be baptized. I will, also Jason, Sue and their two boys, and Matthew. They are treating it as a big celebration."

"Joe, it is something to celebrate when we know all of you are forgiven and a member of God's family. I'm very happy about it. Do you think we could get Preacher Fredericks and his sons to attend Sunday? He says they are all Christians and it would be a good time for him to present them with his life story. He has put a title on it, *My Journey- the end is Heaven*."

"Do you think he is well enough to do that?"

"Yes, I think he will be willing and able. Will you ask him, then call the sons and we'll surprise him."

"Jane, do you think it would be the right time to tell everybody that Mattie has agreed to marry me."

"Yea, she said yes. Sure we'll all be excited about that. Will you two be married in that church?"

"We haven't planned all that yet. I want to sell my farm first so that I'll have some money."

"This is Mattie's first time to be married. I bet she would like a church wedding. She is a Christian, you know. Her family will probably pay for the wedding."

"She said that and she wants to get married soon. We talked about the babies we both want. She plans to keep working at Blue Pond since I don't have a job."

"Be sure that you two keep in mind all the things God wants for you. Just keep his commandments, as Brother Burns always said, and everything will work out well for you two."

61

The trial for Vince Patterson was scheduled to begin in Federal Court on Monday, April 15th. Jason told us that he had bought drugs from him and that he was one of the men demanding the money he owed to Squire Sanderson. He thought that Patterson either set the fire that burned their house or he had it done.

The charges against Patterson were murder, arson, and importing and distributing drugs. The State drug agents and the FBI had been investigating these men and all the charges the State and County had against Vince Patterson and Jose Hernandez. They would be tried in Federal Court because they worked for Squire Sanderson. Finally, maybe we would learn what happened to those three men.

Joe, David, and I, along with Jason, Betty Sue, and Noe Sanchez were sitting together in the courtroom. This was the third day of the trial. It took the first two days of the trial for jury selection. The Defense Attorney Tumlin and the prosecution were very careful to pick the fourteen people, from the eighty called for jury duty, that they thought would give them the verdict they wanted. Now we were waiting to hear from their witnesses.

The jury was seated. None of our group knew any of the jury.

The bailiff entered and announced, "All rise."

Judge Nolan Bradford entered and all were invited to sit again.

Elizabeth Oliver Wooten

The opening remarks from the prosecution and the defense attorney were a repeat of what we had heard at Squire's trial. His trial had ended on the fourth day with a guilty plea from the defendant. Unless the Attorney Jim Tumlin had found a positive way to defend his client, we felt Patterson should plead guilty to something.

The FBI agent that we had met took the stand. His testimony gave information about the recovery of human bones from our well and the discovery of two bodies taken from the cemetery. He described how they had identified the two bodies; told who they were and gave their arrest record. They had been shot in the head with a high powered gun. Both of them had been arrested in Mississippi for possession of illegal drugs and one for possession with intent to distribute. They served time, paid their fines, and were probably doing the same illegal things when they disappeared. Missing person's records showed that one got lost about three years ago and the other one was reported missing a year later. Their families identified them by clothing and other tests. The human bones taken from our well had not been identified. The man had been dead longer and having been in water so long it was harder to get positive results on them.

The defense attorney had questions for this man.

"Mr. Sims, did you find any evidence that connects my client to the deaths of these men?"

"No, They were drug dealers and so is your client."

"No further questions at this time," Mr. Tumlin said. He seemed confused.

The Alabama Drug Agent that had been investigating the drugs in this area for several years took the stand next.

He told about arrest that his department made eighteen months ago. He said "Mac Davis was arrested at that time, but he was not convicted of any crime. I believe he was on probation for drugs and we suspected he was dealing but didn't find any proof. We did not arrest Vince Patterson."

The prosecution called its next witness, Charles 'Squire' Patterson.

After Squire was sworn in The District Attorney said, "State your name, address and occupation."

"Charles Sanderson, I live at Route one, Veeny, Alabama and I'm a rancher." Squire spoke clearly. He was dressed in causal pants and shirt. We knew he was still a prisoner but maybe the jury wasn't supposed to know that.

"Do you know the man seated at the table with Attorney Tumlin?"

"I know him, he has worked with me for about three years."

"And tell us what he did while working for you."

"We transported cattle from Mexico to a ranch I own in Texas. His job was to see that they were taken care of after we got them to the ranch."

"Mr. Sanderson, please be more specific. Why were you and Mr. Patterson bringing cattle from Mexico? What do you mean by—taken care of?"

"Some of the cattle had marijuana or cocaine sewn in their bellies. The ranch is where it was taken out. Their bellies were sewn up again and most of them lived. We fed them for a few months and then sold them to slaughterhouses. My ranch also raised regular Texas cattle. We moved those to Alabama and other states. Most of the time we were also delivering drugs in the bottom of the trailer.

Sometimes the drugs were brought across the border in the bottom of the trailer. The border guards were familiar with us bringing cattle from Mexico."

"We have one of those cows taken from your ranch in Alabama. The DEA agents have had it examined by a Veterinarian. The cattle trailer is in our lock-up and has been tested for drugs. What can you tell us about those two things?"

"Somebody messed up. Those cows were supposed to be kept in Texas. The slaughterhouse there was glad to get them at a good price. They tested them to be sure they didn't have any disease. The trailer was also used to pick up antiques that my wife bought in different places. We also delivered illegal drugs to distributors on those trips."

"Did Vince Patterson go to Mexico and bring illegal drugs back to Texas?"

"Yes."

"Did he distribute those drugs in other states?"

"Yes."

"Did he collect cash money for the drugs he delivered and give it to you?"

"He did."

"Was there ever problems in getting the money people owed you?"

"I think he had trouble with a few of those people. We never discussed it, Vince took care of it."

"Objection, witness thinks."

"Stay with the facts, Mr. Sanderson." The Judge told him.

The District Attorney continued his examination. "We know three men were killed. Please tell us what you know about them. Remember you are under oath."

"I know nothing about those deaths. I recognized the names of two of them as people we sold drugs to. That was a long time back."

"Is there anything else you can tell us about the defendant?"

"No" Squire was visibly upset now.

"No more questions."

Judge asked the defense if there were questions for the witness.

"Yes, I have a few questions."

"Mr. Sanderson, it seems that you have included yourself in those accusations against my client. Are you guilty of importing and distributing illegal drugs?

"Yes."

"What have you been offered for lying about my client?"

"Objection, witness does not have to answer."

"Over ruled, jury needs to know all the facts."

"I have pled guilty to those charges and others and will serve time and pay a fine for breaking the law. I agreed to tell what I know about our operation. If it affects others, I'm sorry." Squire was contrite and looked very tired.

"Mr. Sanderson you stated that you did not know how those men died. Do you think my client had something to do with their death?"

"I cannot testify to what I think. I do not know who killed them."

"Why should the jury believe you, an admitted drug dealer."

"I don't care if they believe me or not. Others know what I told is the truth, maybe the jury will believe them."

"No further questions."

Everybody including the Judge was ready for lunch.

"Court will convene at one-thirty today. Adjourned," the Judge banged his gravel.

Our group had lunch together and nobody had anything to say about the trial.

As we were returning to the courtroom, I voiced my opinion again. "Somebody killed those poor men, will we ever find out who did it?"

※

The prosecution had one more witness, Michael "Mac" Davis. The questions he asked him were the same ones answered by Squire that morning. The answers were almost the same. Mac had been to the ranch in Texas and he knew most of what happened there. He said he worked most of the time in Alabama and only sold drugs in Alabama. He answered one or more question that wasn't asked of Squire.

"Mr. Davis, to your knowledge did the defendant have anything to do with torching a home near Veeny?"

"He told me and Jose to do that. He wasn't actually there."

"Mr. Davis, do you carry a gun and are you a good marksman with a rifle?"

"I sometimes carry a pistol. My hunting rifle is usually in my truck and I can hit a deer in the right spot to kill it. It's not illegal to have guns, is it?"

"No, you can shoot deer in hunting season. It's illegal to carry a gun if you are on probation. I believe you are not on probation at this time.

"Mr. Davis, did you know the men that were found buried in that cemetery?"

"I had seen one of them. Years ago I think I sold him drugs. I don't know the other one, and I have no idea about the one whose bones were found in the well."

"Remember that you are under oath. To the best of your knowledge did Vince Patterson kill these people?"

Mac didn't answer right away. He seemed to be considering what come happen to him or trying to remember what he knew about Vince.

"I guess I don't know who killed those men."

The district attorney had finished and the defense had no questions for the witness.

�~�

The trial began promptly at nine o'clock on Tuesday morning. The prosecution had another witness sworn in, Preston J. Perry. We knew him from Squire's trial. Perry had wanted to talk about the bones then but was overruled by the judge on objection of the defense. Patterson is being tried for murder, surely we'll hear what he knows now.

After the defendant and his attorney, the prosecution team, and court reporter were all in place the jury was brought in. The bailiff then asked all to rise and the judge took his place. We were told to be seated and the prosecution began questioning Perry.

"State your name, address, and what you do for a living."

"Preston J. Perry. I live at Route One, Blue Pond, Alabama. I am currently unemployed."

"Do you know the defendant, Vince Patterson?"

"Yes, I have bought drugs from him. I'm not a personal friend of his."

"Do you have any knowledge of the deaths of three men, one of which bones were found in a well where you had lived."

"I did live in that house. After we moved away, I continued to meet with Vince and Jose there to buy drugs from them. One day while waiting for them I found some bones and a skull near the barn. When Vince saw them, he was mad. The three of us found and dug up more bones and threw them in the well. I think wild animals had dug up the ones I found. They threatened to throw me in the well alive, if I ever told about the bones."

"Did you tell anyone?"

"No."

"This trial is about the deaths of three men. Do you have knowledge of any other killings?"

"Vince called me and asked if anybody besides us ever went to that old house. I told him I didn't think they did. I went there sometimes. He said he wanted to use the well. I thought about that and got scared. If he was putting dead or alive people in that well then I could be tied to that because I had lived in that house. I met him and Jose there that day and told them about another place to bury bodies. It was the little cemetery that I knew about. Nobody would worry about a grave in a cemetery; they just needed to put rocks on the body to keep animals from digging them up."

"Did you go with them to that cemetery?"

"No, I told them to take the log road off Thaxton Road and go to the older trees on right side of the log road. There were grave markers so I knew they could find the cemetery in the woods. We never talked about that day again."

"Did you buy illegal drugs from Vince Patterson?"

"I did, many times."

"No further questions."

Defense Attorney Tumlin was on his feet and quickly asking questions.

"Mr. Perry, did my client tell you that you were putting human bones in that well?"

"No, it wasn't mentioned but I knew it was a human skull."

"Did you see a body when you met them and talked about the cemetery."

"No."

"What gives you the right to talk about Mr. Patterson and dead people if you never saw him kill anyone."

"I know he did, or maybe it was Jose who killed them. Vince and Jose were together both times and they weren't getting rid of dead animals."

"You say they threatened you. Why are you willing to talk about this now?"

"They are both in jail with no bail so I feel safe."

"Have you been promised a suspended sentence for your part in selling illegal drugs?"

"Objection, witness does not have to answer that."

"Sustained. Mr. Tumlin, that is not a part of this trial."

"Mr. Perry, I would like the jury to know what your occupation has been for the past two years. Would you please tell us?"

Elizabeth Oliver Wooten

"I have used and sold illegal drugs for years. I was arrested, served time and am still on probation. I hope to do better than that in the future."

"No further questions."

The judge asked if the prosecution had more witnesses.

"No, Your Honor."

☙❧

The defense attorney called his first witness. We had never seen him, the tall good looking man with a great suntan took the stand and was sworn in.

"State your name and occupation." Mr. Simpson said

"I'm Scott Owens. I own a car dealership in San Antonio, Texas."

"Are you acquainted with Vince Patterson?"

"Yes, he worked for me for about two years. He was our top salesman."

"When was that?"

"It was about six years ago. He left to follow the rodeo circuit that year and didn't come back. We heard that he did well, won lots of prizes."

"Was Mr. Patterson a good employee? Was he honest with you and your customers?"

"Yes. I believe he treated everyone fair. He sold lots of cars and I never heard a complaint from anyone."

"That's all the questions I have for this witness."

"No questions from the prosecution."

"Mr. Simpson call your next witness." The judge said.

An attractive lady of questionable age took the stand. After she was sworn to tell the truth, Mr. Simpson had her tell who she was and her occupation.

"My name is Rita Patterson and I have no occupation. I was married to Vince Patterson eight years ago. We lived together eighteen months and he left."

"Mrs. Patterson, can you vouch for Vince being an honest man? Did he treat you fairly?"

"Vince never did anything to make me think he was a liar. He treated me nicely, except I never got my support payments from him. I sued him and only asked for support. We were never divorced."

"Would you take him back as your loving husband?"

"No."

"That's all I have for this witness."

"No questions from the prosecution."

ॐॐ

The judge called for a recess. We talked quietly about the two witnesses and wondered who else the defense had.

ॐॐ

It was a surprise when Defense Attorney Tumlin called Vince to the stand. The way Mr. Tumlin preceded let the jury and everybody know it was not his wish to have his client on the stand. Vince was dressed in the jail attire, an orange jumpsuit. He gave his name and occupation as a rancher and rodeo star.

"Vince, did you kill the man whose bones were found in that well?"

"No, I did not."

"Did you kill either of the men whose bodies were found buried in the cemetery?"

"No, I did not."

"Did you know those men before their death?"

"I think they were people who bought illegal drugs from the Sanderson gang."

"Preston Perry testified that you knew about the death of at least two of those men. Can you tell us why he said that?"

"Yes, he's a liar, drug user, and a drug dealer."

"Squire Sanderson told us that you and Jose Hernandez collected drug money for him. Did you have trouble getting that money?"

"Sometimes we did. Jose set fire to a home trying to get one man to pay. Nobody was hurt and we didn't get money from him."

"Then you admit to working for Squire Sanderson, selling illegal drugs and arson along with working on his ranch in Texas and Alabama."

"Yes, but I did not kill anybody."

"No further questions." Mr. Tumlin sat down.

Mr. Simpson had questions from the prosecution. He took his time approaching the witness, looked at the jury, then waited a bit before his first question. He reminded Vince that he was under oath and perjury could be added to the charges against him if didn't tell the truth.

"Mr. Patterson have you ever been arrested before?"

"No."

"Do you understand all the charges against you at this time?"

"I think I do."

"I heard you admit that you are guilty of selling illegal drugs and arson. The other two charges are importing illegal drugs and murder." Are you also guilty of those?"

"Squire has testified that I did help to bring drugs from Mexico, but I did not kill anybody."

"Then who did?"

Vince looked at his lawyer, and then looked at the Judge. "Do I have to answer that?"

The Judge answered him. "You are under oath, and, yes, you better answer truthfully."

All the confidence and swagger left Vince. He sank down in the chair and covered his face. He finally answered.

"Jose is the marksman that likes to shoot at anything. When the first one was killed, he claimed it was an accident. He also shot the other men at different times. I tried to stop him but since I knew about all three I couldn't turn him in. I knew I would be charged if I did."

"That's all the questions I have." Prosecutor Simpson seemed pleased.

"Any more questions for your client, Mr. Tumlin?"

"No, Your Honor."

Vince Patterson stumbled to his chair at the defense table. I felt sure he would be found guilty.

"Do either of you have more witnesses?"

Both prosecutor and attorney for the defense said no. Judge Bradford said court would convene at nine-thirty Wednesday with closing statements by both attorneys.

62

Patterson Guilty of all Charges

The murder and drug trial of Vince Patterson ended yesterday. After four days of testimony by witnesses, the jury heard from Patterson when he took the stand in his own defense. The District Attorney questioned two men about the recent activities of Patterson. The testimonies of a former boss from Texas and a wife revealed very little. They both said they thought Patterson was an honest man when they knew him. He proved that he was by telling that he knew who pulled the trigger to kill three men. Patterson gave the name of Jose Hernandez as the man who killed three men. Hernandez, Patterson, and the men murdered were all involved with selling illegal drugs.

The jury deliberated six hours before bringing in a verdict of guilty on all charges. Charges against Patterson were importing and distributing illegal drugs, arson, and murder. He admitted to several of the charges against him but insisted he did not kill anybody.

Patterson is being held in a federal jail without bail. Sentencing will be at a later date.

Benjamin County Times
April 20, 1996

We did not attend the last two days of Vince Patterson's trial. After hearing him admit that he knew Jose Hernandez had pulled the trigger, we knew who was guilty of killing the three men. I think I was afraid the jury might not find him guilty of murder since he told that Jose was the triggerman that killed those men. The newspaper article was the report we were waiting for. There is still one more man, Jose Hernandez, to be tried and then sentencing for all of them. After that, the drug and murder fiascoes might finally be over.

༄༅

The last Saturday of the month was coming up and that meant another auction in Veeny. Since that was a regular monthly gathering and social time, we planned to attend. I thought I could now buy a few pieces of furniture for 'The Homestead', if anyone had the pieces I wanted. I would even put some of my things from our Veeny shop in the auction. It should be fun to participate.

The business in our new-old town was improving every month. The first thing I saw when I went there on Friday was a new store. It was in an old 1950's peddler truck. I was thrilled and immediately went in. The owner said he knew where it was and went and purchased it just for this place. He had repaired the motor, fixed the outer cover, and cleaned the inside. The old shelves were stocked with the some of the items we used to buy when the peddler came by our house in the 1940s and 1950s. He also had lots of other things for sale.

My first question was, "Can I trade a fresh egg for candy?" That's what I did as a kid when the peddler came to our house

"Sure if you have a fresh free range egg."

I didn't and had to admit it. I congratulated him on having an authentic addition to our town.

Memories and Murders

    I learned of other new events that had been planned. One Saturday of each month there was a big grill set up and barbecue venison or beef was sold. This always brought lots of people. The auction had more sellers and a lot of people attending. The committee had plans underway for a big birthday celebration next year. The town would be eighty years old according to the records we found. The shop owners wanted to start giving a ticket, with each purchase, for a drawing once a month. I remember when this was done back in my era. Those monthly drawing had people coming to town to find out if they won. I think the prizes were cash money donated by the merchants.

    I visited each shop and booth, talked with the people, and told them about my book I would be publishing about my ancestors and this town. I promised to be back for a book signing at the big birthday celebration, of the town. I ate lunch at Miss Mary's tearoom and went home to convince David and Joe to come to the auction with me.

    Mattie met us at Veeny and we had dinner at Norman's. We later talked with our group of friends at the auction house. Everybody was happy about the up coming wedding of Mattie and Joe. The city officials were there and all the talk was positive about the changes in our town. Mayor Finks whispered to Betty Sue and me that they had not heard from Rex Arnold. I whispered back that I had begun writing my book and would be back in Veeny for their big birthday celebration.

63

The Pastor of the church told the large group assembled in the church that this was not the usual first Sunday meal. It is our regular monthly dinner but this one is special. He spoke briefly, "We are here for a welcoming party for our new members and a special baptism service. I have not had the opportunity before to baptize a complete family. This number is by far the most I have had the pleasure of welcoming to our membership. We have prepared a new member list for you that will help you all remember each of these people. We also have special quests tonight, Rev. Fred Fredericks, and his family. I have asked David Cotton to tell you about them while I go prepare for baptizing six of our new members, Jason and Sally Pierce and their two boys, Jimmy and Timmy; also, Matthew Sanderson and Joe Burns. Sally and Butch Sanderson are new members, also. We're happy to have their families visiting today. We have lots of food so join us for the dinner after this short service."

  David went to the podium very quietly, but then he smiled and began talking, "I am so happy to see Rev. Fredericks here tonight. You may know he has not been well lately and we have missed him. This is an important event for him and his family, also for Jane. Preacher Fredericks asked me to do this for him. We have a surprise for his sons. Will you three please join me here on the stage."

  David took four slim books from the table behind him. I looked at Preacher; he was waiting to see the expressions on his son's faces when they saw the book he was so proud of. David explained, "This was supposed to be ready for you last Christmas but it wasn't finished. Jane and Preacher have written about his life and printed this just for you and your children. The picture on the front is the original church, which stood here for many years. It was an important part of your life as children. Please accept this book- *'My Journey- The end is Heaven'*- from your Dad. He will sign them and write something for each you.

The Fredericks men were looking at their Dad with tears forming in their eyes. Preacher and I were both trying not to cry. They were happy tears, I knew this was a special day for the old Preacher, maybe the last time he would be in this church alive.

David said, "We have a few more of these books. This is also a book signing for Rev. Fredericks. Please see him at dinner if you would like one. He is giving this copy to the church."

Rev. Parke was in the pool of water behind the stage ready to pray for all of the new members and the Fredericks. Beginning with the youngest boy, he immersed each of the members under the water. He explained that this was symbolic of washing away their old life and rising anew to walk the Christian life. Symbolic only because Jesus Christ had taken away our sins by dying on the cross. We only had to accept his love.

When all six were baptized, the pastor prayed again and blessed the food we were all ready to eat.

The Welcoming Party was a happy occasion. Rev. Fredericks was sitting at a table with his books. The people were very interested in his book and glad to see him again.

I was asked to join him there and autograph them as the writer. His signature meant the most to the people who knew him.

After everyone had eaten and visited with the Fredericks, the new members, and us, David and I begin to feel like this was home. Joe had an announcement that thrilled us.

"Attention, everybody! Mattie has agreed to marry me. We want to be married in this church if Pastor and you all agree." Joe said.

He and Mattie looked very happy. The others began asking questions. When is the big day? Can we have a wedding shower next month? I knew the members and friends would take care of this wedding. I didn't need to worry about helping plan anything. Mattie explained that the date hadn't been set. They would let the members know soon. Yes, a shower could be planned but they really didn't expect them to do that. She seemed so happy and pleased.

The Fredericks family was happy. Preacher Fredericks felt he had led both Jason and Joe to become Christians and was glad they were now members of this church. He was very tired but did not leave early. We left with Mattie and Joe.

ঌ⋞

"Well, now it's official even if Mattie doesn't have an engagement ring. Joe you can't back out of this."

"I don't want to. I just need a job so I can afford to get married. I'm waiting for my farm to sell. Mattie says we can live in her house and we might do that.

"David and Jane, do I need to move my camper? Your little farm has been good for us, Bear, and me. Mattie and I have talked about renting the place. We've even thought about running the restaurant there. "The Homestead" name makes us want to have it become our homestead someday."

"Oh Joe, that would be great. It's almost ready and is looking so good. Why don't you find a chef and we can talk some more about that. David and I did own a restaurant once. We can help get it going, and then it's all yours. What do you or Mattie know about cooking and serving excellent food?"

"Nothing. We can cook what we eat and that's it. I do love to grow things like corn and vegetables and stuff to eat."

"I guess we could learn." Mattie said. She was definitely sounding interested.

"Growing your own organic food would be a great idea for the restaurant.

"Why don't one of you contact the gourmet cooking school in Birmingham. They might have a new chef who would be willing to work here."

"That's a good suggestion, Jane. I'll call and talk to them." Joe was enthused.

David told them, "It's okay to keep your camper here after we leave. Joe, you have been so good to take care of the farm for us and to plant a garden. We appreciate that. We're not leaving until we eat those vegetables."

We talked for a while about the trials. The event at church had been postponed from last month because we were so busy attending the trials. We still had one more to listen to next week. So far, no sentences had been handed out for the homicides.

64

The next morning we had a call from Betty Sue. She was at the church party but we didn't find time to talk. She played with Kaylee while the others visited. Her call was to ask if David, Joe, and I would be here today; she wanted to come tell us something. I said we would be glad to have her come.

We knew we had another trial to attend soon. It seemed that the authorities were waiting to hear more about all the cases that were definitely linked, before any sentences were pronounced by the judge. All we knew for sure was that Jason had been released. Noe Sanchez did not get charged with abetting the drug dealers. Squire or Mac must have insisted that he was innocent and was needed on the ranch to care for the cattle. Mac and Squire had pleaded guilty to some charges. Vince had been found guilty of all charges but had not been sentenced. We had not heard anything about Leon Sanderson since they all were arrested.

When Betty Sue arrived, she wanted to see the house and what we had done in the last month. I told her I was looking for table and chair sets that were wood and would be sturdy and interesting. Maybe antiques or just old, I wanted the chairs to match the table in each set. I needed eight sets with at least four or more chairs in each set, but the eight sets could all be different.

"What are you doing with that many sets?" She wanted to know.

"We are finishing two of the rooms for a gourmet restaurant."

"Oh good, that means you are going to stay here doesn't it?"

"No, we have not committed to living here. Since I think this area needs a nice place to eat I think someone will lease it, or I hope somebody will."

"I can help you find what you want or maybe you could use some sets from the lodge, we are not using it now."

"I did like the look you have there. I plan for one corner of the large room in this house to have some tables with lace tablecloths and be romantic with candles. Other corners can be more casual or have another theme. I'll have screens to section off each area."

"Jane, I think I understand; you like to design things. That sounds like a great idea for this attractive old house. I'll be one of the first customers for good food."

"Let's go sit down with the guys and I'll tell what I've learned from my husband."

I found David and Joe; we were all anxious to hear what Betty Sue knew.

"I have been able to talk with Squire since he testified at Vince's trial. He says he is sorry for the problems we all have and I believe he is trying to tell the truth now. He claims he and Leon did not know that anyone had been killed. He let Vince and Jose take care of people that owed them money. He never asked what they did, most of the time they were able to collect it. He did know that he never saw those two men after they had trouble with them but thought they left the area in order not to pay. He doesn't know what happened.

"I still have to pay the lawyer I got for all of them. Squire tells me that somebody has money that belongs to him. They have not arrested that person and he think he will be in touch soon. I think it might be Rex Arnold since he has disappeared. Please don't mention that to anyone."

"Do you think Rex has been holding cash or laundering it someway?" I just had to ask.

"Maybe, but we don't know that, please don't say anything to the sheriff.

"You all have helped me so much and I think you're doing the right things by helping others. Butch and Sally have told me what you did for them and how Jason and Sue depended on Joe when he was arrested after the fire.

"Mac saw Jason locked up when they all were in jail in Tussellville. Mac knew he disappeared after they set fire to his house, he figured out that Jason talked about him and the others. Mac knew then that they all were in big trouble. Jason knew a lot about their drug distribution since he was part of it. Mac decided he would plead guilty to something and tell what he knew, and maybe he would not have to serve time again.

"Squire wants Butch to come see him. He wants to apologize for the way he treated him when they left Texas. Butch learned about the drugs and moved the next week. Squire was angry and didn't pay him what he should have. Then they were so worried that Butch would report what they were doing that he had Leon and Vince grab Kaylee. Butch says he might go see Squire but not now.

"Squire wants Leon to get his lawyer to work out a plea agreement for him. He thinks his sentence will be less if Leon cooperates with the law. Leon just helped and did what he was told. I know he wouldn't harm anybody."

I didn't know what to say to Betty Sue. She seemed to be finished.

"Well, we still have to go hear the trial for Jose. Preston Perry did tell about the bones in the well and his testifying against Vince and Jose sure didn't help them any. Maybe I really don't want to hear anymore."

David said. "Yes, we all want to know who killed those men. Drug use sure can cause bad things to get worse. I hope these arrests will stop some of these terrible events that we have learned about."

Betty Sue thanked us for being her friends and for listening to her again. I agreed to be in Veeny this weekend and look at the tables she had there.

65

'The Homestead' was almost ready. Betty Sue, Mattie, and I had been shopping for weeks for things it needed. Most of our purchases were old and not very expensive. We were excited to have things like real china plates, even if the sets didn't match. We found estate sales usually had at least one complete set of china and sometimes a complete set of silverware. We found a service for twelve of china. Crystal or glassware was harder to fine in sets.

    We were happy with the furniture, which was all wood or painted and looked great in the old house. The porch had tables and chairs that we painted then sanded off some paint to make them look used. They could stand a little water and sun. The porch had a roof but was not closed in. I knew that porch setting would be my favorite place to be served iced tea and good food.

    We did have to buy some new cookware for the kitchen. Mattie said we should wait to see which small appliances the cook would want. We did install an old hanging rack over the island in the kitchen. If we had groceries we could cook and check to see what else we needed.

    Mattie had asked Betty Sue and me to find some recipes for gourmet foods that would be easy to serve. She was ready to begin planning the menu for our new restaurant. So we had looked and had several things for her to consider. I felt that anything unusual and tasty could be considered gourmet. Of course, the dishes needed to be things that could be made and kept in the refrigerator or at least be able to make the dressings and sauces ahead of time. We both promised to give her our best recipes that could be used in the restaurant.

༺༻

The place was furnished and most of the things needed were in place, so we decided to do a test dinner for about twelve people. David and I, Joe and Mattie, and Betty Sue would do everything, buy the food, cook, and serve in our old-new home.

Joe had almost finished a class for 'cooking in a restaurant'. He was also looking for someone who would cook on a promise of a percentage of the profits. He planned to do the next class on 'finances and management of a restaurant'. We planned our dinner for a weekend that he could be back from Birmingham to help.

The invitation was written, what, date, time, place, and RSVP to Mattie's phone number. No mention of the restaurant was made, just dinner and fun for our friends. We finally decided on our guest list. All of them were people that had helped us and became our friends. Jason and Sue Pierce, Butch and Sally Sanderson, Mayor Finks and husband, George and Beth Cotton, Rory and Joy Cotton, and finally the hardest to decide on was Sheriff Fred Moore and his wife, that was our twelve people. Preacher Fredericks wasn't able to come. Our menu for the evening was written for our planning and shopping. They would all be served the same, but with a choice of drink and dessert.

Memories and Murders

Appetizers
Soup
Bacon Chicken Rollups with Mushroom Gravy Served on Brown Rice
Green Beans Almondine
Strawberry Congealed Salad on Fresh Lettuce Leaf
Homemade Bran Rolls/Lemon Butter
Iced or Hot Tea, Lemonade, Coffee
Pineapple Orange Cake or Banana Pudding

We set three tables for four people and one table for six people. The china and silverware matched on each table and with candles and white napkins they looked very pretty. The guests would be served their choice of drinks. They would all get the same foods for their main course but could choose their dessert from the buffet. Some of the vegetables would be from the garden. David had taken over caring for the garden with Joe gone. He had been gathering and freezing what we didn't eat.

David and I will serve as the greeters, and direct our guest to their seats. One chair will be left for us to join the dinner after serving the others. Betty Sue and Mattie will be the waitresses. Joe will be in the kitchen. We'll all prepare the foods earlier and have it ready to serve as soon as the guest have finished the appetizers and have been served their drinks. I think we can serve food to an empty place. Then one of us will sit at each table. The table for six leaves one empty chair in case a ghost shows up. I think we can finish and go to the porch by dark. By candlelight we can pray and talk. Sounds perfect.

❦

Elizabeth Oliver Wooten

As we settled on the porch David thanked everyone for coming. He told our guests, "This has been a try-out for this new restaurant. We want your comments for Joe and Mattie to consider. Jane and I will be taking the motor home back to Georgia. Joe plans to move his camper to the barn and that will make more room for parking. Joe will be living here and running this business as soon as he learns more about cooking."

"David you have told enough. These friends came to visit. Let's get Joe, Mattie, and Betty Sue from the kitchen. We can have our prayer and then talk."

"We didn't ask a blessing before dinner because you were at a gourmet restaurant. But now, lets all pray silently and I'll close the prayer." David said.

The mayor talked first, "I think the dinner was perfect. David and Jane I think you should live here."

Sheriff Moore said. "I'm not sure how we got invited, but thank you, it was great food. I'll certainly pass the news around. When will 'The Homestead' be open?

"We plan to open as soon as Joe finishes his class, maybe in a month." Mattie was ready to begin promoting their business. "We can begin private events for small groups sooner. In fact, David, Butch, and Jason are doing our rehearsal dinner here. Jane and Betty Sue will cater our wedding reception here. The big day is in two weeks, I hope you all received your invitation."

Joe chimed in, "Boy, Mattie tells you everything. Be sure to come back later as paying guest, we'll need your business."

Jason wanted to know if they had a job for him. He was looking for work.

I had to ask some questions about the recent events. "Sheriff Moore what is happening with the other trials? We can't stay here much longer. We never heard about a trial for Jose Hernandez or about Leon.

"I know Leon Sanderson agreed to a plea agreement. He pled guilty to one count of selling drugs and the other charges were dropped. Hernandez did not have a defense attorney. Mr. Tumlin would not represent him. The State had to assign a public defender, since he didn't have any money to hire one. His trial is held up for months."

"When will we hear about the sentences and fines for the others?"

"Judge Bradford may delay those until after Hernandez's trial. He can do that. The guilty men are already serving time in jail. That will go as time served on their sentence."

"One more question and I'll hush. What about graves in another cemetery?"

"Oh, there weren't any unmarked graves there. Somebody gave us misinformation."

"Okay, everyone, did you believe we could rebuild this house into something so unique?

The other guest began to ask questions about the new restaurant, about the things that had happened here, and what we would be doing next.

66

David and I were back home in Rowley, Georgia. We had made the decision to live there until we found another project to get involved in. Veeny had been our home at one time but now we were devoted Georgians.

The newspaper article from Joe finished our adventure in Alabama.

> **Six Men Convicted of Crimes**
> Judge Nolan Bradford pronounced sentences for six of the men involved in a drug distribution ring. In August of last year, six men were arrested at Charles Sanderson's place in Northwest Alabama and accused of importing and distributing illegal drugs. Trials were held in April for two of the accused and a third man was tried in May.
> Charles 'Squire' Sanderson was sentenced to ten years in prison and six years probation and a fine of one million dollars for importing drugs, distributing drugs, and money laundering. All of his land holding will be sold and any profit will be applied to his fine. Drug money confiscated in the raid will not apply to his fine. Sanderson pled guilty to three charges and asked that his wife be allowed to keep their home.
> Leon Sanderson was charged with distributing and selling drugs. He also pled quilty and was sentenced to serve two years, two years probation, and a fine of five thousand dollars.
> Michael 'Mac' Davis pled guilty to distribution of illegal drugs and testified in the trial of three co-defendants.

> He was sentenced to serve two years and four years on probation.
>
> Vince Patterson's trial ended with guilty as charged. He was charged with importing and distributing drugs and murder. Patterson told the jury he did not kill anyone. He named co-defendant Jose Hernandez as the triggerman. Judge Bradford heard the jury's recommendation of life in prison with no parole. The Judge sentenced Patterson to thirty years in prison and five years probation.
>
> Jose Hernandez trial was much the same as Patterson's. The jury found him guilty of murder, arson, and distribution of drugs. He was sentenced to fifty years in prison and five years probation.
>
> Preston Perry pled guilty to selling drugs. He testified in the two murder trials and gave information about the deaths and involvement of Patterson and Hernandez. He was sentenced to serve three years and five years on probation.
>
> Another man, Noe Sanchez, arrested during the raid was not charged.
>
> Alabama drug agents have been investigating the activity of drug distribution in this area for many years. Three men were killed because of their involvement in selling drugs and failing to pay the men who imported them from Mexico. The sentences for murder should have been life in prison without parole, but the Judge seems to have considered the overall circumstances and gave the two men found guilty of murder lighter sentences.
>
> Benjamin County Times
June 4, 1996

p 242-247

Made in the USA